TRACEY BARSKI

Cassidy Marchand Unraveled

Book Three of The Alternate Chronicles

First edition

ISBN: 978-1-961707-02-3

This book was professionally typeset on Reedsy.
Find out more at reedsy.com

Self—you wonderful, fragile thing—this is for you.

Contents

A Word About Content

If you've been with me (and Cassidy) on this journey for a while, you know what this book contains. But, as always, I want to make sure no one is caught off-guard. Cassidy continues to deal with her PTSD, panic attacks, and the implications of her brush with a serial killer. In this book, however, we see her face down her stalker, which could potentially trigger someone. Take care of yourselves, friends!

With love,
Tracey

1

Slime and Punishment

In theory, I should have been harder to kidnap. Being a woman who was as tall as an average man had once given me that false sense of security. Though I was on the slender side, I had assumed I was less likely to be a target for the usual crimes against women when walking down the street.

But that theory was obliterated when I'd nearly been taken out by a serial killer only a few months prior. Being a veteran of the experience gave me the authority for pegging this place immediately. It had "overabundance of serial killers lurking in the shadows" written all over it.

A creepy crawly feeling rippled along my skin like I was being watched. Which only added to my unease.

I should have immediately gone back, but jumping always took its toll, and I needed at least a short buffer between arrival and departure.

I should have made an exception. Because this place. . . Dark and dingy, cold and damp. I was afraid to talk to anyone or touch anything. It was like there was a greasy film on every surface. Even the few people I'd already encountered had an oily layer of grime all over them. And now the slimy feeling of their eyes like fingers over my body made me pick up the pace.

There were so many dark, cave-like spaces along the street that it was very probable I was being tracked by multiple pairs of eyes. It was worse that I couldn't see them and wouldn't know if I was about to be attacked. I hadn't witnessed any overt violence since arriving, but the way this place made me feel put it in the very-likely column.

I pulled my jacket more snugly around myself in an attempt to block the cold and keep from brushing anyone or anything. I wanted to make myself as tight and compact as possible until I found a spot to make my jump home.

There was no way to know what had landed me here, and the question of how any of this worked blinked like a neon sign in my head. I was still feeling my way blindly, making jumps whenever I had spare time or the itch to get traction in the stalled-out search for answers.

But this was the first place I'd jumped to that was vastly different from anywhere else I'd been. It wasn't discrepancies in my own life throwing me off this time. Being in a world that was so disparate from the one I knew made fear tangle inside me and kept me hyper-alert.

There was no obvious rhyme or reason to what timelines I went to, and I found very little when I arrived. I had no connections to use for research, and in places that were backward and confusing like this one, I had no idea where to start.

So here I was, slinking down the street in the creepiest setting I'd yet experienced, thinking that I was put off horror films for life when I heard movement behind me.

My nerves jumped, and my steps faltered for a moment. It

would have been an advantage to hide that I knew someone was following me without alerting them to the fact. But I'd probably flubbed the opportunity. I hoped whoever it was hadn't noticed my change in stride.

The panic still licked at my heels, and I picked up my pace again, hunching my shoulders. As if that would actually help.

I caught the shuffling sound of a foot along the sidewalk like someone had tripped over an uneven slab of concrete, closer than I would have liked, and my breath hitched.

They probably knew by now that I was aware of them, so I didn't see much point in trying to hide it. I broke into a run, the movement lopsided and slower than it used to be. Damn the still-healing leg injury.

The footsteps behind me picked up too, and—Oh, God, there were two sets.

Terror lit a fire inside of me, hot and blazing as adrenaline pumped hard and fast, limbering up my muscles and spurring them on.

It wasn't enough.

I felt one hand on my back, followed by another, then a shove from behind sent me stumbling, and I went down. I caught myself before hitting my face on the damp sidewalk, and my attacker grabbed me by the shoulder to flip me over.

I swung out in a panicked punch while my heart hammered against my ribs.

The sound of my fist hitting flesh dissolved the image in front of me. The grimy surroundings melted away until the dim light of a bedroom pushed into my awareness.

Drew stared at me with a question glimmering in his dark eyes, his hand still raised to block a possible second blow. It was his palm my fist had connected with.

My breath came out in a rush of shock. "Oh, God. Drew, I'm so sorry." I sat up straighter, struggling to extricate my legs from the tangle of sheets ensnaring them.

He lowered his hand slowly, giving his head a shake. His eyes never left my face. "It's my fault for trying to wake you up from a dead sleep like that."

My stomach clenched at his tone. His attempt at shrugging it off didn't mask the worry I still heard in his voice or the way he was staring at me. There was something else there, too.

It set fear dancing in my stomach, and the haze over my brain made it hard for me to decipher why.

"How long was I asleep?"

He hesitated, shifting on the bed. "It's been close to eighteen hours now."

Needles prickled along my skin. I didn't even remember coming home, let alone being tired enough to sleep that long. I pressed the heel of my hand to my forehead. Had I even been in the timeline I'd been dreaming about? Or was that conjured only in my mind?

Eighteen hours.

"Wait, did I miss my doctor's appointment?" I squeezed my eyes shut, trying to fit the passage of time into my mental calendar. I was supposed to get my cast off.

"I rescheduled it for tomorrow."

"Crap." I rubbed my hands down my face. "I'm so sorry. That shouldn't be your responsibility."

He reached out to brush the hair behind my ear, then trailed his hand down my arm. All of the anxiety firing in my nerves died away like his touch was a balm.

"It's okay," he murmured. "I don't mind." His eyes traced my face again before he tugged me to him.

I sighed, melting into his embrace.

"But are *you* okay?" he asked.

"I am now." Which was true for the moment. But the doubt nagged in the back of my mind that this was beyond the already *not normal* of my situation. I had made a few jumps since finding the necklace, but this was the first time I didn't remember making a return. Or had slept so long afterward.

He pressed a kiss to the top of my head, giving me a little squeeze. "Are you hungry? I make a mean bowl of cereal."

I pulled back to look into his face, giving him a sly smile. "No pancakes this time?"

He lifted a shoulder. "Not today. I don't have enough time. I only stopped over on my lunch break."

My smile fell away, and I swallowed. It had been evening when I left. Usually when I jumped, I came back to the time and place I'd been when I left. I touched my forehead where a slight headache throbbed, overly aware of Drew intently watching me.

I offered another smile, though it was a weak attempt to dispel the unease that bounced between us. "Cereal sounds good."

He waited a beat longer before standing and offering his hand to help me up.

A wave of dizziness accosted me, but I worked to keep it from showing. "I'll be there in a sec. Bathroom."

His eyes narrowed as he studied me. Too incisive, this one. He could tell something was off.

I fumbled for a distraction. "What? Am I not allowed to pee on my own?" I hoped the sarcasm masked my breathlessness.

He rolled his eyes. "For your well-balanced breakfast, do you want Cocoa Puffs or Golden Grahams?"

"Surprise me."

I watched him go, waiting until he was out of sight before staggering to the bathroom. Placing my hands on either side of the sink, I took several long, deep breaths and looked at myself in the mirror. Dark circles smudged under my eyes, more obvious because I was so pale. Not my best morning look. But certainly not my worst either.

There'd been a time that a blackened eye or a split and swollen lip greeted me first thing in the morning. I experienced an echo of that feeling I'd get back then, like I was looking at a stranger and not my own reflection.

The question would always be there in my mind: *How did I let it get this far?*

I pushed down the uncertainty, then turned the water on to splash my face.

I simply needed a break from jumping, that was all. I'd been going too often, and I hadn't made any progress in finding my family, Louisa Lee, or Professor Thibald, anyway. Everything would be fine and back to normal after a break.

Right?

I brushed my hands through my hair and tied it in a loose bun at the nape of my neck before heading out and down the hall.

Apprehension always crept through my body when I left Drew's room, anticipating an awkward interaction with Evan that had become the norm since he'd patched the gunshot wound in Drew's shoulder. It was always a possibility until he closed on his house and moved out.

"He's not here," Drew said, leaning against the archway as I approached the kitchen.

I didn't think my anxiety was that obvious. But it was also a

Drew and me thing—he practically had Cassidy ESP. He knew how annoying I found it, which was why he grinned when I scowled at him.

"Cereal's on the table." He tipped his head toward the dining room, still smirking.

Despite my ire, my body reacted to the sight of him—long and lean, his biceps flexing as he folded his arms across his chest. That crooked smile, the raised dark brow had desire unfurling inside me in a way that electrified my skin.

So instead of heading for the table, I gave in to impulse and hooked my finger into one of his belt loops to yank him toward me. He didn't even seem surprised as his body collided with mine, and I tipped my face up to his, waiting for his lips.

He obliged my unspoken request and lit a fire in my core with a kiss that curled my toes. His mouth danced with mine in a tango of give and take that made me forget any other physical needs I may have had.

When I pressed against him, he let out a groan, breaking the kiss and pulling back enough to make me feel suddenly and irrationally angry. I clenched my teeth and clutched at his shirt. Then his hands clamped around my wrists to stop me even as his breathing remained ragged.

"I have to go back to work soon," he said, his voice husky and irritated.

"We have time," I insisted, breathless.

I felt his wavering resolve through the conduit of his palms, the electricity like a live wire sending a charge along my skin. But he gave his head a quick, decisive shake. "Not if we do it right."

My lip protruded in a pout.

"You need to eat, anyway." He pried my hands from his shirt

but didn't release me. "How would you even have the energy?"

I scoffed. "I just slept for eighteen hours. I'm well rested. If you're worried about it, I'll let you do all the work."

He gave me a wolfish grin. "If I'm doing all the work, then we definitely don't have enough time."

My breath hitched. "So take a sick day."

He released a guttural sigh that bordered on a growl. "Don't tempt me." He shook his head again. "I can't take another one right now, anyway. Not after taking those other days off."

The flame of lust sputtered out, doused by the icy guilt that poured through me. I pulled my hands from his grasp, the intensity of the electricity between us dying so suddenly it was almost painful. He'd tried to skip over actually saying it—that he'd missed days to recover after he'd been shot. But I filled it in anyway. Because it had been my fault.

I backed up.

"Right." The word scraped up my throat like a blade. I moved toward the table where my Cocoa Puffs were now soggy mush and avoided looking at him.

The intensity of his gaze was warm on my back as he watched me put distance between us. Eventually, he followed me. Probably because his ESP was telling him how much self-blame I was still wrestling with.

I sat and didn't acknowledge him as he came closer, but he rested his hands on my shoulders, anyway. Always reminding me of his unwavering presence with a touch. He pressed his lips tenderly against the side of my neck, sending a wave of goosebumps cascading down my body, and I closed my eyes.

"I should be home before dinner," he murmured, his nose skimming my ear.

Home.

The word echoed in my head as both an inducement of panic and a comfort beyond explanation as I worked through the meaning behind it. He meant home to me. Like it was ours *together*.

I reached up to touch his hand, steadying myself with the feel of his skin under my fingers. He always would be my anchor in the chaos, even that of my own mind.

He shifted to the side, and I looked up at him, my heart and mind more settled. He leaned down to kiss me again, a light brush of lips.

And yet I still had to push. "You could be late from lunch. . . "

He grimaced. "You're going to be the death of me."

I raised a brow. "Infuriatingly stubborn, remember?"

He laughed and pulled away to head for the door, muttering something that sounded like, "Who needs a job, anyway?"

I watched him go, nibbling my lip as a new wave of guilt washed over me. He was letting me live here, rent-free—another reason I was sure Evan made a habit of shooting me borderline hostile looks—jobless while I jumped timelines in search of my answers.

Maybe I shouldn't be taking a break. At the very least, I needed to be doing *something*. I focused on eating my soggy cereal, rushing as a plan started to form in my mind.

I hadn't had much luck with getting any answers, and there was no real rhyme or reason to the timelines I went to—none that I could find, anyway. Maybe I needed to regroup while I was here.

I finished my breakfast and put the bowl in the sink, a new resolve driving the speed with which I went through the process of taking a shower and getting dressed.

It occurred to me that if I jumped from one timeline then back to my own in between, maybe Louisa Lee was doing the same.

Time to pay her a visit.

2

An Unexpected Pull

At least I didn't have to rely on Drew for a vehicle anymore. Not that I needed it most of the time with all the jumps I'd been making. Still, it felt good to slide behind the wheel of the Beast and hear that familiar protesting growl as I started her up.

Even if I eventually got a job and really settled in, I was attached enough to the Beast I wasn't sure I could give her up. She'd been my protection, my home for enough time now that even sitting there while the engine warmed gave me a sense of calm and safety that had always been so fleeting in my life.

I gave the dashboard a little rub of affection before putting the car in gear and heading out.

Since my last visit to Louisa Lee's house, where I'd been chased down by the two goons who'd almost killed Drew, I'd done some more research. Creating new social media profiles gave me the kind of access I needed to get a glimpse of the life she'd curated online.

Louisa Lee had the almost black hair and high cheekbones of someone with Asian heritage. Her studious, serious appearance felt like such a contrast with the sleeve of tattoos that covered her entire left arm. Which might have been the point. Holding a bachelor's degree in English literature and a minor in creative writing, she taught both subjects at the local high school.

With the sudden death of her uncle, though, she'd abruptly taken the semester off and seemed to fall off the grid.

She wasn't terribly active online in the first place from what I could tell, but she'd made a brief update about taking the break after a slew of friends posted messages of condolences on her various profiles. She hadn't posted since.

The last thing updated was her profile picture. It was an old one of her with her uncle, no doubt as a tribute to him after his murder.

I slowed as I cruised past her duplex, sucking my teeth. Last time, I'd opted to park around the corner, some premonition of self-preservation inspiring caution. I still didn't feel comfortable parking right in front, but choosing the same spot as before didn't seem smart, either.

Considering that there was still at least one person who knew my face and what timeline I was in, I needed to remain cautious about who saw me and where.

Not to mention that the ongoing case against my would-be killer had inspired a celebrity-like obsession with every move I made in the media, and I was second-guessing my gratitude about having my own—very recognizable—car back.

So I parked farther down the street, though not around the corner like last time, and got out.

Apprehension skittered through me, and I didn't bother trying to will it away. Being on high alert would work in my favor when there were still so many things threatening my safety. I hadn't forgotten the note that no longer existed except in my memory, which reminded me that more than one person was intent on finding me.

There had been no sign of Callum in the last several weeks since his little love note. We had been diligently watchful for any sign that my ex was lurking. Callum had found me at my parents' house before, but no one knew I was now living at Drew's except for Evan. And we planned to keep it that way for as long as possible.

The day was unusually warm, the sun blazing in the bright, cloudless sky. The higher elevation meant that on a clear, sunny day, even smack dab in the middle of December, it was warm enough to need only a light jacket.

The rope of wet hair swished across my back as I walked toward the gate that opened into Louisa's half of the yard. The townhouse was conspicuously missing the Christmas decorations her neighbors had started to put up, giving away her regular absence.

I didn't experience that nervous uncertainty about approaching the front door like last time. I'd never thought about it before, but my tumultuous life had given me some sort of a sixth sense about danger on occasion, and right now, no alarm bells were ringing in my head that something nefarious waited for me inside.

Still, I took quiet steps up the stairs and across the porch to the door and knocked. I waited a few minutes and knocked again. There were no sounds of movement inside, even of someone avoiding visitors. Though I'd figured it would be a long shot, I deflated in disappointment.

Not ready to give up, I scooted to the side to look in the front window. The curtains weren't as tightly shut as they had been the last time I was here, and a tingle of excitement went through me. I could see into the living room, and my eyes traced over the small space, trying to recall how it had looked before. Sparse. Tidy. Very little out of place.

I froze when I saw it. A mug was perched on the corner of the desk across the room from the window. That hadn't been there before. I remembered seeing the neat stacks of papers on the desk but nothing else.

That must have meant she'd been back. But how recently?

I squinted to see if I could make out any steam coming from a hot drink—tea or coffee—to give me a hint, but I couldn't tell from this distance.

And then a shadow shifted and a slender hand took the mug from the desk, making my stomach lurch. Someone was there, and that feminine hand gave me a glimmer of hope that it was her.

I moved back toward the door but felt the prickle of awareness along my skin and froze. It was more than a sense of being watched, and I shut my eyes for a split second, wishing this wasn't what I knew it probably would be.

Listen to your instincts.

The warning words tickled my mind, and I opened my eyes so I could turn and survey the neighborhood. It didn't take long to figure out what had alerted my senses. He wasn't even bothering to be sneaky, his hardened expression zeroed in on me.

Edwards jogged across the street with an intensity he hadn't possessed the last time I'd seen him, and I knocked on Louisa's door again, this time with more urgency. I didn't have enough time to run, so getting inside was the next best thing.

There was a muted thud from inside the house. Then:

"Mother—"

"Louisa?" I called, panic snapping up my spine as Edwards made it to the sidewalk. Now we were both in danger, considering she had been the original target before they'd known of my existence. "Please!"

I pounded at the door, not caring how much noise I was making or how I might draw attention to myself. Which was probably why I didn't pick up on it at first. It wasn't until the pressure built on the air, and the ringing started in my ears that it registered.

"Crap!"

I spun to sprint down the stairs, vaguely aware that Edwards was still headed my way, his eyes going round as he picked up speed. I knew the force was too strong for me to outrun, but would he get pulled with us? It rippled like a wave in water against my back, pulling like some unseen hand yanking me back. Bulbs burst behind me, the porch light throwing the shards like glitter onto the top of my head, and my eardrums threatened to pop under the pressure.

I tried to take comfort in the way that Edwards faded out as the world shimmied, then blinked out when my consciousness dipped into darkness.

* * *

Awareness came slowly, every sense buried deep underwater. It felt like I was swimming slowly to the surface against a current threatening to pull me back down.

"Is she awake?" The words broke through to me, muffled and heavy with suspicion.

My mind registered that he was outside of the room, but even half-conscious, my body reacted to that voice.

Wait, I hadn't been in a room when I'd made the jump. My sluggish mind tried to work through the possibilities. Had I lost time again? Or had I jumped directly somewhere?

The fear sent a wave of sharpness with the adrenaline, and my eyes shot open the same moment Drew walked through the door. He froze, staring at me with widened eyes, his mouth falling open a fraction.

His shock confused me. But so did the room I was in. This wasn't his house. White-washed walls, wires and equipment hanging all over, that overly sanitized smell that burned my nose. It was a hospital room.

"Cassidy?" He tripped over my name, still not moving.

My gaze shifted back to him, and I realized something else was off. He looked different. Haggard. Dark circles under his eyes, a hollowness to his cheeks. His hair was longer and disheveled, the usual five o'clock shadow was fuller and unkempt—an actual beard. He looked like he'd spent the last month in a dark cave and had only recently emerged into daylight.

"What is going on?" I lurched into a sitting position before thinking better of it. My head throbbed in protest, and I let out a moan without meaning to.

My hand shot up to press against my skull as if to hold my brain inside. I winced, taking stock of the rest of my body. No additional pain. My usual faded muscle soreness in my thigh from the healing stab wound was ever-present but negligible. The wrist rarely bothered me anymore, which was why I was supposed to be getting the cast off.

"Cassidy?" Drew said again, moving slowly into the room

like a hunter sneaking up on a deer in the woods.

I squinted at him, taking in his cautious movements, the burgeoning hope igniting in his eyes. I couldn't puzzle it out with the pain stabbing into my cranium.

"Drew?" I tried to match his tone, but the headache and my frustration gave my voice a sarcastic edge.

"Oh my God." He collapsed into the chair next to my bed, his hands clutching at the blankets. He looked like he was about to cry as moisture gathered in his eyes, a wondering smile pulling at his mouth.

All of which made the panic flare through me like wildfire, and I grabbed his hand. "What's going on? How long have I been out?"

His brows knit in confusion, and he shook his head. "I think they found you earlier this afternoon. When they checked your ID and found the death certificate, they called the station."

Death certificate? Ice water flooded my veins. Somewhere behind me, a machine registered a spike in my heart rate.

"They put them through to me directly because of. . . Well. . . I didn't think it could really be you, but I had hoped. . ." He shut his eyes, running a hand over the scruffy beard on his face, and blew out a tremulous breath.

The disheveled mountain man look was appealing, but it was another puzzle piece in the realization that hovered on the edge of my comprehension. My mind stuttered and stumbled as I struggled to grasp what he was telling me, to knit the fragments together to form a full picture.

"I need to call Skylar," he muttered.

"Skylar?" I yanked my hand from his grasp, and it finally slid home. Death certificate. Hospital room. Pounding headache. My last memory being pulled through dimensions again.

And him. . . I had felt no simmering charge of electricity at his touch, the grief that hung palpably, compounded and more violently taking its toll than the last time. This wasn't *my* Drew.

Was I back in that original timeline?

3

Complications Compounded

"I'm fine," I insisted. "Can you please clear me to go now?"

The doctor flashed a light in both of my eyes, checking my pupillary reaction. "By all my estimations, you do *seem* to be fine. No concussions or unusual brain activity, signs of tumors, or other abnormalities. But the fact remains that you were found unconscious and unresponsive on someone's front porch."

He clicked the light off and tucked it into his pocket, his frown carving canyons into his weathered face. "You've clearly been through a lot recently. Healing leg wound and the wrist fracture. That looks like it should come off soon." He touched the red cast lightly with his forefinger. "Not to mention you're carrying the ID of a deceased woman." The suspicion tightened his eyes, and he shifted his focus to Drew who stood on the far side of the room, arms folded over his chest.

He gave away very little in his expression, and the tension in his body was unmistakable. But his demeanor fit the bill of tough-guy cop that I hoped would play in my favor.

I gestured in his direction. "Then release me into Detective

Seward's custody and let him figure it out." I turned in Drew's direction, begging with my eyes for him to back me up and get me out of there.

Thank God he took the hint and lurched into action. "Yeah, Doc, if she's clear on your end, I can take it from here."

The doctor's mouth pinched. "I'll make sure they get the paperwork ready." He sighed. He wasn't happy, but there wasn't much else he could do.

I knew I was fine. Or fine enough.

Too much of this was a reminder of my experience only a couple of months prior. A low, simmering anxiety buzzed through me as I thought about the reason for it. My mind didn't want to go there—to the aftermath of my brush with Creedy.

The doctor walked out of the room, the irritation pulling his shoulders taut.

His frustration wasn't my concern. Getting out of here was. And, more importantly, getting home. I had planned to rest for a while. Being in this hospital room was more proof that I had been jumping too often.

"Where are my clothes?" I muttered, looking around.

Drew moved toward the door. "I'll go find out."

My eyes followed him out of the room. I hadn't said anything, but the way I'd pulled my hand out of his grasp right before the doctor came in must have alerted him that something was off.

And it was causing him pain.

I rubbed at my rib cage, getting another dose of guilt squeezing in my heart. I was going to hurt him, there was no doubt. We'd selfishly given in to the desire and attraction we'd felt for each other, and he was still there mentally and emotionally.

Worse, he'd been mourning that other version of me, and now the loss of me-me. And here I was, back and half in love with another version of him.

I flinched, that thought solidifying in my mind with frightening clarity. I hadn't admitted that much to myself before this moment, though I'd vaguely acknowledged it more than once.

I put my hand to my forehead where my headache had settled from stabbing agony into a dull throb. Everything was about to get more complicated again. My timeline had seemed to simplify for a bit. No alternate versions of people whose existence wounded me or turned me into a weapon as a defense mechanism. Though I still needed to keep my eyes peeled for those out to get me, all that remained was my investigation into the professor and Louisa Lee.

I jolted at the reminder. Louisa Lee.

It had to have been her inside the house. It was definitely a woman's hand I'd seen, and the half-spoken expletive had been a woman's voice. It wasn't likely anyone else would be using one of her mugs. So she'd pulled me here. Which meant she was probably in this timeline too.

But it was also possible that Edwards made the jump as well. I wasn't sure how any of that worked, given that Edwards was out to get me, and I was still alive and unharmed. So maybe he hadn't come with us. Did that mean he *couldn't* follow wherever we went?

I rubbed at my temples.

Either way, I couldn't just leave and miss the opportunity I had to find Louisa. She ran from me earlier, meaning she was probably as spooked as I was about being chased down by Edwards or anyone else who worked with him. If I could prove to her that I was on her side, maybe we could join forces. It might offer us both a fighting chance. And the opportunity for my answers.

"I got your clothes. And the paperwork. Flashing a badge lights a fire under the sloth-like administrative side of hospitals."

I flinched at Drew's words. Even his voice sounded ragged despite the jocular tone, and guilt stabbed into me again. The last few months since I'd been unexpectedly pulled back to my world had not been kind to him.

"I appreciate it," I murmured.

It was like my presence compressed him because he seemed to shrink as it all came crashing back. He must have felt it, the barrier between us, though he wouldn't know why it was there.

And yet I still felt a pull that I had to fight. Not quite the anchor I had in my version of him. But a compulsion to move closer all the same. In some twisted way, I was grateful for this grieving version because of how different it made him look and sound. It kept me from forgetting who he wasn't.

I took the bag that held my clothes from him and hurried into the bathroom, holding the hospital gown closed at my back. I made quick work of swapping, irritated that I even needed to do it in the first place.

Someone *had* to find me unconscious. Why couldn't I wake up where I'd lost consciousness? Or, better yet, jump and stay alert like the last several times?

Except. . . I hadn't remembered coming back from the last jump. How had I gotten home and into bed? Things were already spinning off-kilter there. Sleeping for eighteen hours definitely wasn't normal.

But what part of *any* of this was normal?

It made me want to scream. Instead, I pulled my boots on and checked my hair—in decent shape, given the circumstances. My face was pale, as it had been this morning, but I was less hollow-looking. Not as much a stranger to look at.

Drew was standing by the window, staring into nothingness when I came out. An ache spider-webbed through my chest at the sight. I moved carefully back toward the bed as if I were treading on ice.

He finally came away from the window, saying nothing as I went over the paperwork and handed it to the nurse who came in a few minutes later.

I made a mental note for the next time I was in this situation to have him on hand to get the process rolling so much faster. But then I mentally crossed myself, warding off the possibility of ending up in a hospital again. If I could skip another stay for the rest of my life, I would die happy—hopefully old and in my own timeline.

The silence continued as we walked to the elevators and rode down to the main lobby. The weight of it grew heavier and heavier, almost painful, and my grimace became more entrenched—enough that I noticed myself making the face in the distorted surface of the elevator doors.

I grappled for something to say to ease the rigid tension. He'd mentioned Skylar, and I clung to my need to know as a lifeline. "How is Skylar?"

He looked down at his feet. "She's been better."

I couldn't help feeling like the answer encompassed more than her well-being.

"Her grandma passed away."

I'd forgotten all about her grandmother's stroke and hospital stay. It seemed like a million years ago. I'd had so much more on my mind since going back to my timeline, so I tried not to let the guilt for this take root.

Still, my heart clutched. "Oh, no." Heartache wherever I went—my fault or not.

We walked through the lobby, and it was disorienting to find that it was nighttime when we approached the front doors.

Right. Because I'd woken up in Drew's room during his lunch break. But how many hours had I lost? At least four, based on how dark it was.

Enough to feel like my stomach was going to start eating me from the inside. Cocoa Puffs hadn't made a lasting impression on my digestive system. I hadn't noticed how famished I was until now, when my mind had shifted from confusion to re-calibrating my expectations.

As we headed out into the night, I was thrown again when I spotted the snow on the ground. I'd left sunshine and warmth in my timeline, and this snow had been here for at least a day—half-melted, but here all the same. A different timeline could mean different weather. Of course. But it was hard to reconcile, and it magnified my disorientation.

And everything was made more jarring by the man walking beside me. His uncertainty and questions buzzed through him so that I felt the vibration, and my mind and my body warred with what they were supposed to do.

"Drew." I touched his arm before thinking better of it.

He recoiled as if I'd burned him, and I snatched my hand back. I didn't know what I wanted to say, how to alleviate the pain, what answers to give. I didn't know where to start with any of it.

His eyes flashed to me. "After we arrested Creedy, and I got back, Skylar was hysterical, saying how you just *disappeared*."

Both hands raked through his hair, and I was reminded of that first day I'd woken up in this timeline, how off-balance he'd been because of my presence. Except this was exponentially worse.

He stopped in front of his car and turned to me, a determination sharpening his features. After only a brief hesitation, one toke of oxygen, he slid his hand across my cheek. And I let him for the moment because I saw how the touch comforted him.

"I'm so sorry," I murmured. "I had no control. I mean. . . I still don't even know how it happened."

His eyes searched mine. I couldn't tell if it was that he didn't believe me or if he was waiting for permission to do something—because he still didn't know, didn't understand. Maybe he even hoped it had merely been the confusion that made me pull away earlier.

He brought his other hand up so he was cradling my face. "Please tell me you're real."

I was frozen, rooted by the whispered words, the desperation laced through each syllable.

He brought his face closer, and I realized he was going to kiss me.

"Drew," I warned, breathless. "Don't."

He stopped, his brows knitting low over his dark eyes, and there was agony in their depths.

I sucked in a breath. "I—we can't."

Even though my mind knew he wasn't my Drew, my body didn't fully comprehend the difference. After all, those hands, strong and warm, felt like the ones that belonged to me, the ones that had already memorized the curves of my body. Having to look up at exactly that angle, the way his coffee-colored eyes bored into mine with that intensity and depth—it was all too familiar. Had it only been a couple of months since I'd pivoted my life to include him?

The time stretched before my words seemed to land, and he jerked back, his hands leaving my face. "I-I'm sorry."

I shook my head to deny his apology as he backed away. It wasn't his fault, and I wanted to say so, but I was incapable of speaking. He turned abruptly to go around to the other side of the car, and I released the breath that had been trapped for too long in my lungs.

I opened the passenger side door and climbed in. In the time it took after my rejection, Drew's wounded expression had turned into his Cop Face, though it wasn't as impenetrable as it usually was. He really was struggling.

"Tell me what happened after you left here," he said. "Did you go back to your universe?"

Down to business. It stung, but it was for the best. I needed that sting to keep it clear in my head. It didn't matter that Drew was Drew. He wasn't *my* Drew.

"Yes. I woke up back in the jail cell. Like nothing had happened." I shook my head. "I sent Keener to go find. . . other you."

I shuddered thinking about what would come next. Maybe I could skip it for now. I hadn't prepared myself to talk about it, hadn't built up the walls of protection. So I brought it back to him. He'd said they'd gotten to Creedy before I'd disappeared.

I turned in my seat and forced my hands to stay in my lap instead of gripping his arm in desperation. "Drew. Please tell me you got to Creedy before he hurt that girl."

He rubbed a hand down his face, and my stomach twisted. "She survived."

Those two words. They were not spoken with the relief I was

hoping for. "Oh, God. How bad?"

He grimaced and shook his head. "I can't." He ran his hand over his chin this time. "Maybe later."

Had Creedy been punishing her because of me? I knew from my experience with him that he'd had a special fixation on me. Here, he'd taken one version of me out, but then I'd arrived, another iteration appearing as if to haunt him. If he was as obsessed with me as he seemed to be in my timeline, he was in a more tortured and frustrated mindset, and that poor girl probably suffered for it.

If it was equal to what I'd been through, it was too much. Especially for someone so young. No one should ever suffer that kind of cruelty.

I settled back in my seat and looked out the window. "Where are we going?"

"Skylar's."

I glanced at him again.

"She would want to see you. I don't know about anyone else." He swallowed hard. "Not if it's going to be. . ."

I knew how he wanted to finish it. Silently, he added *like this*. Because it was already torture for him. I certainly wasn't eager to see anyone else. I'd said my piece to my father, and after my recent experience, I needed some space. And I would be happy to never see this Evan as long as I lived. The Evan in my world was plenty.

But I hadn't replaced Skylar in my timeline. That was essentially what I'd done with Drew, wasn't it?

If this opportunity to get to Louisa and Thibald wasn't successful, I would be making my jump home before I did any major damage. I wouldn't be able to take what this would do to us all.

4

Skylar's the Limit

Skylar hadn't answered Drew's calls or texts on our drive over, so she opened the door with an irritated and exhausted expression when we knocked. Dark circles under the eyes, a haggard appearance like Drew drove home how sucky things had been for them both. She even seemed thinner.

When she registered who stood in front of her, she released a sob so heavy with grief it dropped her to her knees. My heart broke to hear it, and it lashed tears into my own eyes.

How could I allow this to happen? To wound them so deeply yet again made me feel like a monster. What if they never recovered?

Drew ushered me in so we could shut the door before neighbors started getting curious.

I took Skylar's hands to help her to her feet and led her to the couch while she clung to me like a lifeline. I blinked back my tears as she cried. After a few minutes, while Drew stood as far from us as possible, his jaw working, she had calmed enough to speak.

"How?" She sniffled. "How are you back? What happened?

Where did you go?"

I smiled a little, not knowing exactly where to start. "A lot has happened in the last few weeks. I'm still figuring some of it out."

Skylar looked at Drew, whose face was too guarded to know what he was thinking. His arms were folded across his chest again like he was prepared for an attack. After getting a bit blindsided when he'd come into the hospital room earlier, I didn't blame him for wanting to keep it from happening again.

I hoped he wasn't turning to stone like Evan had started to. Like my father had in my world. Walking away from the pain and anything that reminded them of it was all they could do. The possibility that it could happen to him, that he would let it happen, made all of it almost unbearable.

"What happened to you?" Skylar asked when no one said anything else. Her eyes were on the cast on my wrist. "You were limping too."

I wet my lips with my tongue. It was better that I would get to tell them now, together. I'd started to prepare myself, knew I would have to walk them through it all. At least this way I wouldn't have to talk about it more than once.

I rolled my shoulders back to steel myself. "Creedy was ready for me when I got back home. Took me right out of the jail. To his. . . torture chamber."

Both of Skylar's hands flew up to cover her mouth, and her big eyes swam again with tears that magnified her horror. Drew's guarded expression broke then. The unmitigated rage made a flush creep up his neck and his hands became claws against his biceps.

I couldn't look at either of them anymore. "He stabbed me in the leg. I broke my wrist in my struggle to escape. But I did escape. And he was caught before he could hurt anyone else." There was a measure of pride there, but it died quickly. I hadn't been able to spare the girl here that pain.

"Oh, Cass," Skylar breathed, grabbing my hands. "I can't even imagine."

I shook my head, trying to dislodge the lingering feelings about it. "I don't know yet what pulled me back to my world. But I've started to get answers about other things. It's why I'm here."

"How *did* you get here?"

The question was Skylar's, but my eyes were drawn to Drew, who still hadn't moved. "The professor."

Drew had the slightest reaction to that, a coiling of muscle in his shoulders, but he still didn't open his mouth. The beginnings of irritation started within me.

"The professor?" Skylar repeated.

I turned to her, trying to ignore my frustration. "He was murdered in my world. The day I was transported here the first time."

Skylar finally took her eyes off me to exchange a look with Drew. "That doesn't seem coincidental."

"It definitely wasn't. Drew—uh, the other Drew—said he was shot executioner style."

Skylar didn't hide her confusion as it wrinkled her brow.

"Point-blank," Drew put in, finally moving a little closer. "A pro?"

I shrugged. "Still figuring that out. But he has a niece. And when I went to talk to her, two men were searching her house. And they were talking about jumping to alternate universes."

Skylar's confusion gave way to a flare of excitement.

"It's not good news," I put in quickly. "There is someone

who's messing with timelines and looking for those of us who don't belong. Those guys chased me, pulled me to another timeline with the intention, I think, to kill me. But I made it out. With this." I lifted the necklace from under the collar of my shirt.

Skylar leaned in to inspect it, and Drew came closer still.

"I've been able to use it to jump when *I* want to." I grimaced, amending silently that it was *mostly* when I wanted to. Today was obviously an exception.

"Can you control where you go?" Drew asked.

The tension he held hinted at what was underneath the question—it was more than the desire to understand how it worked. It was like he wanted to know why I hadn't come back sooner if I could control where I went.

I shook my head as if his true question was spoken aloud. "Only when I jump home. I don't really know how it works or why I end up going where I do." *I didn't abandon you*, I wanted to add, but the words remained trapped. Because he hadn't asked, I wouldn't answer.

"How can you control jumping home but not the other jumps? That's weird." Skylar seemed to be musing more to herself than actually asking me, but Drew watched me with an intensity that was one of his universal traits. He wanted that answer.

I didn't want to get into the other Drew stuff now, not in front of Skylar. The last thing I wanted was to hurt him with an audience. So I went for vague.

"When I was with the two men, they mentioned something about an anchor. I think I'm tethered to the reality I belong to." Okay, it wasn't a total lie.

He lifted his chin a fraction as if he were acknowledging the slight fudge in my answer.

Skylar sat back against the couch, her eyes going to the ceiling while she processed. "Well, I guess that makes sense. But who knew there would be rules for this kind of thing?"

Drew gave a mirthless snort.

"Today, though," I continued, ignoring him, "I got dragged through with the professor's niece. I went to see if I could talk to her, and she panicked and made a jump. She probably doesn't realize she can pull people through. I'm pretty sure she was the one who pulled me the first time."

"What makes you think that?" Drew asked.

I lifted a shoulder. "It's a theory, but it seems the most likely. She was at the police station the night I was there. And the two men confirmed that she'd made her first jump there."

He scraped his bottom lip with his teeth, considering.

Skylar lifted her head. "So she's here too. Do you think she's trying to find the professor here?"

I shrugged. It was such a casual movement, but I felt so far from it that my empty stomach was churning toward nausea. "I don't know if she can control it any more than I can. That's where I've hit a wall. But I still need to take the opportunity to find her. At least we have some common ground. Maybe find Professor Thibald, see if he has more answers now."

I looked at Drew, and he pulled back, guarded again.

I tried not to let that discourage me. "He disappeared on us before. And I didn't ask then. But you can find out where he lives. We could go see him, and maybe he could connect me with his niece. Maybe he even knows more now."

Drew made a face. Because, of course, the rules. He had no reason to investigate Thibald, and it wasn't exactly ethical for him to look him up for us and pass out that information.

"Drew, beyond my own selfish reasons, I genuinely think the professor might be in danger." I scooted to the edge of my seat, allowing my intensity to bleed through. "The men who chased me, who took me to another reality to *kill me*, were looking for something. I saw them in the professor's office illegally, then looking for his niece. I think they might be the ones who took the professor out in my universe. They could very well be planning to do that here, too. We could be saving his life."

He narrowed his eyes. "And we could be breaching his privacy for no real reason. He didn't have much to offer the first time. What makes you think that's changed?"

Frustration flashed through me, and I stood up, balling my hands into fists. "Even if he doesn't have answers for me, he is the connection point with his niece. I need to talk to her, and we should at least warn him that he could be in danger. Louisa might not even know *she's* in danger."

I didn't realize how loud or intense I had gotten until I felt Skylar's fingers wrap around my wrist to calm me down. It was a good reminder that this Drew was the one who'd pushed back all the time. I gritted my teeth and turned away, breaking Skylar's hold on my hand.

"Drew," she said. "Please consider it. I know you always like to do things by the book. But this is more important than breaking a little rule."

Out of the corner of my eye, I took in her earnest expression, a warmth spreading in my core that she was on my side. Like a true friend, something I hadn't had in so long. There had been some potential with Molly, but with so much tied to the background of that relationship, I'd never been able to let my guard down.

It made me want to connect with the Skylar in my timeline. Would she be as open to this whole craziness? Even if she wasn't, with my plans of permanence there, it was an opportunity to lay more roots.

I turned to see if her words had struck a chord with Drew at all. She had always been the one who could bridge the gap between everyone, the peacemaker who could soothe the conflict. I'd forgotten in the time I'd been away.

Drew's steely expression held for a long moment. Then he broke, rubbing both hands up and down his worn face, and my frustration melted away. I finally saw him for the mess he was, the mess I'd seen when he first walked into my hospital room.

The last few weeks had been absolute hell, and I wondered if he'd been taking care of himself at all. One blow after another and, with the case against Creedy—I had no idea how that was going here—he was probably at the end of his rope. He wasn't ready to get into details about the teen girl Creedy had taken, so it must have been bad.

"I would appreciate your help on this. But. . ." I bared my teeth for a moment, making sure I truly meant what I was about to say. "I understand if you have to say no."

He blew out a breath, looking heavenward. "I can't make a decision right now."

I softened a little more. He looked like he would break if even one more thing was laid on him. "Okay," I said softly. "Sleep on it then."

"Are you staying here?" Skylar asked, not bothering to hide how eager she was for my answer to be yes.

I gave a soft laugh. "I take it you don't mind."

"Hell no. It will be the couch, as usual," she warned.

I shrugged. "You know I've had worse."

"I'll let you ladies catch up," Drew muttered, moving toward the door. His voice was so defeated.

I swallowed. "Wait." The word dropped into the air, soft but insistent.

He stopped with his hand on the knob, but he didn't turn, his shoulders scrunching.

Skylar got to her feet. "I'll get you some blankets and stuff."

I didn't watch her go, but I knew she would take her time to be sure we had a moment. Being understood so implicitly made my heart ache for what they had lost. For what I'd never had.

Earlier, the barrier between Drew and me had been there. Knowing that anything between us had to be pushed down for the sake of the man who waited for me at home. But, right now, I needed to care for this Drew. Because he did still matter to me. He had opened that door, and I wouldn't have a home if it weren't for him.

He still didn't turn as I approached, but he was breathing hard with the weight of emotion.

"Who is he?" he asked, pushing the words through his teeth.

I flinched, and it was an agonizing slice through my chest to hear it in his voice.

He knew. Of course he did. I wished I didn't have to hurt him this way. But wouldn't this hurt less? To know I hadn't moved on completely, not really? He thought he hadn't mattered at all, but it couldn't be further from the truth.

"You."

He turned his head just enough to look out of the corner of his eye, his jaw working. His expression didn't soften, and the pain raked at my heart.

"I know that sucks," I started. "I don't want to hurt you,

and you did mean something to me. You still do. More than you know. But I don't belong here. I never did. We never could have. . ."

He shook his head and laughed without humor. "I know. Never could, now never will. I get it."

I sucked in a breath, the pain of it burning my throat with bitter regret. I touched his arm. "Drew." His name came out choked because seeing him in pain would always hurt me, too. Any version, anywhere.

He turned suddenly and pulled me into his arms, and I hugged him back, tucking in perfectly like I always did, always would. It was not a lover's embrace, though. Not quite. It was comfort he needed, and I was willing to give it to him, even as he held me tighter, burying himself against me.

I pulled back after a moment, though he didn't release me, nor would he look at me. I put my hands on either side of his face to make him meet my eyes. His beard tickled my palms.

"It really is better this way."

He tried to look away, but I didn't let him.

"It doesn't feel like it. And I know you don't want to hear it."

He scoffed, a pained, twisted sound. "Yeah, it hits differently knowing you have what you want, and I don't."

I gave him a sad smile. "You could tell me to go to hell. It would only be fair."

He didn't smile back. Because the moment I'd said that to him hadn't exactly been sunshine and rainbows. And that memory would undoubtedly lead to others.

God, it felt like a lifetime had passed since I'd been here, dealing with the first anomalous family, grappling with the emotional whiplash that came with seeing my father for the first time in twenty years.

I brushed a wayward lock of his hair back from his face. Apparently when it was this long, it started to curl. "I am so, so sorry."

He took a deep breath. And because I knew him so well, I could tell he was working to slam some protections into place. He released me and went for the door.

I dug a thumb into my ribs and sucked back a sob as he disappeared into the night.

5

My Dead Best Friend

I stared at the closed door for a long time, my chest aching from the effort of holding my emotion in. This felt like it was meant to be a fractured reality, one in which everyone suffered. Even I suffered when I was here.

"It's been bad," Skylar said from behind me.

I flinched but didn't turn right away. "I can tell. He was barely holding himself together before, wasn't he?"

I turned then. She stood next to the couch, a blanket and pillow in her arms, dwarfing her. She plopped them onto the arm of the couch, her lip trembling a little.

She gave a tremulous sigh. "I didn't even realize it. When you disappeared, he broke. Worse than any of us, I think. Because. . . he thought you were his." She tried not to look at me. Maybe because she didn't want to show that she kind of blamed me.

Hell, I blamed myself. I took a shaky breath and pressed my fingers to my eyes until fireworks exploded against my eyelids.

I told him back then. Tried to fight him and myself. But that pull had been strong, my desires getting me into trouble again. And now he was paying for my selfishness and lack of self-control.

"I hate this," I murmured, moving toward the couch.

"Me too." Skylar sat next to me. "But this is also good. It's good that you're back, that we can see you're all right." She gripped my hand to drive her point home. "I think that's what we worried about most. At first, we thought maybe Creedy had gotten to you somehow."

I felt her residual fear through her hand on mine. Or maybe it was her worry mirrored in myself as I wondered about my family, my sister, even their version of me. Were they all in danger? I had no way of knowing whether they'd all made it back. Considering the focus on Louisa and the professor and myself, my worry wasn't unfounded.

"It didn't make sense, though."

Her voice brought me back to the conversation.

"You had been in the station with officers who knew Creedy's face, knew he was the suspect." She looked at me. "We watched security footage. You were there, then you were just. . . gone."

I remembered watching the video of my first jump, knowing what they would have seen. Like some bad editing job on a cheap film. "I'm sorry you went through that. I don't even know how or why it happened. That's why I'm looking for the professor and his niece. They've gotta know a little bit more than I do."

It was a desperate hope that Louisa might know something, even if it was only a small piece of the puzzle. She had to since her uncle—the man who'd raised her—was the one who'd been killed because of what he knew. Maybe the version of Thibald here knew more than he realized when we'd first talked to him too. If Louisa had found him, I'd bet he did now.

I prayed Drew's reluctance was the only wall in the way of what had become the most crucial step in the process of finding answers. But I wasn't holding my breath. Which meant I'd have to find another way.

Skylar watched the anxiety morph my face. "I'm sure Drew will come around. He just needs a little time. He's barely begun to pick up the pieces to even try to put himself back together." She paused, seeming to debate about what she said next. "He's been on a leave from work. Not voluntary."

I pressed my lips together. In all honesty, he probably should have been on one before. He hadn't taken much of a break after the other Cassidy's death. The grief was so evident in his face that first day I'd seen him. But he wouldn't take the time, of course. Not with the killer still at large. He probably would have broken eventually even if I hadn't been here.

But this felt worse because I'd brought another element of grief with my presence. Everything inside me twisted and churned and felt toxic. It was a reminder that I was often the poison that ruined things, making me want to shrink, erase the fact that I'd ever been here. It didn't matter that it had healed some parts of me if I was hurting the others around me.

I pressed my palms against my face. "God, this is all my fault." The words were half-muffled behind my hands.

"Don't do that," Skylar said.

I looked at her, shocked, having forgotten for a moment that she was there.

"Don't blame yourself. It wasn't your fault you got dragged here."

"No. But I let this happen. Even after I told him it couldn't work, that I had to leave. I didn't know that I'd go home, but I knew I couldn't stay. And I let him kiss me anyway."

"Excuse me," she interrupted with a hand in the air. "Did you say you forced him to kiss you?"

I blinked. "No. I said—"

"Exactly." She held my eyes for a long time. Long enough that the intensity made me uncomfortable. "Drew is a grown man. He's broken and hurting. But he can heal, if he lets himself. He would have needed to whether you'd been here or not."

The truth of her words rang in my head. But head knowledge didn't translate to heart knowledge easily. It was like going from English to Japanese. There was no word-for-word equivalent, no quick changeover.

Skylar pulled me in for a hug. She could probably tell I was about to cry. "I'm still glad to see you. It's been a shitty few weeks."

I hugged her back. And for the second time, I thought about looking her up back home.

Home.

That word sang through my blood and bones.

She pulled back and searched my face. "You want something to eat? I have some leftover Chinese in the fridge."

I nodded absently, my mind elsewhere, though I knew I desperately needed to eat something.

I'd accidentally left, had had no way to warn *my* Drew that I was going anywhere. Had he arrived at his house to find my dirty bowl in the sink and the house empty, wondering where I was? Would he panic?

I always told him if I was making a jump, always promised to come back. Since finding the necklace, I'd been in control of when I went. It didn't occur to me that morning that I'd be sliding realities, and I'd had no way to prepare.

The pull was there in my middle, a constant, gentle tug even now, assuring me that I'd make it back. But Drew wouldn't know.

He might jump to the conclusion that Callum had found me and start a manhunt. We already knew Callum had missed his last check-ins with his parole officer, so there was some coordination happening between their two departments.

We'd seen no sign of him, but that didn't mean he was gone. I doubted he'd given up. Not when he'd made the effort of traveling all the way to where I was. So it was a logical assumption for Drew to make. If only there was some way to warn him. If I'd only known, I could have at least left a note.

I nibbled the inside of my cheek, wishing there was some kind of inter-dimensional communication system. It sounded stupid, but not any more than sliding dimensions did. If someone figured out how to make *that* happen, they should have figured out a way to communicate between planes.

Skylar came back with two plates, setting them on the table for us.

I got up and moved in that direction, shaking my head at the ridiculous thought.

"You look tired," she said, watching my face.

I snorted, giving her a wry smile. "Thanks."

She flushed a little. "I mean, you look good, too. Different. More peaceful." The words tumbled out in quick succession. "But you also look kind of run down. You said you've been making jumps?"

I nodded, sighing as I dug into the food. At least this would be more sustaining than children's cereal. "Yeah. In the process of trying to get a lead on someone who can answer my friggin' questions about it all." I rubbed a spot above my eyebrow where the headache still throbbed. "I thought the professor or Louisa would be the ones, but I haven't been able to find them."

"I can't imagine it's good for you, doing that many jumps. Are you taking breaks in between?"

I looked at her, shocked she would make the connection so quickly.

She lifted a shoulder, but she held my gaze. "I saw the video—the way every light bulb in the room burst. The kind of pressure that can do that is the same pressure being exerted on your body." The depth of her concern was obvious then as she leaned forward.

"Jeez. How crappy do I look?" I asked, trying to downplay it even as my mind began whirling down a hypochondriac rabbit hole. Aneurysms, heart attacks, strokes, internal bleeding. . .

DeMarco and Edwards had said that Louisa Lee didn't know what she was doing. And neither did I. Maybe there was some sort of protocol, some standard resting period between jumps we were ignorant of. Drew had even been worried about it, had voiced that concern more than once.

"Not crappy," she amended. "Exhausted."

I swallowed, bringing my attention back to her. "I'm fine. There are a lot of things on my plate right now is all."

"Besides feeling guilty, what else?"

I blew out a breath, looking heavenward. "My ex-boyfriend stalking me. Preparing to testify in court against Creedy. My Drew says—"

She held up a hand. "*Your* Drew?"

Heat crept into my cheeks, and I lifted tense shoulders. "I meant the one from my universe."

She gave me a knowing smirk, a sly look in her eyes. "No,

you didn't."

I stared at her. I had the absurd flashback to when Molly tried to get me to dish on that first kiss I'd shared with *my* Drew. But it was easier to ward her off. She'd had that weird little sister reverence for me. Not to mention that I'd had some more pressing information to share. But Skylar was practically my best friend. Or the closest thing to it.

I grimaced. "Now you know why Drew was being extra Clint Eastwoody this evening."

She put her palms flat on the table. "Shut up. For real?"

I almost laughed at her reaction. But I was too embarrassed about having this conversation. Like some high schooler with her first boyfriend.

"I know it's only been a couple of months," I started, looking down briefly. "But I pretty much live with him. The whole back story is pretty complicated, and that would *not* have happened if not for the insane circumstances."

She squinted at me, no doubt picking up on my defensive tone.

"Okay, rewind," she said, twirling her finger around in the air. "We need to start at the beginning. Tell me everything."

6

Extant

That was the clincher. I was going to look up Skylar when I got home. Maybe after all this mess was over, so I wouldn't have to try to explain and convince someone new about the whole reality jumping thing and all of the complications that came along with it. Since I was still making a jump every few days to a week—accidentally or not—it seemed like too much to dump on a new friend.

Plus, it sounded crazy, and that didn't bode well for a budding friendship.

But divulging every last detail of what happened to me after going back to my reality had been cathartic in a way I hadn't anticipated. Skylar listened, dumbfounded, as I recounted the moment my father and my dead mother had walked into my hospital room.

She'd even gotten misty-eyed when I told her about the strained relationship with my mother, and how badly that had sucked. How shocked I was to find that I missed Molly and the possibilities her presence had engendered.

Having someone like that in my corner permanently gave

me a sense of hope about the life I wanted to start in my own reality. For once, I saw myself wanting to go back to my life, to move forward in a new direction that had promise.

A little twinge of fear echoed in my heart briefly. What if the new Skylar wasn't like this one? I had experienced enough rejection in life to want to avoid it at any cost.

Drew was still teaching me that my expectation of abandonment wasn't always the truth of the situation, but I had no idea what this other Skylar would be like. She might not have the patience to hang on when things got tough. And by things, I meant me.

I stared at the ceiling in the dark, the sound of me picking my nails a soft *click-click* that permeated the silence until I forced myself to stop. I flexed my hands and turned over, smiling grimly at the light peeking through the missing slat from the blinds and all the memories associated with it.

All the times I'd planned to run and had been thwarted in some way, though I could admit in hindsight that I'd been a little too paralyzed by all the things happening around me. How often had I let myself sit back and not *do* anything about it all? I'd let myself become a victim of my circumstances more often than I should have.

I remembered that moment, waking from the depths of a nightmare, when I'd found Drew sitting in the chair in the darkness. How close we had come then to letting what was building crash over us. I knew now why stopping it had been the smartest move. If only I'd been wise enough to do that the second time. Maybe he wouldn't be hurting so badly.

No matter what Skylar said, I would always blame myself for how far I'd let it go. Because there was no way around the fact that I *had* been selfish. I was angry at the other Cassidy for having what I didn't, and I had to admit that some part of me wanted revenge for that, at least back then.

But what did that mean for a relationship with my Drew? That had nothing to do with her. I'd tried to chalk it up to the residual feelings—real enough, though misguided—from the Drew here. And then he had become something more, my mooring in the insanity of everything around me. I had no explanation for that. Not really.

I pressed a hand to my stomach where I felt that little tug, realizing I needed to make this impromptu separation worth it. Since I couldn't sleep, I sat up, throwing the blankets off of me.

The silence in the apartment was stifling, the darkness heavy with memory, but I forced my way down the hall to the extra bedroom that housed Skylar's desktop computer. The room held a bitter tang of nostalgia from my time debating about stealing from the murdered version of myself and everything that had led to that moment.

I hesitated just inside the door, tilting my head as I took in the empty desk chair. My mind conjured a faded image of when I'd driven myself half crazy looking at the life I'd never be able to have.

Turning away from the phantom in my memory, I shut the door softly and flipped the light switch in hopes that Skylar wouldn't notice. I had no idea how light of a sleeper she was.

I woke the computer up, glad that she never took the time to fully shut it down, and pulled up the internet browser.

I knew Professor Eli Thibald existed in my world and this one. But was there another Louisa Lee?

When we'd researched alternate realities last time, we'd only focused on experts. It had never occurred to us to look further than their expertise. Not that we'd needed to think about that, anyway. But it was an odd thing to approach now, thinking we'd only been one step removed before.

I typed in the professor's full name and scrolled down, bypassing the articles on parallel universes and the backlash he'd gotten from sharing his theories. It took a little digging to find anything more personal. The connection was loose enough that it took me a while to find it.

Two birds, one stone, luckily. It was an article linking him with his niece.

Louisa Lee had a career in the literary world which had taken off at a young age. She'd blown the critics away with her incisive wit and observations on society. Apparently.

In this timeline, her hair was cropped at her chin, and the picture showed her next to her uncle. The article mentioned the conspicuous absence of her father, a big tech magnate whose company was dabbling in experimental medical technology. He'd recently come under fire for some of his experiments injuring employees.

I studied the low-res picture on the screen, noting the shadow in Louisa's expression. In my timeline, she'd been raised by her uncle, hinting at the permanent absence of both parents. But she'd seemed healthy and even like she was thriving.

This picture and the article intimated that it was only her father and uncle in her life, so I assumed her mother was not around in this timeline as well, and I wondered about the reason.

Something about the stiffness in the way Louisa and her uncle were standing told me there was some tension between them. They stood close but weren't touching, and her smile was muted, no teeth. He, too, was rigid, smile tight and not reaching his eyes. The fact that Louisa's father was nowhere to be seen told me there might have been some strain in that relationship as well.

I clicked out of the article, curious about any other family information I could find. Pulling up Louisa and her father, David Lee, I eventually came across an article about her mother, Patricia Lee, née Thibald—so that was the connection there—and how she'd passed away from some rare illness. It had been the impetus for David's foray into experimental medicine.

His company, Warp Corp, had been both lauded and criticized for its innovations and experiments. But still, very little of this was helpful to me. Nothing about parallel universes, and even an article about Lee's company briefly mentioned a disdainful remark made by Lee about his brother-in-law's outlandish theories on dimension jumping.

There were some other articles about Thibald's recent issues with the college, which I'd almost forgotten about. His sudden firing and the scandal that ensued reminded me that it was still in question whether it was an unhappy coincidence or something to do with the parallel universe stuff and the fact that his life was in danger.

After my experience with the whole science fiction mess, I couldn't afford to overlook or dismiss any possibility. Nothing could be a coincidence at this point.

I pulled my bottom lip between my teeth and worked my way through more articles.

Outside of Louisa's more public social media pages in this reality, which only focused on her literary career, I found very little that would give me insight into either the professor or his niece or information I could use to find them—this reality's versions or mine.

I doubted I'd be able to directly contact Louisa via any of her available channels with how much recognition she'd been getting. At the very least, she probably screened her emails. And if she was as popular as she appeared to be, it was more likely that her emails were regulated by a personal assistant. Either way, she'd likely never get anything I sent. What would I say, anyway?

"Hey, my mom's dead too. We should talk."

Creepy and morbid.

"Hey, I am trying to find an alternate version of you. Seen her?"

Nonsense.

"Can you help me get in contact with your uncle?"

Less creepy, but it definitely wasn't a message I would have responded to in her position. It still fell distinctly under the *weird* category and would surely go ignored. Especially since they didn't appear particularly close here.

I placed my elbows on the desk and scrubbed at my face. If only I could guarantee that Drew would help us out. Skylar's assurance that he would come around didn't give me any sense of confidence, so I had to assume it would be a no-go and make other plans to cover my bases.

But I still had no idea where to start. Louisa likely didn't live in the same house as my reality. It didn't sound like she was teaching in this world, so I couldn't very well try to locate her near the school.

That would more than likely get me in trouble, if not arrested, anyway. Strange adults with no children lingering around a school were usually frowned upon.

I sat back and blew out a breath, willing all frustration and jitters to leave through the loud exhale. If only it worked that way.

Figuring I'd done as much as I could for now, I put the computer into sleep mode and headed back out to the lumpy couch in the living room, missing Drew's king-sized bed and the warmth of his body.

I put my hand against that tug in my core, feeling it more keenly, like that connection was being yanked on some invisible line.

Soon enough, I thought, hoping he wasn't too worried about where I'd gotten off to. There was always that little anxiety, always the thought of how little he approved of my adventures into the unknowable number of timeline splits.

We'd fought it once or twice. His admission that worry was eating at him made his testy behavior make sense. That was in those early days when I'd first started jumping. He was afraid there would be a day that I didn't come back, and he'd never know what had happened to me.

Though he'd never let it get to that point again, I could tell he still didn't like that I used the necklace to bend the laws of physics. The fact that he'd been so wound up, clamping so hard on the worry, still touched me in a way that gave me a tangling mix of excitement and fear because it meant that I mattered that much to him.

I'd pointed out how similar it was to him going in to work every day in a dangerous industry that never guaranteed his return home. I'd already been through him getting shot once, and I didn't care to relive it.

But he'd healed quickly, no worse for wear, and assured me that he spent more time behind a desk, following up on leads, piecing together facts, and making endless phone calls than chasing down bad guys. But still.

"*You would know what happened to me,*" he'd argued. "*You could die in an alternate reality, and I'd never know what took you away from me. Not the same thing.*"

I shut my eyes against the memory of that conversation and imagined his arms around me instead. He liked to fall asleep holding me against him, and that thought settled a little bit of peace over my stirring emotions. My mind started to drift toward unconsciousness, lulled by phantom comfort and the steady sound of warm air blowing through the vent.

And then the sensation of falling, the drop of my stomach as I became aware of the nothingness beneath me, sent a shattering jolt through me.

7

Fall Into You

I lurched upright in the darkness, heart hammering against my ribs as if it wanted to escape from its cage of bone. Movement—a man's shape against the inky shadows that filled the room—triggered a chain reaction of terror that clawed up from the pit of my stomach.

My hand shot to the bedside lamp and clicked it on, suffusing the room with dim light.

Drew froze in the act of taking off his shirt, only half the buttons undone, his startled gaze taking in the terror on my face.

"Sorry. I didn't mean to wake you up," he whispered.

My rapid breathing didn't slow as I registered his scruffy—*not bearded*—face. My mind wheeled when I took in the dresser behind him, noted the bathroom door in the corner that stood half open, and the familiar ticking of the clock on the wall drove home where I was. My hands clutched at the blankets over my lap of their own volition.

How did I get here? *When* did I get here?

"Cass?" he said when I didn't respond, worry lacing his tone.

I wanted to answer, but there was not enough oxygen to form the words. My breathing was still jerky, air shooting in and out of my lungs too quickly for me to catch a breath.

I shook my head and jammed my thumb into my sternum where the pain twisted like someone was tightening a screw into the bone.

He took slow steps toward me, his head cocked a fraction, one hand splayed in front of him.

"You're safe, Cassidy," he said, low and soothing. "Just breathe. No one is going to hurt you."

Oh, right.

I was having a panic attack. That's why my head was spinning, my fingers were tingling, and my vision was going spotty. I should have recognized the symptoms by now.

Sitting gingerly on the bed next to me, Drew pried one of my hands from its stranglehold around the blankets and placed my palm against his cheek, laying his own hand over it.

"What do you feel?" he whispered.

I sucked in a breath and forced myself to catalog the details of his skin to steady myself. The prickle of his stubble was like sandpaper, and my hand molded to the shape of his cheekbone; even the way his eyelashes brushed the tip of my finger when he blinked had a stabilizing effect on my nerves. All of it in combination with the tingle of electricity that made every touch we shared almost addictive helped focus my mind.

"What do you hear?"

I blinked at his words. My own heartbeat in my ears was all I could hear at first. Then his breath, faint and calm, in and out slowly. The ticking of that clock, perfectly synced with the rhythm of his inhale and exhale.

I focused on matching it. And finally, the oxygen broke

through the haze of my near-hyperventilation, clearing my vision and loosening the torquing of my chest one breath at a time.

I stared at him, amazed that he'd known the physical contact would stop the avalanche of panic. Or at least keep me from suffocating under it.

My confusion didn't abate, though. Because I still didn't know how I'd gotten here, tucked in his bed like I'd never left. For the second time, I wondered if I'd been dreaming everything before this moment.

But it had seemed so real. Going to Louisa's house, being pulled through, waking up in the hospital. The other Drew and then Skylar, their arms around me in turn.

"What do you see?"

I focused on the dark eyes before me now. Free of the very real agony I'd seen in the gaze of that other version of him. The gaunt cheeks I'd felt under my hands, hidden by the fluff of the beard he'd allowed to grow unchecked in the midst of his grief—there was no comparison.

Only concern stared back at me now.

"You okay?" Drew asked, noting my breathing had returned to a somewhat normal rhythm.

I nodded, not trusting myself to speak yet.

"That's twice now I've startled you awake." He gave me a wry smile. "At least this time, you didn't punch me in the face."

The indignation gave volume to my voice. "I didn't punch you!" As heat rushed into my cheeks, I realized that had been his goal.

He laughed softly. "Close enough." He took the hand from his cheek and pressed my palm to his lips before lowering it.

"You're extra jumpy lately. Something bothering you?"

I stiffened before I could stop myself, and a glimmer of suspicion sharpened his gaze.

I glanced away and back quickly. "Probably all this jumping stuff. It's getting to me."

He watched my face for a stretch, probably sensing my evasion because of that freaking ESP. But he also had this obnoxious tendency to respect my space and didn't push for more.

I plowed ahead with a subject change in case he decided it was worth pursuing. "What are you doing sneaking in here in the middle of the night?"

His brow furrowed. "Didn't you get my texts?"

I glanced around for my phone. It wasn't in its usual spot, plugged in on the nightstand. My eyes lit upon the dresser, but it wasn't there either. Unease slithered through me as I searched the floor next and found no sign of it.

I frowned.

He mirrored my expression. "Sorry I missed dinner. Something came up with a case. We were all pulling overtime."

So that was why he hadn't noticed me being gone. It didn't explain why I was back, though. I hadn't even been gone long, and I certainly hadn't been ready to return.

What was happening?

The more frightening prospect was that I'd gotten back here without consciously deciding to. Was my car here? I had been pulled through at Louisa's house. Had I jumped back there and driven my car home? Something pulled tight in my gut that I didn't remember any of it. How much danger had I put myself and others in?

When we'd had the conversation about me using the necklace, Drew had expressed his concern about the fact that I didn't know enough about how it worked and how dangerous that could be. As usual, he'd been right.

"You're pale," he murmured. His hand brushed hair away from my face, then settled at the nape of my neck where he began to massage the tension that coiled in the muscles there. "I'm sorry I scared you. Again."

I flashed the ghost of a smile. "It's fine."

It wasn't the first time since I'd been staying with him that I'd woken up entrenched in a panic attack. There were plenty of times I'd startled him awake in the middle of the night. He was already used to calming me down in the dark and even seemed to know exactly what tactics to use and when.

My dreams were often vivid enough to seem real, which was why I woke so frequently in terror. So maybe this had been one too. That was a much more palatable prospect. I reminded myself that it was the middle of the night, not the time to be dwelling on it or trying to figure it out. Or so I told myself.

In desperation, I searched for a distraction. My eyes dropped to Drew's half-unbuttoned shirt, and I hooked a finger where he'd stopped, brushing the skin of his chest.

His gaze followed mine. "You interrupted me."

I gave him a slow smile, undoing the next button. "Well, now I get to finish for you."

He huffed a laugh and leaned forward to kiss me, gently at first, then with more intensity as I parted my lips to invite him deeper. His hand was still resting on the back of my neck, but it had stopped kneading the muscles as he fell into the diversion.

I wanted to fall too, lose myself in the physical sensation so I didn't have to dwell on the new questions that made anxiety writhe in my stomach.

Once I finished undoing the rest of the buttons, I slipped his shirt off and slid my hands over his shoulders, down his back, and up again to pull him with me as I laid back against the pillows. An ache to feel the weight of his body on me, to have the tangible reminder of what was real and right in front of me, called for relief. I didn't care that our clothes were still a barrier between us. Not yet, anyway.

Not when losing myself in the feel of his lips on mine, our mouths moving in an exhilarating and familiar dance, made my nerves sing. The lightning storm that started at our touch amplified any reaction I had to him, burying any concerns I may have had under waves of electric sensation.

It was a gradual descent into the eye of that storm as our clothing came off in stages, layers coming away to reveal swaths of skin calling to be devoured by mouths and hands. One by one, each barrier was removed until the cold air nipped at my exposed body, raising goosebumps along my skin. Drew seemed impervious to the chill, his own skin flush with desire.

His throat bobbed with a swallow as he took me in, eyes raking over every inch with deliberate and studious slowness. That kind of visual exploration might have made me self-conscious, but the open appreciation in his gaze simply started a pool of warmth low, low in my stomach.

So I was ready when his hands began exploring the contours of my body, his calloused palms rough against my bare skin, creating a delicious friction that sent bolts of need charging through me. My own hands were hungry as they traced every edge and plane of him in turn, pulling him closer, inviting him deeper.

Slowly, we began a rhythm of give and take that had an immediate pressure building inside of me, an ache that started at my core and radiated outward until I felt it in every cell of my being.

His lips painted me with electricity, driving my thrumming pulse faster as he bathed my skin with his breath, whispering compliments like secrets all over me. I wanted to drown in his words, sink into his scent, immerse myself in the feel of his body sliding along mine. Every move he made sent shocks of sensation through me, chaotic and unrelenting, and I felt myself careening toward that edge, ready to crash at any moment.

My muscles coiled in greedy anticipation, and I clutched at his hair almost involuntarily. My sudden intake of breath was sharp, the sound lashing the silence in the room with the violence of pleasure as it broke over me. Unraveled, my arms fell limp at my sides with the last wave that pulsed through me, and his own shudder of release came with my name as a sigh on his lips.

His nose skimmed along the column of my neck and across my jaw before he stamped my mouth with his and rolled over to collapse onto his side of the bed. Only the sound of our rapid breathing filled the room.

Then he reached over to tug at my arm to get me to scoot closer and tucked me against him when I complied. His heart thundered a wild rhythm that matched mine, and I rested my head over the pulsing pattern with a smile.

We laid like that for a long time, his fingers trailing up and down my bare back. I noted, distantly, that my attempt to distract myself worked—my mind was as loose as my body. I drowsily counted each heartbeat that fluttered under my ear, lulled toward unconsciousness.

Footsteps in the hall pulled me back from the brink and

stilled Drew's hand. I had no idea what time it was, but generally, Evan returned well after midnight. The fact that Drew had come home only a bit before this told me that whatever had kept him late must have been a big deal.

And thinking of the time made me wonder again how *I'd* gotten here, if I had, in fact, gone to the original alternate reality and returned already. It hadn't been late when Skylar and I called it a night, and even after my brief internet research, it hadn't been anywhere near midnight.

Calculating how long I'd lain unconscious in the hospital, I was probably there for a mere eight or nine hours total.

"It's just Evan," Drew murmured, his gravelly voice rumbling beneath my ear. He was reading my tension incorrectly for once.

Tell him, an inner voice chanted, but the words remained locked behind hesitation.

"I know," I said instead.

My fear was an attentive jailer. It wasn't that I was scared of his reaction. Not entirely, anyway. But I was afraid of acknowledging it out loud—as if giving it voice would make it what I was hoping it wasn't. I didn't want to admit how dangerous my situation might actually be.

Because I knew that I wasn't going to stop. Not yet, anyway.

I took a breath and sat up, my long hair dragging across Drew's chest, the red a flame against his bare skin.

He stared up at me, a question in his eyes. The faint smile tugging at the corner of his mouth told me he wasn't concerned and, thus, hadn't picked up on the unrelated source of my anxiety.

I paused, distracted by the angry scar on his shoulder, and traced my fingertips along the gathered skin, pink and puckered where it had roughly sealed. He should have gotten stitches. Even these months later, I felt the stab of guilt, the shadow of fear the sight of his blood had elicited.

He caught my hand in his, now reading me right. "Stop."

My eyes cut to his face. Of course, the reminder of his gunshot wound would always trigger my self-blame, and he knew it. But being aware of Evan's proximity in the house also gave me a sense of unease. He still watched me with distrust, especially because Drew had never given him any of the details.

The actual explanation probably would have made things worse than whatever Evan believed about me since it sounded like absolute lunacy when put into words. So we left him to his own conclusions, however wrong they were.

I couldn't blame him for his poorly veiled wariness though. The fact that Drew and I were together under the circumstances would arouse suspicion in anyone's mind, though it wasn't like I had bad intentions. But it wasn't the wisest thing, considering Drew was the lead investigator in the case against a serial killer who'd tried to end my life. Not exactly in line with ethical practices.

The urge to cover myself and hide from Drew came on strong and unbidden. I leaned down to kiss his shoulder near the scar to ward off further discussion before abruptly climbing out of bed to slip my clothes back on. He pushed himself to a sitting position and watched me, his eyes too sharp as they took in my tension.

"I hate it when you pull away like that."

I glanced at him over my shoulder, working at keeping my voice neutral. "I get cold."

"That's not what I mean."

I pulled my shirt over my head and spun to face him, knowing full well it wasn't. I braced myself. "I'm not—"

"You are. There's something you're not telling me." A muscle in his jaw rippled.

I crossed my arms over my chest, fumbling for a defense. "You knew I was difficult. It was your choice to take me on."

He sighed, rubbing his hands down his face. "Can we not make it about that?"

My chin jutted forward. "About what? The fact that your patience has run out? Like I told you it would."

He bared his teeth, climbing out of bed to pull on the sweatpants he'd discarded onto the floor the morning before, evidence of his delightful tendency toward disarray. "Cassidy. . ."

"Don't *Cassidy* me. This is who I am." My tone sounded dangerous enough that I knew I was spinning out of control, but I couldn't stop myself. Fight or flight had been tripped, and it told me I needed to protect myself. Strike first before he could, or cut and run.

He stilled, though his chest moved with the force of emotion coursing through him. "I know this is still new, and that this is your first instinct. But I'm not going anywhere, Cass. Get used to that."

My chest tightened. I had no barbs to hurl, no defense against kindness and understanding. I'd already used my usual tactics: anger to cover my fear, cutting words to drive him away.

"I'm a patient guy." His smile was soft and a little sad as he repeated the same words he'd spoken during another fight. Another time I'd gotten ridiculous.

I gave a weak laugh and turned my face away to hide the tears gathering in my eyes. "Damn it, Drew." There was no anger in my words now.

He held up his hands. "Why don't we just sleep on it? You can tell me in the morning."

I raked my fingers through my hair, trying to dispel the last of my frustration. "You are the *worst*," I said, smiling darkly.

He clutched at his chest like he'd been struck by Cupid's arrow. "Be still my heart."

I threw a pillow at him, which he caught, laughing. But there was an edge to it, so I knew he was still frustrated too.

I almost broke down and told him everything then. Because he was so freaking understanding and deserved better from me. But I didn't know *what* to tell him since I still wasn't sure if I'd actually made the jump I thought I had. Until I could figure out *if* it had happened, it wasn't worth worrying him.

At least that's what I told myself as I watched him walk to the bathroom to finish getting ready for bed.

8

Apology Bacon

I woke before Drew the next morning and slipped into the bathroom for a shower. I'd half-expected to wake up back on Skylar's couch, doing another frightening mental search of how and when I'd returned, panicking about whether my time with Drew had been conjured in my mind.

In the light of day, the jump to *that* reality seemed more like a dream than it had even seemed in the middle of the night.

I went through the motions of showering, distracted enough that I couldn't remember if I'd washed my hair or not. So I did it again just in case, focusing on each step to be sure it stuck mentally.

I walked back out to the bedroom to get dressed, stepping lightly to keep from waking Drew, though he hadn't even moved. I left my hair damp, the wetness soaking into the back of my shirt, and headed down the hall to the kitchen.

I found the usual supply of eggs and bacon in the fridge and set to work making breakfast for myself and Drew. He didn't have to work, so I knew he would sleep in a bit, but I felt like I owed him for the things I'd said the night before. An apology breakfast of sorts.

He liked his eggs over easy, cooked in the bacon grease for added flavor, so I did the bacon first. I absently watched the meat bubble in the pan as it crackled and spat and thought back to my possibly real, possibly dreamed jump.

If I had actually gone to the original alternate timeline, would I be able to get back there if I tried to jump again? Since Louisa had been the one to initiate that slide, she had pulled me there with her. Was she still there? Or was her return the reason I had come back? Was there some kind of tether to her too?

I gripped the tongs in my hand with unnecessary force as I flipped the strips of bacon, frustrated that I'd been sent back without answers.

The lack of understanding was starting to drive me crazy. It seemed almost pointless to keep jumping timelines if I was going to hit these walls over and over again. Of course, that wasn't enough to make me stop. But it gave me a reason to be more strategic.

I choked back a gasp when the hands slid around me from behind, the warmth of a male body enveloping me in an embrace that I leaned into only a fraction of a second later. The planes and edges of his body were too familiar for me to truly be scared. But I'd been deep enough in my own thoughts that he'd snuck up on me.

I placed my free hand over the arms wrapped around me and tilted my head back against his shoulder. Accepted and safe.

He leaned forward to glance over my head at what I was making.

"Apology bacon," I informed him.

"Hmmm. Looks like regular bacon to me."

"Just wait. It's all in the taste."

He pressed a kiss to my temple and pulled away to rummage in the pantry for the tin of coffee he kept there. "Liquid sleep?" he offered, holding it up.

I shook my head, placing the bacon on a plate, then reached for the eggs. "I think I've had enough sleep for a while, even if interrupted."

He nodded with a yawn as he scooped the grounds into the coffee maker. "No regrets, but I definitely haven't had enough."

I cracked the eggs on the side of the pan, raising my voice to be heard over the sound of the sizzle as they met the hot bacon grease. "You could have slept longer."

He moved around me, placing a hand on my hip as he reached over my head for a mug. It wasn't an absent thing, like a habit or like he thought nothing of the touch. It was deliberate and reassuring, a reminder to him that I was still here, and to me that he was still in this.

After his overly understanding words in the middle of the night, though, it was impossible not to read insecurity in the gesture. After all, his father had left too.

And maybe that was where his understanding nature came from, his tendency not to push me too hard. My reaction was to put up walls and drive people away with my words to keep myself from getting hurt; his was to be overly accommodating.

I turned abruptly just as he lowered his hand with his chosen mug. It was always the same one—matte black on the outside with a glossy emerald green on the inside. It appeared to be handmade.

He looked down at me, his brows raised in surprise as I pressed myself against him. His arms went around me without hesitation.

I laid my head against his chest, noting the uptick in the rhythm of his heartbeat. "I'm sorry I'm such a pain."

"You're not a pain," he murmured.

I clicked my tongue. "You need to stop being so nice to me."

He laughed, and it rumbled against my cheek. "I think you deserve to be treated nicely for a change."

The words forced a lump into my throat, but I swallowed it down, determined to apologize. "Not at your own expense. It's not fair for me to lash out."

He was quiet for a moment. "No. It's not."

I stiffened, but I talked myself down, throwing out the reminders of all the times he was undeservedly patient with me. "Okay, I was expecting at least *some* push-back on that one. But fair enough."

He pulled back slightly and tipped my chin up. "You're not a pain," he repeated. "And this will get easier as we get used to each other."

I shook my head, aiming to get back to the point.

"I know you think I'm being too nice," he said before I could start. "And you think I walk on eggshells to keep the peace."

His Cassidy ESP really pissed me off sometimes. I glared at him.

One side of his mouth tipped up in amusement. "That's not entirely it, though I'll admit that is sometimes the case. I've learned, though, that calling people out on their bull is less effective than getting them to call themselves out."

I squinted at him. "Why do I feel like that's a cop move?"

He kissed me lightly. "Because it is. You're burning my apology eggs."

I jerked out of his arms, hissing a curse, and snatched the spatula off the counter, frowning. "Your eggs are not going to be over easy."

"Neither are we," he shot over his shoulder as he poured his coffee.

"Ha-ha," I dead-panned.

He grinned into his mug as he sipped, slapping my butt on his way out of the kitchen. My gaze followed him to the living room where he lowered himself onto the couch and laid his head back. He rested the mug against his thigh and rubbed at his eye sockets with the fingers of his free hand.

I put all the food onto a plate and walked out to where he sat, standing over him. "A helping of burnt apology eggs with a side of apology bacon, cooked *not* crispy for the bacon heathen that you are."

Used to the lighthearted jab, he chose not to acknowledge it and patted the spot next to him instead of taking the plate.

I obliged and held the food out so he could take a strip of bacon.

He took a bite, chewing for a few seconds. Then: "So. You gonna tell me what's going on, or do I need to whip out some more interrogation techniques?"

I gave him a dark look, turning my nose up at his wobbly bacon when he offered. I stalled by lowering the plate to my lap before answering. "I made a jump yesterday."

He froze for a second then put the strip of bacon down. He took the plate from me to set it aside with his mug so he could give me his full attention. "You're supposed to let me know before you jump."

I winced at the reproach in his tone. "It wasn't on purpose."

His skepticism narrowed his eyes, but he waited for me to continue, silence stretching. Cop move.

"I went to Louisa Lee's place." I looked down, using a hand

to guide my leg as I tucked it under me. "I thought maybe I'd have some luck and find her. Sure enough, she was there."

He opened his mouth, but I plowed on. "Instead of answering her door, she made a jump and dragged me with her." Some instinct made me keep the part about Edwards to myself. The omission torqued my stomach, but I swallowed against the guilt.

He took a steadying breath, reaching for calm. "Did you catch up with her there?"

I shook my head. "I. . . woke up at the hospital."

He lurched forward, the concern an instant spark in his dark eyes. "What? Why didn't you tell me before?"

I put a hand on his shoulder to keep him from physically checking me over. "I was fine. I *am* fine. But someone found me unconscious on her front porch. Or, rather, the alternate version of her porch."

He pinched the bridge of his nose. "Cassidy. . . "

"I'm fine," I insisted. "You came to the hospital to get me."

He tensed, dropping his hand. "*I* came to get you," he repeated dryly.

I lifted a shoulder, glancing away. "Other you. . ."

"Which other me?" His tone was flat like he already knew he wouldn't like the answer.

I braced myself and answered in a subdued tone, "I went to the original alternate timeline."

He shook his head, exhaling loudly through his nose. "I can't believe the phrase 'original alternate timeline' is a regular part of my life now."

I waved that away with a hand. "It doesn't matter. What does is that I need to go back."

"Why?"

"Because of Louisa Lee."

He didn't speak for a moment, his silence was stifling as it stretched. I shifted under the weight of it.

Finally, he looked toward the ceiling like he was working through something in his mind. "This is the weirdest thing."

I shot him an incredulous look. "You're going to have to be more specific. The number of weird things in our lives is at an all-time high right now."

He clenched his teeth. "I can't stand the thought of you with that other me."

I almost laughed but thought better of it when I noted how serious he looked. "You can trust me," I assured him.

He scowled. "I trust you just fine. It's me I don't trust."

I tucked my tongue up into my cheek to suppress a smile because he sounded genuinely jealous. It wasn't entirely unfounded, to be fair. I *had* kissed that other version of him, had wanted him at one point. Admittedly, I was currently halfway to what might be love because of what had started there.

That other Drew was mourning the loss of not only the version of me that had been his lifelong friend, but the possibility I had presented when I'd been there. He would realize what I'd told him in time—that it was better this way—but he was still hung up on me for the moment. It didn't make him untrustworthy, but the jealousy made sense in that light.

Even though *I* knew where my heart lay, I couldn't entirely blame the man in front of me.

He watched my face, his scowl getting deeper as I processed.

I reached up to run my thumb over the line between his brows. "Please relax. That other you is honorable."

"Oh, is that why he kissed you even though you were engaged

to Evan?"

"That was *her*," I ground out. Even in this reality, I had to have this argument.

"Were you even different in his mind?"

His words stabbed into me. Because that had been my fear and greatest heartache while there. The fact that hearing him say it and having it hurt made me pull back, uncertain. That probably wasn't a good sign, was it? Or did it bother me because of something else? The still-bleeding wounds of rejection from childhood, perhaps?

I decided to cling to that as my explanation. I didn't want to analyze it any further.

"Let me tell you something," I said, determined to drive the point home—for both of us. "That other Drew touched my hand. Do you know what I felt?" I took his hand then, my grip tightening when the zing shot through me at the touch. Neither of us had grown used to it, but it didn't shock us quite as easily as it once had.

His lips parted, but he said nothing as he watched me lace my fingers with his.

"Nothing."

His eyes flashed to mine.

"This. . . " I lifted our clasped hands. ". . . is uniquely us." I turned them so that I could rest the back of his hand against my cheek. "*You* are the one I feel tugging at my core, calling me home."

His glare smoothed out, his mind no longer on that other version of himself but on me and our touch. His fingers tightened between mine. "How are you planning to get back there? I thought you couldn't control where you went."

I sucked in a breath, grateful that at least he sounded more subdued than before, even if he was asking the question I frustratingly didn't have an answer for yet.

"I don't know. But I feel like maybe something about Louisa being there will help me get back."

Skepticism pinched his expression. "You and your feelings."

I could hear the humor in his tone, so I knew not to take him too seriously. "Well, if you don't want me to follow my feelings. . . " I stood up as if to leave, but he tugged me back, rolling his eyes.

As soon as I was sitting again, he turned serious, searching my face in earnest. "I really need you to be careful. It's obviously taking a toll on you."

More than he knew. I fought to keep my gaze from sliding away from his.

"I'm being careful," I said, though my voice lacked any real conviction. But that might have been because I knew it wasn't entirely true.

This was my opportunity to tell him. I knew I should, and the war erupted inside of me. I needed to keep the communication between us open. He deserved that. But I also nursed the fear that he'd fight me on going if he knew what was happening to me. And I couldn't give up on this quite yet.

"When are you going?" He sounded distinctly disapproving about the prospect.

It felt like a confirmation of my suspicion, and I pressed my lips together.

As my hesitation lengthened, his expression got darker. "Can we at least make out before you go?"

I blew out a surprised laugh. "Last night wasn't enough for you?" I placed my hands on either side of his face to brush my lips against his.

He grinned between kisses. "It's never enough."

I leaned back, but his hands grappled for purchase on my waist in an attempt to pull me back.

"I have to go to my doctor's appointment first, remember?" I laughed. "You were the one who rescheduled it for me."

He grunted. "Bad timing on my part. If I had known, I never would have scheduled it for such an inconvenient time."

"And your apology breakfast will get cold," I warned.

He growled, sending a shiver through me while his hand slid over my thigh, scorching through my jeans. "I don't want an apology breakfast."

I tilted my head back to laugh, and he took the opportunity to bury his face against my throat. "Stop it!" I gasped. "I seriously have to go. I'd really like to get this cast off."

He muttered something unintelligible and pulled away, his mouth turned down. "I guess I support that." He looked down at the cast on my wrist, and his frown deepened. "I'd like this thing gone, myself."

It was one of the most glaring reminders of all that had happened, particularly the worst parts. Tangible evidence of what Creedy had done to me that we both wanted to erase.

Even though there would always be one memento, it wasn't something anyone else would see on a regular basis. The ugly, red scar in the fleshy part of my thigh would be mine to cherish for the rest of my life, even if it would fade over time. Only Drew knew the mark in my skin as intimately as I did. But it wouldn't be a constant reminder the way the cast had been thus far.

Drew tensed up, his eyes drawn behind me.

I twisted to look at Evan walking into the kitchen, and even though he seemed fairly zombie-like as he shuffled along, I found myself stiffening up as well. We pulled further apart, both of us probably thinking about the fact that in some world, a version of me had been engaged to a version of him. Not to mention his dubious acceptance of my presence here.

Or maybe that last part was only me. Drew didn't feel it as acutely as I did. Largely, of course, because he wasn't on the receiving end of the cool, appraising looks from his cousin like I was. Thinly veiled suspicion and aloofness was Evan's favorite way to interact with me.

Mostly, I avoided him whenever possible, and Drew ran interference as much as he could. But it was a matter of biding our time until he moved out.

"Don't mind me," Evan said, his voice flat. He didn't even look our way, but it was overly deliberate, so he was clearly more aware than he wanted to let on. Not that there was anything he would catch at this point. I'd already put a stop to it.

Drew sat back with a huff and took his plate of apology breakfast, grudgingly picking up his abandoned bacon.

"You let him stay here. And this is public domain," I reminded him in a low voice.

He grunted in response, making me chuckle. I put a hand on his shoulder to help get myself to my feet. He stared up at me, unhappiness carving lines into his face. I touched his cheek in reassurance.

"I've gotta go. I'll be back before I, um, jump." I slid a glance at Evan. "Promise."

The muscle along Drew's jaw rippled at my whispered words, but he didn't argue. My heart squeezed a little as the guilt washed through me and the doubt nagged. I could stop right here, right now.

But then I wouldn't have my answers. And I might not have my freedom anyway. Someone knew I could slide dimensions, and they knew I was in this reality. I wasn't safe to live my life. Not completely anyway. Especially when I'd already encountered Edwards again.

And so I needed to go.

I walked toward the closet to grab my boots and my jacket, nibbling the inside of my cheek. Stewing in the shame of concealing pieces of my current circumstances from Drew made me reluctant to come back because it meant I'd have to keep it from him longer. But I'd promised to say goodbye before I jumped again, and I'd stick to it.

Then I'd execute my plan, which was to make my jump closer to Skylar's apartment. That way I could easily knock on her door as soon as I arrived—assuming my guess was right, and I'd get back to that timeline.

There were no guarantees.

I zipped my jacket as a cold fear wended its way through my gut, uncertainty solidifying like an ice block.

I strode to Drew and planted one last kiss on his mouth, putting a force behind it that was almost bruising. He watched me walk out the door in silence, his eyes narrowed with suspicion.

9

Doctor, Doctor

My car was not outside. I stood on the porch for a stretch, mentally grappling with that fact and what it meant.

I prayed that it was at Louisa's, that I wasn't losing my ever-loving mind. If I found it there, it would confirm that I hadn't dreamt my adventure into that original alternate reality. But it also meant I didn't know how I'd gotten back.

I pushed those thoughts from my mind before they paralyzed me with panic. There was no time to explore the questions when I couldn't get the answers now anyway.

It wasn't too far to walk to Louisa's, and it wasn't that cold out. If I had my phone, I would have called for a ride because I was definitely *not* going back inside to ask for the keys to Drew's car. That would open up a whole line of interrogation that was best avoided.

But I didn't have my phone, and so I had to risk being late for my appointment. It couldn't be helped. Not when I wanted to keep these complications a secret until I figured them out.

It confirmed more fully that I needed to get back to Skylar's timeline to look for the professor. Assuming I *could* get back.

And that the other Drew would give up the address. And I could even find the professor, let alone talk to him.

As much as I felt that sinking sense of pessimism that none of it would work out, it would be stupid of me not to try. Or so I convinced myself.

I rounded the corner to Louisa's street, freezing when I caught sight of the Beast parked at the curb where I'd left it. It was odd to be simultaneously relieved and rattled about that. There was my proof that I hadn't dreamt anything, but my stomach twisted into knots with the confirmation that I'd come back without my permission.

No one was around, the street was quiet, but I didn't move. The memory of Edwards hurrying across the street when Louisa pulled me through planes struck me motionless and fearful.

The fact that he hadn't been pulled through with me didn't make sense. I should have woken up in some kind of laboratory or a weird prison for dimension-jumping delinquents. And since I hadn't, there was no way he had followed me. Which told me there was still too much I didn't understand about how this worked.

I forced myself to keep walking, my trepidation about Edwards popping up out of nowhere again making me cautious as I scoured the area for unusual activity. I made it to my car unscathed but still jittery and unsettled as I started her up and drove to my appointment.

I arrived just in time for check-in, then sat to wait for them to call my name, though I'd been informed the doctor was running behind. I should have known that would be the case. Weren't they always running behind? This would be the one time it worked in my favor.

But still time pressed against my mind with every tick of the clock, the sense of urgency emanating from my core causing me to wiggle unceasingly. With the new questions, my desire to make the jump was a pressure I couldn't alleviate, and part of me regretted telling Drew I would come back before I jumped.

But I'd promised, so I would follow through.

The receptionist shot me furtive glances every few minutes, but I ignored her. It was probably because of the news story that played on the TV in the corner of the room. The volume was muted, but I could read the captions just fine.

Not that I needed to. Or wanted to.

The reporter was standing in front of what used to be a version of my parents' house, now a different color and with a For Sale sign out front.

Several stories had been run by news outlets about the "disappearance" of Cassidy Marchand and her family. Some were speculating that I'd skipped town and that my family had folded under the scrutiny of the media and moved to help hide me. All the wild theories had started out amusing because of how ridiculous they were but had settled into irritating as the stories continued to spin out of control.

I'd opted not to watch if I could help it. It was enough to know that they were all still so obsessed with the story of my traumatic experience as a serial killer's escaped victim. In all honesty, it was likely my alleged disappearance had renewed the fervor over my experience.

It was something I'd have to roll with, even if I couldn't truly get *used* to it. Drew had warned me that the attention would flare up any time a development arose in the case, which was likely to happen periodically for some time.

The sight of the house, so different than it had once looked while I'd briefly stayed there, sent my mind swirling with the fear and worry that had been part of the catalyst for my forays into alternate timelines of late. Searching for answers had been my biggest motivation. But finding out where my family had gone and if they were safe was always in the back of my mind.

I'd made no progress on that front, and admittedly, it was somewhat naive of me to think I would have found some clue thus far. Nothing was ever that simple.

Getting pulled through with Louisa had been the best break-through I could have gotten, and it hadn't even been inten-tional. But it was a step in the right direction. If only I could get back and, if the other Drew would cooperate, I might very well be several steps closer after being stuck in limbo for weeks.

"Cassidy?"

A female voice broke into my reverie, and I jerked my eyes from the TV to look at the woman in scrubs holding a tablet. It was good timing since the camera had cut to a shot of Creedy's defense lawyer speaking to a mob of reporters. I didn't want to relive that or see what lies he was spinning to put Creedy in a better light.

The nurse glanced up only briefly when I stood to walk toward her, trying to exhale the jitters that one shot of the defense lawyer set off in me.

"How are you doing today?" she asked.

I couldn't dredge up more than a borderline polite tone. "I'm fine. How are you?"

She didn't notice my lack of enthusiasm as she clicked through all of the information on my electronic chart and led me down a hall. "I'm well. Looks like you're losing the cast today."

"Yeah."

"Bet you're ready for that," she said, finally turning to give me a smile.

"Definitely."

She gestured for me to precede her into a small room, then followed, shutting the door behind her.

She went through the standard questions and weight and height checks, then she left me alone to wait for the doctor. I opted not to sit on the paper-covered table and took the chair instead so that my nervous jiggling wouldn't make so much noise.

Waiting was agony, the pressure to be onto the next thing on my agenda a physical weight. I jumped when the door swung open and the doctor came in.

He didn't look up from the tablet he held in his hand, taking a page out of the nurse's book, who shuffled in behind him.

"And how are we today?" His voice was falsely cheery, and I doubted he would even remember my face when he walked out of the room.

I blew out a breath. "Fine, thanks."

"Cast removal," the doctor muttered, then finally glanced up. "Exciting times."

I forced a brief smile. "Very."

He clapped his hands and rubbed them together. "All righty. Any concerns with the wrist?"

"Nope. Just ready to have it back." I was proud I kept my voice in check despite the anticipation tightening up my entire body.

He glanced back to the tray the nurse was setting the instruments on for him, and he clicked his teeth together. The drill was intimidating to look at, but he assured me that its vibration would only saw through the plaster and no farther. Specially designed to not break skin, apparently.

"Have a seat." He gestured to the bed and pulled the tray with him as he rolled closer in his chair.

Once I sat, wincing at the crinkling sound of the protective paper, the nurse draped a disposable cloth over my lap, and the doctor held his hand out for my arm.

The process was quick, and the immediate relief that came with the release of my wrist was beyond anything I had ever experienced. It was more intense than I thought possible given that it was only my wrist, but it even elicited a gasp of surprise from me.

The doctor actually smiled before he had me rotate and move my wrist up and down to be sure it had healed properly. There were questions about pain, mobility, hand strength. He felt the bones and tendons as I moved and flexed and bent it.

Once he was satisfied with my answers, I was released back into the hallway to find my own way out of the maze of rooms and corridors and back to the elevators.

I always hated the way doctors' offices made me feel. My clothes smelled anesthetized, and a grogginess always settled on me afterwards, like I'd been locked in an overly bright cave for hours. But the buoyancy that came with my newly-freed wrist dulled the feeling.

The office was on the third floor of a larger medical complex, so it was a short ride down to the lobby, made shorter by my lifted mood. I was too busy rotating my wrist, watching the movement with gleeful appreciation, to notice anything else.

That was what kept me distracted enough not to detect what I should have and would have under normal circumstances. I'd always been proud of my sense for impending danger, but I was too entrenched in enjoying the movement of my wrist to pick up on the ambush waiting for me outside of the automatic doors.

"Cassidy!"

My head jerked up at a man's voice, panic shooting through me like an electric current, fraying my nerves in one second flat. My fingers curled into my palm as I reflexively started to back up, totally freaking out the automatic doors as they whipped back open.

<h1 align="center">10</h1>

A Question of Paranoia

I didn't recognize the man who was moving toward me, but his demeanor screamed journalist—eyes bright with eager anticipation, the dogged advance even as I moved back into the building and away from him. Not to mention the small digital recorder he held in his hand, which solidified my guess.

"Ms. Marchand, how does it feel to have the last physical evidence of your ordeal removed?"

My mouth opened and shut like a fish on land, but nothing coherent formed in my head, let alone came out of my mouth. He was referring to my cast, I realized. His eyes flashed down to my wrist and back to my panicked face. I continued to stare at him without saying anything.

It didn't seem to deter him as he plowed on. "The defense for Gavin Creedy is requesting a competency hearing. How are you feeling about that?"

The question hit me with the impact of a bullet, and I staggered back another step. My thrown equilibrium must have shown on my face because the reporter's expression changed. It was like a predator sensing blood; he'd cornered wounded prey, and he had the upper hand.

He almost smiled. "Were you aware that the trial clock is being put on pause for an evaluation of Creedy's competency to stand trial for his crimes?"

A bead of sweat rolled down my spine as tingles shot through my limbs. The discomfort of being caught unawares and getting ambushed with new information triggered the adrenaline response.

Wait, I told myself, trying to logic the illogical response into submission. I started counting the seconds for each inhale and exhale as I tried to process what he'd said to me.

Evaluating Creedy's competency? As in, checking if he was mentally fit to stand trial? Of course, anyone would think he was seriously unhinged to unleash the kind of violence he had on me and those other women.

But he had also been fully aware and intentional about what he had done. Meticulous in his execution, reveling in the results. Premeditated and calculating.

I swallowed the bile that rose in my throat, recognizing on some level that this must have been why the TV in the doctor's office was playing an interview of Creedy's lawyer. That wasn't old, rehashed footage. It was recent.

Normally, Carla Ojeda, my victim advocate, let me know about any changes in the case, but she had no way to get a hold of me since I didn't have my phone. It never crossed my mind that her inability to contact me would be an issue; nothing major had happened in a couple of weeks. Apparently, that was all about to change.

But what did this reporter want from me, really? Did he want me to tell him that it made my stomach turn inside out if I gave it any of my mental energy, which was why I'd been spending my time sliding dimensions, torturing myself with an entirely different uncertainty?

No, I couldn't very well say that, especially the last part.

A flash of anger ignited in my chest, sending shooting sparks into my fingers. I wanted to tell him it was sickening that he would approach me with these kinds of questions, that he was a despicable human being for sneaking up on me the way he had.

But I knew opening my mouth to unleash any of what crossed my mind was unwise.

Something spoken to me during a different media attack—was it Drew? Or maybe Carla?—came back to me then, solidifying my decision to clamp my lips shut against any response.

Hit them with "no comment." Put your head down and walk away. Don't feed the sharks.

A frenzy was not something I needed right now, and I couldn't believe I'd gotten so complacent with the last few weeks being more peaceful and the interest in me dying down. I'd shifted my focus too fully on the jumping, and I'd been way less diligent in this area.

I had no choice now. This experience would bring my priorities back in line.

The reporter persisted despite my continued silence. "Ms. Marchand, do you have anything to say about this new development?"

"No comment," I muttered, ducking my head and pushing past him. A thrill of worry skated up my spine that he would follow and pester me with questions.

I tucked my chin to look over my shoulder, but he stayed put, staring after me. A speculative look pulled at his features as he watched me weave through the other cars in the lot.

Even though he didn't follow me, paranoia settled deep into my bones. Absently rotating my freed wrist, I scanned the lot in unending sweeps for any other reporters or possible threats. My muscles clenched whenever my eyes landed on a person, but none of them paid me any attention as they made their way to or from their vehicles and the buildings around us.

The fact that I'd so easily been ambushed, even by someone who wasn't intending to physically hurt me, set off a diatribe in my brain of how stupid I was for not paying more attention.

It would keep me jumpy for longer than I would care to admit, but it was better to be on high alert than caught off my guard again.

As soon as I climbed into the driver's seat, I slammed my locks down before even starting the engine. When I checked for the reporter, he was gone, and I frantically searched my surroundings in case he decided to follow up after all.

I pulled out of the parking spot faster than I should have and almost hit a car backing out of its space opposite from me. I slammed on my brakes, letting the vehicle go ahead of me, and took my time checking for other cars or people before venturing out again. It didn't occur to me until a few seconds later that the driver of the car could have been the reporter, and he might follow me out of the parking lot and to Drew's house.

So I drove through the lot, weaving up and down rows to pull into a totally different spot and wait a few extra minutes. The car didn't follow and no others passed by, and I told myself I was being ridiculous now. But I couldn't stop the intrusive thoughts from circling around my mind like a vulture preying on a dead animal.

The whole drive back to Drew's house, I was so wound up that I sat forward, white-knuckling the steering wheel as I shifted my gaze from the road before me and the rear view mirror repeatedly.

"No one's following you," I muttered, reaching to turn down the heat when it got to be too much against my nerves. Even the sound of my own voice out loud made me feel like I was about to crawl out of my skin.

I went around the block once when I reached Drew's street, just in case. No cars appeared out of nowhere on the sleepy stretch of older homes. From what I'd seen in the few months I'd lived here, most residents were middle-aged or older, making appearances only when clearing snow from walkways or getting mail. Most kept to themselves, thankfully.

I pulled to the curb in front of the house, still checking the street in both directions, though the tension in my shoulders loosened the longer I went without spotting a tail. I debated parking around the corner in the alley behind the house, but I knew I would be leaving again soon, and parking back there was overkill.

I sat in the car for a few minutes longer to try to settle my mind before going inside.

11

Sketchbook

I smelled something warm and savory when I walked inside the house. Garlic, butter, and toasted bread. The jump in temperature as I put my jacket in the closet was like a warm blanket around me.

This was the kind of welcome I could spend my life appreciating, especially if it consistently chased away anxiety like the kind that still simmered within me.

Drew peeked around the edge of the archway between the kitchen and living room, one brow raised. "How'd it go?"

It wasn't apparent whether he had been apprised of the situation with Creedy. Had Grace called Drew in the time I'd been gone?

Instead of bringing it up, I lifted my hand, twisting it for him to see. "Fully functional."

Even with the comforting warmth enveloping me and the slowly dissipating jitters, I still moved to the front window to peer out as a precaution.

A car made its way slowly down the street, and I squinted at the driver even though I couldn't make out any features. It neither slowed down in front of Drew's nor did it speed up once it was passed. Could go either way. Still, I made a mental note of the sleek, dark sedan—a Toyota Corolla.

"What are you looking at?"

I spun to face Drew, wrapping my arms around myself. My lip remained trapped between my teeth as I debated. But why delay the inevitable?

"Did you know about the competency hearing?"

He pulled his head back, wincing.

Not a surprise, then.

"I knew it was being tossed around," he admitted. "Grace called not long after you left to let me know they'd filed. I figured Carla would have called you."

My hands clenched around my arms. He knew it was a possibility. I tried not to be bothered by that, walking myself backward from that edge. Carla *would* have let me know if she'd been able to. And it wasn't his fault that she hadn't had the chance.

"I didn't want to say anything until it became official." His expression twisted, maybe as he recognized how it sounded. "There was no reason to stress you out unnecessarily."

I clawed at my arms again, trying to hold back the emotional response, but I couldn't keep the bite from my tone. "It's only stressful when I'm accosted by the media because of it."

He took a step forward. "What?" The word snapped on the air with sudden anger.

Seeing that reaction placated me a little.

"Outside the doctor's office. Somehow, he got an early scoop," I said dryly.

I thought back to the woman from the front desk at the office and the way she'd stared at me. Could she have tipped him off about my location?

"Someone must have alerted him I was there."

He ran a hand down his face, blowing out a breath of frustration. "Are you okay?"

I considered for a moment, taking stock of my mental state. "I'm fine," I answered, knowing it was the truth now that I was here.

He barely moved, but I could feel him drink me in from head to toe, measuring my appearance against my words. "Have you talked to Carla?"

I shook my head. "I misplaced my phone."

He pulled his out of his pocket. "You can use mine."

I took it from him and made the call. Half the time was spent assuring Carla that I was all right, that it wasn't her fault she hadn't warned me. And then we got to the nitty-gritty, which was to set up a meeting for all of us to go over what would happen next.

When I hung up, I wrapped my arms around myself again and chewed my lip, turning to find Drew watching me again.

"The meeting is set for Thursday at ten."

He nodded. "I know it seems stressful, but it's likely a ploy to delay the case. He'll get the evaluation, but there's no way he'll get flagged as incompetent."

I squeezed myself tighter for a moment in an attempt to banish the remaining anxiety that bounced inside of my body like a pinball. I didn't want to talk about it any more. Especially not right before a jump. I would need to focus, not worry about something that was out of my hands, anyway.

"What are you cooking?" I lifted my nose into the air to get another whiff, hoping he would take my change of topic in stride.

He stared at me for one long beat, probably to see if I was really ready to move on. "Spaghetti."

"Hmm." I moved toward him, handing him his phone before sliding my hands around his waist to press my body to his. My tension already fell away at his proximity. It reminded me that I should have sought that comfort much sooner.

He seemed more than willing to let the topic drop. One of his arms went around me to keep me attached as he walked backward into the kitchen. He half-smiled down at me as he picked up the slotted spoon to stir the noodles.

I glanced at the pot, raising one skeptical brow.

"Stop it," he warned, his tone playful. "No disparaging comments about my cooking."

"I would *never*." I pressed my lips together to hide my smile. The last time he made pasta, he hadn't let the noodles cook long enough, taking the term *al dente* a little too far.

Checking the rest of the kitchen in search of the garlic bread I smelled, my eyes bouncing from spilled garlic powder, the empty packaging from the noodles, and bread crumbs littering the counter to something that made my breath catch. My gaze had landed on a brand new, still in-package notebook on the counter beside the little bowl where Drew dropped his keys and loose change at the end of the day. On top of it sat a new box of chai.

He knew the moment I registered what I was seeing because his grin grew in wattage.

I released him, my eyes not leaving the two new items. "What is that?"

He jerked his chin in that direction. "Go see."

With halting movements, I walked over, my mouth dry. I picked up the box of tea first. It was my favorite brand.

"You were almost out," he said softly from behind me.

I smiled a little, then set it aside, a warmth building in my middle.

The second item made me hesitate. The purposefully worn look of the leather, a rich teal color, called for the gentle brush of my fingertips. I knew it would be soft and supple. But I was afraid to remove the plastic protection around it. I wanted to drag out the moment, take in every detail of the precious gift. If Drew weren't watching in eager expectation, I might have taken more time to process.

Instead, I picked it up, gently pulling the plastic off like it was a sacred relic. The label indicated it was a sketching notebook, and my heartbeat stuttered. The leather was smooth under my palm as I caressed it, and I could almost feel it calling to me through my skin.

"I noticed you've been doodling."

I looked at him leaning against the counter, trying to appear more casual than he actually was. I could see the nerves in the way he held himself overly still. He cared very much about my reaction to his gift.

My breathing became shallow, as if a full exhale might scare away this moment, like some part of me thought it was a dream that would dissolve as soon as I realized it.

"I thought maybe it was a nervous habit or something to keep your mind occupied during those meetings with Carla and Grace." He lifted one shoulder. "I know they can be hard sometimes, for obvious reasons."

I placed the notebook against my chest, hugging it as if it could help me hold back my emotions while a lump formed in my throat. I had no idea he'd noticed something so small about me.

"But I saw your doodle at the last meeting, and it was. . ." He sucked a breath in through his teeth. "Amazing. A woman's face in profile—Grace's face. You'd captured her expression so well."

I blinked at the moisture that stung my eyes. He hadn't even seemed to be paying attention.

His teeth flashed in his brilliant grin. "I finally found the perfect notebook. I knew teal must be your favorite color."

I shook my head. I'd never told him that. "How did you know?"

He turned to stare at the pot of noodles, stirring absently. Or maybe to give himself something to do because he was embarrassed. "Every time we go somewhere, it's like you automatically gravitate toward anything that color. Those earrings we saw at that store one time. The fake flowers at the DA's office. The scarf you always wear. You touch it constantly. It's like it's magnetized, pulling you in."

I couldn't keep my tears at bay if I looked at him any longer, so I opened the cover to look inside at the blank pages, ideas swirling in my head for what to fill the empty space with.

His hands, the artist in my mind said, and I stole a glance at them while his eyes were still turned away.

The drawings I'd found tucked in boxes that belonged to another version of myself had inspired me to pick up sketching again, but I was woefully out of practice. I'd been taking any opportunity to doodle, dredging up the sleepy skills with my earnest attempts at capturing likenesses.

And he'd noticed.

There was a raw sharpness to the realization that I'd been *seen* on such a level, and the sense of vulnerability was hot and stinging and scary as hell. Without warning—for either of us—I threw myself against him, burrowing my face against his shoulder to hide the feelings I knew I wouldn't be able to conceal otherwise.

He stumbled back a step in surprise, chuckling, then wrapped his arms around me again.

"Thank you," I choked out. It was all I could manage with the emotion clogging my chest and throat.

He sighed and rested his chin on top of my head. "You're welcome."

I heard the smile in his voice, which sent a wave of warmth through me. I knew exactly what it would look like—that particular smile. Soft and subdued, his genuinely pleased grin that didn't quite show any teeth, but it felt deeper than his other smiles.

It felt special—just for me.

12

Ricochet

I wanted to stay and enjoy the meal with Drew. To bask in his warmth and the fuzzy feeling the gift he'd given me had created. Maybe even start on a new drawing. It was enough to make me forget about the competency hearing and the junk associated with it.

But even though my fingers itched to get a pencil, to scratch out mindless doodles while I acquainted myself with the texture of the paper in the journal, I still had answers to search for.

As if to drive the point home, the cloud of gloom that Evan dragged around with him any time I was in the vicinity made its appearance on his return from a workout in the garage, where Drew had a home gym set up.

The way Evan's chin jutted out at the sight of Drew and me together made me bristle, and his presence lit a fire under me so that I opted to leave before the food was ready just to get away from his judging stares.

Which put Drew in a mood, since he hadn't wanted me to go in the first place. I wondered if he'd have it out with Evan

95

while I was gone.

And because I now seemed in the habit of feeling guilty, I added causing more strife amongst the people around me to the pile of never-ending shame and blame I lugged around. I was counting down the days until Evan moved out, and I could have a little bit of peace for once.

I jogged down the porch steps with my shoulders hunched inward as if shielding myself from his judgment. To be fair, it was natural that he would be that suspicious of me, but it didn't make it easier to deal with. I thought by now he would have gotten over it, but he remained aloof and distrustful.

The tension sent my already high-alert senses into overdrive as soon as I was out in the open. Sweeping the street up and down did nothing to calm my nerves. It may have even added to my anxiety.

I regretted that my car was so recognizable. It was bad enough that my hair was a beacon of recognition. Add to that my limp, and I was a magnet for attracting the eye.

I'd almost forgotten about my limp until Skylar asked about it. Though I still felt the aching twinges, it was an old pain that had become part of my life, negligible background noise. It was way less pronounced by this point, but it stuck out to anyone else who didn't expect a young, healthy woman to have a hitch in her gait.

It was warm enough out by now to let my coat hang open to the breeze, but I knew I might need it when I jumped now that I knew the weather was variable between timelines. I scanned the neighborhood again but convinced myself everything was fine and climbed into the Beast. It was less of a mess since I'd gotten the front end repaired and practically moved in with Drew, but I checked the interior anyway. My recent brush with a skulking journalist made it feel necessary to cover all my bases.

Satisfied, I started the engine and headed for Skylar's apartment complex, too nervous to pay much attention to whatever played on the stereo. Eventually, even the background sound of it became too much, and I twisted the knob until the sound died.

I couldn't do much about the volume of the engine, but its steady growl was more soothing than irritating. Probably because I'd spent so many hours in the cab of this car, fleeing across state lines. That sound had meant distance, if not true freedom.

I pulled into the parking lot and cut the engine in front of the building that would be Skylar's in the other reality.

A full minute passed after I shut off the car while I worried my lip with my teeth. The possibility that I wouldn't get back to the right timeline weighed on my mind and kept my hands clamped on my steering wheel.

I'd never know if I didn't try, and I took comfort in the fact that, regardless, I could get back *here*, where I belonged.

That word reverberated in my head, amplified by my sense of culpability in concealing and misleading Drew about the whole situation. All these things happening to me were signs that I should have stayed here, not go sliding through dimensions.

Instead of turning around and letting it all go like I should have, I got out, locking the door out of habit more than necessity, and walked into the covered hallway.

A shiver swept over me when I remembered the cameras here that had picked up Creedy's sinister smile when he'd been stalking me in that other universe.

Would the cameras catch me making this jump?

Searching the corridor led me to the little black devices perched inconspicuously in the corners of the hall. We'd watched video of me before and after a jump, and it had been an eerie sight. But it was a weird ripple that could go unnoticed so easily if you weren't looking for it. A person could even explain it away as a glitch. I wasn't sure who saw the video these cameras caught, if anyone, and decided that it wasn't something worth looking into or worrying about. It wasn't likely they'd be able to do anything about it even if they noticed.

Still, I turned my back to the closest camera when I pulled the necklace out, not bothering to look at it as I rubbed my thumb over the design. I kept my focus on each of the doors that lined the corridor in case someone picked that moment to walk out and catch me in the act of sliding timelines. That would be a hard one to explain to a stranger.

The world wobbled and shimmered, the buzzing pressure building from my core. When it got thick enough, the air compressing to flatten me like a pancake, I slammed my eyes shut, trying to hold the air inside my lungs, but the weight of the atmosphere squeezed it right out of me.

I didn't fully lose consciousness this time, but I wanted to.

Oh, I wanted to be engulfed in the darkness and lost to the peace that came with it. But instead of blacking out, I caught myself with a hand on the concrete floor, the pressure inside my skull radiating with every throb of my heartbeat.

I pushed to my feet and staggered to the door to knock, leaning against the frame to keep myself upright as the world spun wildly around me. I had stopped moving, right?

Skylar yanked the door open with eager expectation as if she knew who would be on the other side, though she still looked shocked at the sight of me.

"Cassidy?" She took a step back, her eyes wide.

I stumbled forward and inside, barely making it to the couch before my legs gave out, fighting to stay lucid. Darkness prowled around the edges of my vision, and I blinked hard to keep Skylar in focus.

She stared at me from the door like she hadn't fully processed my presence. Her stillness made her sudden action when she moved seem inhuman by comparison as she shut the door and rushed into the kitchen. Or maybe that was an aftereffect of whatever was happening to my brain.

I closed my eyes while listening to the sounds of her slamming a cupboard, filling a glass with water at the sink, then her footsteps as she came back out to me.

She took my hand and put the glass into it. It felt warm against my palm, but I realized that was because I was freezing. My teeth had begun to chatter.

"What happened to you?" she asked, sitting next to me.

I lifted my head then felt a tickle on my top lip. When I reached up to touch my nose, I was unsurprised to find my fingers come away wet with blood. Skylar's eyes widened again, and she leaped from the couch to get me a paper towel.

If I had been questioning jumping timelines so often before, now I was certain. My brain was probably shredding itself from the inside, and I was about to stroke out right here on the couch.

I couldn't dredge up the appropriate panic the thought should have inspired because my head was hurting too badly, the room still rocking unsteadily like a boat on stormy seas.

"Do I need to call someone?" Her voice was tight with worry as she handed me the paper towel. "Take you to the ER?"

I shook my head, then regretted it, groaning as I pressed the towel to my nose. "I just need to rest for a minute." If I slipped into a coma, I'd certainly get the rest I craved. It didn't seem far-fetched at this point.

Her concern was like a physical presence, rolling off of her in waves that buffeted me with a worry that didn't penetrate my mental fog. I laid my head back and shut my eyes again.

"Cassidy." There was a warning in her voice. Somewhat like a mother cautioning her child away from something they knew they shouldn't touch.

"I'm jumping too much," I replied, but my voice was thready. Probably should have listened to my own concerns about jumping again so soon. My questions had seemed too important to ignore at the time. The most important thing to me now was getting the continuous throbbing of my brain to stop.

"How often are you going?"

Of course, she had to ask a question I couldn't answer. Not with the missing chunks of time I was experiencing.

"Every few days? I haven't been keeping track."

"That definitely seems like a lot," she said softly.

I lifted my head to look at her, still holding the paper towel to my nose. I blinked hard but considered it a good sign that the world had stopped whirling. I was starting to get my equilibrium back.

"I had to get back here. I need to know if Drew will give us the address."

A beat passed as she weighed her answer. "He sent it to me, but he was pissed you'd left again."

I took the paper towel from my nose to check the bleeding. It seemed to have stopped. "I didn't mean to." At least that I knew of.

She gave me a puzzled look.

My sigh was more tremulous than I would have liked, but my head wasn't protesting quite so violently. More good signs. "I went to sleep here on your couch and woke up at home. I don't remember how I got back, let alone deciding to."

"Are you serious?" She put a hand on my arm. "Cass, that seems dangerous."

The fear finally started to manifest, the first coil of unease tightening in my belly. "I don't know how to stop it." I almost didn't say the next part because it would confirm what she'd said. The words came softly as if that would keep her from hearing them. "It's not the first time recently that I didn't remember going back."

She gave me a shrewd look. "What does Drew think?"

I pressed a clean corner of the towel to my nose to double-check but also to give myself time to plan my evasion. "He's never been a fan of me jumping." It wasn't a lie, but it also wasn't a direct answer to her question. Judging by the look on her face, she knew it.

"Does he know what's been happening?" There was definitely reproach in her tone.

I stiffened, struggling to fight off the defensiveness that made me curl my fingers into a fist.

"It's fine," I snapped. "I just need to slow down a little."

She frowned at me. "Well, at least making you mad brought the color back to your face."

She was right. I felt the warmth in my cheeks, though I didn't know what I'd looked like in the first place. If my appearance was any reflection of what I felt, it was not a pretty sight.

I didn't want to keep talking about me, or Drew's disapproval, because he *was* going to be upset with me for not telling him what was going on. Especially when he found out how bad it really was. And I didn't want to dwell on what all of it was confirming.

Since I had already made the jump, why not make the complications worth it? I needed to redirect the conversation.

"So you have the address?" I winced as I shifted, but it wasn't as bad as I thought it would be. My headache was calming down to a dull throb.

She regarded me for one long moment, debating whether she wanted to go with the subject change or not.

"It's why I'm here," I insisted. "I swear I wouldn't risk it if it weren't important." Possibly now more than ever. If they had any answers, or at least a connection to an answer, I might find out what was happening to me and how to eradicate the problem.

"Drew sent me the information this morning. Before I told him you were gone." She stood. "Which reminds me."

I watched her walk into the kitchen. She came back, holding something out to me.

My phone. Not that it did me much good here. I'd had it with me on previous jumps and discovered how useless it was in other timelines. The process of whatever happened when I changed realities shorted it out until I went home, and even then, it took a while for it to come back to life. I didn't want to think about what that might mean for what was happening to me physically.

Still, I took it from her and stuffed it into its usual pocket inside my purse. "Thanks."

"As soon as you're feeling better, we can make a trip over to Professor Thibald's house," she said grudgingly.

"I feel fine now." I sat forward but didn't have the energy to stand up, breathing slowly through the flood of hot and cold that rushed over me in alternating waves.

She raised a brow. "Yeah, right. All the color drained out of your face just now."

It was just as well, considering that we might have been walking right into danger if whoever DeMarco and Edwards worked for was after Thibald. I hadn't confirmed if they were looking for him officially, or if it had only been the version in my timeline. But it wasn't worth the risk. So I needed to be in better shape, if not in top form.

She plied me with food, which did wonders for my complexion and lightheadedness, and I half-convinced myself that I was probably not eating enough. The bloody nose was a fluke, maybe even a coincidence.

Skylar chewed the inside of her cheek as I stood, watching my face for signs of an impending fainting spell, most likely. But my equilibrium remained steady, and I was almost more surprised than she was by the fact.

"Should we wait for Drew?" she asked.

I paused in the act of pulling my hair up into a messy bun. Her question was legitimate on the surface, but it seemed like a stall tactic to me.

I continued with my hair. "I'm not sure it's the best idea for him to know I'm here again."

She made a face as she put on her coat. I couldn't tell if it was because she agreed, or because she didn't like keeping it from him. Maybe it was both because I felt those things simultaneously as well.

My ultimate motivation was to avoid having to watch him in pain. It seemed like every interaction we had would drive him further into the shell of grief. Now that I had seen how I affected Drew when I knew him as well as I did, I had a lot more sympathy for the Evan here than I once had. Even my own father garnered more of my forgiveness than I'd previously extended.

All because someone I cared about was struggling with unimaginable loss, and I could see grief for what it was.

Admittedly, it was out of self-preservation to keep my return a secret from Drew. The guilt would swallow me whole if I spent more time with him, knowing how much agony I caused just by existing.

Skylar led the way out the door and to the parking lot for her car, and I made a face remembering she had that little sporty thing that barely had head and leg room for me. I cringed as I folded myself in, my body protesting every second after my rough landings the last few days.

We rode in silence for a while, and I wondered how much I was hurting Skylar by being here. She was grieving so much more right now too, but my presence almost seemed to bring her comfort.

It struck me then that it was probably because I wasn't off-limits to her. There was no element, outside of the things I wouldn't remember about her relationship with the other me, that was unavailable to her. We'd always connected, and I had never given her credit for being able to keep the two of us separate in her mind. Since I'd had so much trouble accepting that I was not their Cassidy, I hadn't seen it as clearly the first time.

But in this moment, I was coming to realize that I couldn't come back here after this—not with knowing what it was doing to everyone, including myself. I worried about how much *that* would hurt her. Would it be enough that I was able to show her I was all right? To know that I was doing okay in my own world—healing, if not whole? Or would my not coming back make her have to start over, grieving the loss of me all over again?

"Here it is," she said, breaking the silence, and I turned my attention to the house.

It was a one-story brick deal that clearly dated back to the sixties. It had a distinct Brady Bunch feel to it with a big front window and a one-car garage on the right-hand side. The roof hung low over the front, casting the entry in shadow.

Skylar pulled to the curb two houses down, in front of a two-story house whose Christmas lights hung haphazardly, blinking on and off in broad daylight. I was grateful she was being cautious, though I wasn't sure why the impulse had struck her. She had no reason to be constantly on alert like I was.

We sat for a moment, staring silently at the house. And then I saw it—movement across the open window. A shadow that could easily be explained away, if it was even noticed by passersby in the first place.

I might have even dismissed it if it weren't for the desperate hope that answers might be within my reach.

"Did you see that?" I asked to be sure, looking at Skylar.

The wide-eyed look she gave me was answer enough.

13

Seeing Red

We crept toward the house. We probably looked more suspicious moving that way than if we walked up normally, but the sense that we needed to sneak up on whoever was there made it feel necessary.

It was midday, so most people wouldn't be home or looking outside, right?

I peeked in through the front window in an attempt to determine who might be inside—whether it was someone we wanted to find or someone we very much wanted to avoid.

A flash of red caught my eye, and I froze. Someone unfamiliar could be even more dangerous than someone I knew, and no one I knew had red hair.

I held my hand, palm out, toward Skylar. She took the hint, leaning back against the house to keep herself out of view, eyes locked on me.

I considered our options. Could we sneak back to the car to regroup? Maybe sit and watch the house longer? Or was that too big of a risk?

Skylar could pass herself off as a teenager if we were caught, but I would not be able to lie my way out if we were.

We thought someone had broken in?

Weak.

My mind screamed to abort the mission, but I could very well be on the other side of the door from my answers. It was a now-or-never scenario if there ever was one. A ripple of anticipation danced through me, and I fought a shiver.

In the three seconds that passed while I deliberated, the front door swung open. The person on the other side froze as she caught sight of us. Her baffled expression was a literal mirror image of my own as we stared at each other for one suspended moment.

Skylar made a weird choking sound from behind me as she registered what we were looking at.

"What the hell are you doing?" The harsh stage whisper sent a burst of goosebumps rippling across my skin, chased by a drop in my stomach.

Hearing my own voice come from someone else—even if she wore my face—was the eeriest experience, and I swore my brain fell out of my head for half a second.

I blinked hard—because this was surely a hallucination—and licked my lips, debating the likelihood that being honest would work in my favor.

It was worth a shot. "Looking for Professor Thibald."

The other version of myself snorted before sliding a glance toward the street. "Who isn't? Get in here before your ninja poses get us in trouble. You're being suspicious as hell."

I swallowed and glanced back at Skylar, who seemed to be in a daze as she stared at the other me. Apparently, neither of us was fully capable of processing this moment.

I pulled the storm door open, and we joined the other Cassidy inside the house. Ancient wood floorboards creaked under our weight as we shuffled through a narrow entryway to a rectangular living room.

Other Cassidy looked around as if someone else might show up at any moment, and I forced myself to take note of the layout too. It was small and cramped, sparsely but tastefully decorated, which was a cursory summation since it was hard to keep myself from looking at Cassidy, taking more time to note her appearance than the house we currently occupied.

She was dressed in all black, which was not that far of a deviation from me, but her hair was barely shoulder length, waving in that perfectly casual, effortless style I'd seen some women pull off. Knowing my own hair, I bet it was not as effortless as it appeared. Her eyes held a flintiness that rivaled mine, which seemed impossible given all the things I'd experienced in life. But whatever she'd lived through might have made her shell even thicker, and I didn't want to think what that might have been.

"Who's your tiny friend?" Other Cassidy asked, turning to give both of us a cursory glance.

Skylar made a sound somewhere between a grunt and a growl.

Other Cassidy smirked, and it was borderline malicious.

I stepped forward, partially blocking Skylar from view. "Here's a better question: what are *you* doing in a timeline you don't belong to?"

Her eyes slid to my face then did a slow appraisal of my body, up and down like she was sizing me up. If she weren't a clone of myself, I would have felt a little threatened. "I could ask you the same thing, precious."

I stiffened.

She smiled again when she saw that her words had affected me. So she could tell I wasn't supposed to be here. But how? To be fair, there were very few reasons I would be seeking out Thibald if I didn't at least *know* about jumping.

She was watching my face closely. "Oh, yeah. I know about you, little miss anomaly." She winked as she walked the room, perusing items on shelves, pictures in frames. Her movements were overly casual, but she moved with the slinking grace of a mountain cat on the prowl. Something pinched in her expression as she took in the photos.

I forced myself not to look at Skylar, so I wouldn't alert Cassidy that she was getting to me. My initial thought was that this other version of me would be an ally, but she might have been a new kind of enemy, and I was putting us in dangerous territory. And it rankled.

"We *all* know about you," Cassidy said as she picked up a trinket from a shelf, examined it, then looked at me without raising her head.

"Who's 'we'?" My voice was stronger than I expected, considering how off-balance I felt.

She smirked at me again, and it was clear she enjoyed having the upper hand, knowing things I didn't. "You're lucky it was me and not Edwards you ran into. I have bigger fish to fry than chase after little loose ends like you." She set the trinket back down, turning away for a second.

Her words sent a stab of ice through my middle. "Like Thibald?"

She turned back toward us, still with deliberate slowness, and moved in my direction. Did I catch a slight hitch in her step at his name? Or was that my imagination?

"He's a puzzle piece," she admitted.

Her equivocation was irritating, but I watched her intently with my next words: "Louisa Lee, then."

She cocked her head, her expression pulling a little too tight. "Is that whose charm you have?" Her eyes dropped to the necklace I wore.

I fought the urge to wrap my hand around it and hide it from view.

She stopped moving toward me. "That's why you're here, in this split, you know."

Realization dawned as she spoke, and my eyes widened.

That smug look crept onto her face again, and it was clear how much she relished her advantage over me. "Don't you know how these things work?"

Irritation spiked my blood at her patronizing tone. "You know the answer to that," I snapped.

She surprised me by laughing, but it was dark, a little twisted. I thought I had been the messed up, distorted puzzle piece, but she was next level.

"You're here because Louisa Lee is here. Somewhere," she added with a hint of irritation. "This necklace is linked to her. Any jump you make brings you to whatever reality she's in."

Skylar's intake of breath was slight enough that I barely registered it. She'd been so still and quiet, I'd almost forgotten she was there. But even as Skylar seemed to make the connection, my mind struggled to absorb Cassidy's words.

I blinked once, slowly, as the pieces clicked into place. All those other random realities I'd jumped to before this were because Louisa had been in them. Of course, that made sense. And she was still in this timeline, which is what had brought me back.

That was one answer, but I needed a million more. "So, if I

have her necklace, how is she jumping?"

Cassidy's mouth pinched in displeasure, though she tried not to show it. It would seem like a weakness in her mind, the fact that she didn't know. "She must have someone else's."

"Or more than one," Skylar suggested.

Cassidy narrowed her eyes as she shifted her attention. "Possible. But doubtful. There are very few of us who have more than one, and *Louisa* is not one of us."

There was that collective pronoun again, and the question itched to be voiced. I figured she wasn't likely to give up the information since she didn't the first time. But there was something else in her tone, a question that was dogging her, and that seemed like a more viable track to take.

"Is Thibald?" I asked, monitoring her reaction closely.

Her mouth pinched and the slightest twitch of her muscles as they clenched was noticeable, if only to me, though she tried to play it off. "Not technically."

Not exactly a clear answer, but it seemed honest enough. "Is he an enemy then? Turned on you guys?"

She closed the last few feet between us before I knew what she was doing and yanked the necklace from my neck so quickly, I almost lost my balance from the force.

Panic was lightning hot through my gut as she backed away, my hand shooting up to my now naked throat. I had no idea if she had a weapon somewhere on her or what kind of training she had. Her behavior told me she wasn't to be trusted, so I didn't attempt to get the necklace back. Not yet, anyway. She could rethink her stance on me not being her primary target at any moment or see me trying to get it back as a threat.

But desperation was like daggers under my skin.

A thought, like an old friend showing up unexpectedly,

ghosted through my mind. I had once gotten by on pickpocketing, and it seemed like a million years ago that that was how I'd met Drew in the first place.

And though I'd sworn off my old life and my old ways, I had to admit that this seemed like an appropriate time to fudge on my promise. It didn't hurt that the idea of pulling a fast one on her gave me a dark sense of satisfaction.

"I don't belong here, remember? I need that to get back to my timeline." I didn't have to fake the nervousness in my tone, but I leaned harder into it to keep her attention on that.

She palmed the necklace and grinned at me, dark and vicious. "Oh, you'll snap back there eventually. It only takes, like, a week."

"Please," I begged, taking a step toward her, my hand outstretched. "I have to get back before then."

I let the desperation in my voice, the absolute *need* crawling through every molecule of my being, permeate the air. It was so molten that I was sure it heated the atmosphere, the intensity of it bleeding toward her.

Her chin shifted forward just a fraction, and it was jarring to see that look of defiance on her face. Knowing what others saw when that edge came into my demeanor made me realize how difficult I must have been to deal with sometimes.

Cassidy clenched her teeth and gave a soft growl. "Fine." She pulled a bracelet from her wrist. "I need the necklace to find Louisa and Thibald. You can take my bracelet."

I held my relief in check, focusing on the logistics instead. "Will that tether me to you?"

"Cassidy, don't," Skylar warned from behind me, but I ignored her as the other Cassidy took a few steps forward to hand it to me. Her body wasn't close enough for me to swipe the necklace she'd pocketed.

She gave me a disgusted once-over, choosing to ignore Skylar as well. "Technically, yes." And she was none too pleased about it. "Don't be stupid. They're looking everywhere for you. If it gets back to them that I helped you, I'm in deep shit. And you're going to get yourself killed."

The warning made sense given what I'd already experienced, but I tried not to think too hard about it for the moment. It would paralyze me, and I needed to focus. "Thank you."

She rolled her eyes, then strode forward, taking our arms in turn and shoving us toward the door. "You need to leave. We can't be in close proximity or I'll drag you with me. You haven't learned how to block someone else's jump."

"Wait," I said, trying to dig my heels in. I turned inward a little, dropping my hand into her pocket with the bracelet she'd just given me, switching it for the necklace as lightly as I could, pulling it with two fingers. She was less likely to notice the necklace was gone with the bracelet resting in its place. "I have questions."

At least I didn't have to lie about that part.

Her expression pinched. "No questions."

I slid my hand out and curled my fingers around the necklace, continuing with my diversion, and pushed against Cassidy. Was it my imagination, or was she seriously stronger than me? Like, girlfriend worked out.

"Please."

"No. Don't ask questions, lay low, and for God's sake, don't jump too often or you'll liquefy your brain."

My thoughts stuttered over that last part, my mouth opening and closing like a gaping fish as she shoved Skylar and me out the front door. I flinched as she slammed and locked it before we could do anything else.

I stood there, staring out at the street.

Liquefy my brain?

My hands were numb, and I almost dropped the necklace I'd stolen back.

"Cassidy, let's go before she jumps and takes you with her." Skylar's voice was shaky, and I heard the fear in it because it echoed the very real terror brewing inside of me.

Skylar tugged my sleeve since I seemed incapable of forming a coherent thought, let alone making my body move as it should. I let her lead me back to her tiny car, and I obediently got in while my dazed thoughts rambled in panicked circles, absently stuffing the necklace into my pocket.

Skylar wasted no time pulling away from the curb and taking us as far from that house as she could get us. As if she could outrun what was happening or what this all meant for me, for us.

My shoulders curled inward, and I wished I could form a protective shield around myself. I didn't want to deal with what was building inside of me—what was compounded by what Skylar was feeling.

The urge to fill the silence became overwhelming, an itchy pressure against my skin.

"Well. . . that was interesting."

Skylar glanced at me with the most incredulous look on her face, I would have laughed out loud. Which triggered my next thought.

Humor, my brain reminded me. *Divert, diffuse, deflect.*

My fingers curled into my palm. "I mean, we all know *I* can be a bitch. But that was next level."

My attempt fell flatter than usual.

She scoffed with disgust and turned her attention to the traffic ahead of us. "Seriously? You're going to talk about her attitude? How about the fact that she just warned you about something I think you're already starting to experience?"

"What do you want me to say?" The edge in my voice was so sharp even I flinched. "'Oh, right, I'm melting my mind with physics-defying leaps through dimensions. Gotta head home, bye?'"

"Cassidy—"

"I get it," I interrupted. "I've been losing time. Like, literally, waking up with no memory of how I got home, sleeping way longer than normal and missing important appointments, and I know how I must have looked today when I showed up at your place."

Her palms slammed against the steering wheel, making me jump. "You looked like you were dead, Cassidy. Literally, gray and cold. Your lips were purple. You got a bloody freaking nose."

The volume she'd reached was way too loud for the small space, but I didn't dare tell her to lower it. That, coupled with every added description, gave fear a foothold, cold tendrils infiltrating like black vines through my insides. It would suffocate me if I let it, squeeze the very life out of me.

"I still have to go home," I insisted, telling her as much as the terror.

"You're going to kill yourself." The words were half-strangled by what sounded like a sob.

"*They* want to kill me!" I lurched forward, prodded by the heat of anger. Heat to kill the cold. It was my way. "My life is not my own until I make it *stop*. What's the point of preserving it if I have to run or hide?"

"What will there be to hide if you're brain-dead?" she fired back, each word a bullet to my body.

I clenched my muscles against the onslaught and turned to look out the window. If only Cassidy had given me the chance to ask all of my questions.

How often was too often? How did I make them stop chasing me? Did she know anything about the other version of my family? What training did she have that I didn't? Could I train as well? How much did Louisa know? Why did Cassidy need to find her and Thibald? How many other anomalies were there? Should I warn them? Could I protect them in some way?

No one had mentioned any other *known* anomalies, but there had to be more out there. One percent of the population wasn't zero. But they'd at least had the benefit of anonymity to a point. If the people that were part of Cassidy's "us" were aware of *my* existence, then I would never be able to live in peace.

Not when taking me out was their ultimate goal. They had to clean up the mess someone else had made, didn't they? If it were only the questions, I could have made peace with it and given up on answers. But my life was still in danger.

If only I could convince Cassidy to do something about it, help me disappear or fall off their radar somehow. . .

She hadn't been overly helpful, but she certainly wasn't out to get me. Not yet, anyway. If she'd been fully committed to whatever mission the "us" had, she would have taken me in or taken me out.

Was her loyalty more fluid, or was it that she didn't have it in her to eliminate a version of herself? That would probably give anyone pause. Having to watch yourself die at your own hands was a paradox that would send anyone into an existential tailspin. Even the hypothetical scenario would make the average person consider committing themselves to an institution.

I was honestly considering it right then, driving myself absolutely bonkers trying to hash this all out and sift through the emotions that were rioting in my brain.

The pull to get home as soon as possible nagged at me, though. If I had to stop jumping for a while—or indefinitely—I wouldn't want to get stuck anywhere else. And certainly not here.

How much danger was I putting myself in by making that last jump?

14

Sideways

Frustration simmered and crackled between us as we returned to Skylar's apartment. She stewed in her fear and worry over me, and it was amplified by my own anxiety, threatening to drown me.

Wasn't it enough to have Callum on my tail and Creedy still obsessed with me?

It didn't seem fair.

Not that much was. It had been a long time since I'd raged at the world for all the wrongs done to me. The jumping I'd been doing and the experiences I had seemed like a special kind of hell designed specifically for me. Why *not* throw me into a world where my father had never abandoned me? Or show me what an awful person my long-dead mother would have been had she lived?

And now, fry my brain just for trying to figure the whole thing out?

Why not?! I wanted to shout as the bitterness coated my throat and tongue. If only the words would burn the taste away. But they wouldn't. Nothing would.

"Cassidy," Skylar started as soon as I sat on her couch.

"Give me a minute." I leaned back, rubbing my hands over my face. "I just need a minute," I repeated in a whisper.

She sat next to me, resting her elbows on her knees and clasping her hands. She chewed a lip as she stared at the floor. Her desire to speak spiked the air with strain.

I slid my hands into my hair and gripped, the faint sting along my scalp reminding me I was here, that this insanity was, in fact, my life.

How did I get here?

I took a deep breath. "Okay," I finally said.

Skylar lifted her head a smidge but didn't look at me yet.

It was an effort to still my racing mind, to force my clenched hands from my hair, and to sit forward to talk it through calmly. "I got some answers, and I have a connection point if I need it."

"And you were told not to jump anymore," she put in, her tone dry. But I didn't miss what was underneath. The censure put barbs into the words.

"Not forever," I countered. "Just not too frequently."

"Cassidy, why are you even doing this?"

I stiffened, reading an accusation where there might not have been one.

"Things are going well for you now, aren't they?"

I scoffed.

She rolled her eyes. "Okay, not perfect. I get that. But things have turned around for you, right?"

I clenched my jaw, thinking through what she was saying. Did I have a more permanent living situation? Yes. Was I in a relationship that was relatively healthy for once? Seemed to be.

But I had two men on my tail, one of whom was tied to this entire thing and who was still on the hunt to take me out. Edwards was a wild card I had no way of predicting. That meant stopping wasn't the end of the whole thing.

"You should go back and stay put for a while," Skylar said. "Putting your life in danger isn't worth the answers you want."

The stinging rush of anger filled my body, and I ground my teeth. The urge to give the energy somewhere to go forced me to my feet. It felt too much like she was reducing the whole thing to a selfish need for answers, as if it were about questions on a math test and not the explanation for a freaky phenomenon that shouldn't be happening to anyone, let alone me.

Skylar watched as I paced her living room with barely contained rage. Though it wasn't directed at her, the frustration was a building heat that made my muscles ache from restraining it.

Why couldn't this be something easy? If only I could hop back and forth, get my answers, and go home. But of course not. My life had to be fraught with complications.

"You have to weigh the worth of what you're doing," Skylar continued. She apparently thought it was a point worth pursuing, even though I was obviously almost at my limit.

"Getting freaking Edwards and whatever weird ass organization he works for off my back isn't worth the effort?"

She didn't flinch at the edge in my voice. "It's your *life*, Cassidy."

I sucked in a breath and pressed my palms to my forehead. "But I never get to just live it."

She grew very still at my words, like she'd stumbled upon a rare bird and didn't want to scare it away.

It was probably the despair in my voice, the abject desolation and tragedy this whole thing was. My life was.

"I honestly don't know how much more I can take," I murmured, finally lowering myself to the floor in a crouch, wincing at the flash of pain in my leg.

She let me have my moment to wallow in the misery and the pain and the absurdity of everything that was happening. Or she simply didn't know what to offer as comfort. I wouldn't blame her for tapping out at this point. This was certainly where I was out of my depth.

After a few minutes, she spoke. "I know so much of this has been out of your control."

I fought the urge to fling a sarcastic comment at her, to cut her down with my derision. Make her hurt like I did.

She must have sensed it because she softened her next words. "This is the part that you *can* control. You stand up and you walk away. If Edwards is after you, you take him out when he comes. But go home. Don't throw away what's going on there by trying to go on the offense. Offense only works when there's a plan, when you can see what's in front of you. And you're feeling your way through the dark."

I lifted my head, her words both fanning and suffocating the flame of anger and bitterness inside of me. The juxtaposition was unnerving as I vacillated between wanting to scream at her and hug her.

She was giving me permission to give up on this road. No one would think less of me for walking away and taking what came after if needed. If only Edwards would give up, too.

Believing he would was a false hope that I could not allow to grow. Wishful thinking had never gotten me far.

But I wished all the same. That it had worked like I'd wanted it to, that I could feel safe, that I could control something in my life for once. This had seemed like something I could grasp onto and pursue, to do for myself. I could make jumps when *I* wanted to. But even when I'd thought I was sticking it to whatever force was at work, it was working even harder against me.

And some small part of me acknowledged my unwillingness to give up was probably a form of self-sabotage. After all, I'd been keeping all of this from Drew. If he knew, he'd be saying the same thing as Skylar. And he'd fight me a whole lot harder.

It was the first time in so long anyone would force me to put my well-being above anything else. And I was resisting that—pushing back against the people who cared if I lived or died. How backwards was that?

I'd fought off Creedy because I wanted to live. I'd opened myself up to Drew, to the possibility of a life. Why was I willing to throw all of that away for this? When it was all pain and confusion?

I wanted to live. Not hide. Not run.

"It's up to you," Skylar finally said. She must have sensed I'd come to some sort of conclusion in my own mind.

Indeed, my frenetic movements and breathing had slowed, and I became more aware of the other sounds in the room again. The refrigerator that hummed from in the kitchen, the clunk of the heater coming on, and the sounds of neighbors coming or going outside of her apartment.

The ordinariness of it all seemed absolutely absurd, and it made me want to rage again. It was an affront that there was such a thing as "normal" for anyone when I'd been denied anything so rational.

"I think you know what the right choice is. Obviously, I'd

hate to give this up—seeing you again. But I'd much rather you stay alive, even if it's somewhere else." Her voice hitched on the last two words.

That almost broke me. This would cause her more grief. But if I didn't stop, it would be worse. For her but also for my Drew. And I couldn't willfully hurt him like that. Not when I could see what was happening to the Drew here.

I pushed to my feet again, fighting to keep my emotion in check. "You're right. Of course."

She didn't look relieved at my admission. If anything, I could see the grief ripping her open right there.

Or maybe that was because I felt the rupture in my own heart as I watched her face. Nothing could ever confirm my instinct not to tell the Drew here that I was back quite like the agony that bounced between Skylar and me.

It was all too much. For both of us. For everyone.

15

Old Wounds

With all the time I'd spent in this town, even though I'd done little of the driving, I didn't have trouble finding the house I sought. Maybe it was some sort of emotional beacon that called to me.

I slowed and pulled to the curb a few houses down and watched the front of the yellow one. Its farmhouse charm permeated the phantom ache that sent throbs through the fissures in my heart.

I'd needed some space to think after the events of the day before, not to mention time, before I made my jump home, so Skylar had offered her car to me. She'd had to meet her mom for something to do with her grandmother's estate anyway, and I was grateful for the opportunity. Even if it meant cramming myself into this tiny clown car.

And it was probably a stupid impulse to come here, of all places.

Because "addicted to torture" sounded morbid, I decided to blame it on what I had recently dubbed "Little Orphan Annie Syndrome."

Not just because of the red hair.

Technically, I *was* an orphan. It was weird to remember that fact, given that I'd only recently learned my father had died many years before. Even though he'd been gone for a long time, he still existed in my mind.

The Hard-Knock life played in my head in annoying little girl voices, the refrain twisting my insides tighter and tighter. Though it seemed cheesy, it also felt embarrassingly accurate.

So if I was little Orphan Annie, this house could only be that dream mansion—the full physical representation of everything I wanted but didn't have.

But there was no Daddy Warbucks to rescue me from the mire of that life.

Just a father who'd lost a better version of me and who deserved to be left alone in his grief.

And still, I sat in the car, replaying the scenes in my head from when I'd used my words to protect myself from the pain we were all experiencing but couldn't assuage, wishing I could go apologize.

But after my last adventure with an alternate version of my family—and I felt a pang knowing that this was the end of my search for them too—I fought the urge.

It would never, could never, happen.

Like Skylar said, I needed to go home and stay there, focus my energy on what was in front of me. I could go on the defense if it came to that. But at the moment, neither Cassidy nor Edwards knew where exactly to find me, and I needed to use that to my advantage.

A sense of defeat and disappointment blocked any rightness I should have felt at the prospect. Maybe because it was too much like giving up. I had pushed through so much to get to this point, and there was a part of me that felt like I'd made some sort of promise to that other version of my family. I was breaking it if I walked away now.

Or maybe I was just breaking a promise to myself.

The insistent thought that I needed to get home pulsed in my brain, but my hands didn't move from the steering wheel. The desire to turn off the car and go inside to see Jane and my father warred with my determination to leave bad enough alone.

It was strange to know that I'd done enough healing in the last two months to even consider going to them in search of the comfort I was sure they could provide me.

After all, the iteration of my family here seemed the most whole. But it pained me to know that they were now fractured too, sliced apart by the loss of the best version of me I'd never be.

That reminder glued me to the seat.

And so I stayed where I was, letting the wave of longing crash over me unhindered because I did not wish to cause them any more pain. Skylar had experienced some form of comfort by my reappearance. But the agony I was causing the Drew that belonged here made me wary of deepening anyone else's grief.

It would be selfish of me to seek my own comfort over theirs.

Still, I didn't move for a long time. I merely stared at the front of that house, my eyes tracing the front porch like an old friend. Memories accosted me of the night emotions had swamped me and sent me out in tears, aching in a way that felt permanent.

Drew had followed me, comforted me. Kissed me.

That moment had been so defining. I could maybe even say that was the moment some of my fractured pieces had been fitted back together. Not fixed. Probably never fixed. But the beginning of a repairing process that I was still navigating.

I reluctantly put the car in drive and turned it around, absently chewing my lip as I made my way back to Skylar's apartment, a question simmering in my mind.

Would it be easier for her if I left without saying goodbye? I'd had a sense last night that this goodbye would be our final one. Part of me hoped she was still at that meeting with her mom when I got back because I wasn't sure *I* could face what I knew this would be.

I was giving up.

It was still an effort to convince myself this was the right course. But I didn't belong here. People weren't meant to travel between alternate timelines; we weren't meant to see what lives we could have had, who we could have been, good or bad.

I would have agreed absolutely with that sentiment in my first go-around with sliding dimensions. But now, it was undeniable that there were ways my life was irrevocably changed for the better.

I tried to take comfort in that—that I had gained more than I had lost, even if it was the end of the road now.

The sound of a horn honking bit through the emotional deluge that cascaded inside of me. I slammed on my brakes, realizing that I'd almost blown right through a stop sign. The driver of the car I'd almost hit flipped me off as they drove past, and I willed my heartbeat to slow.

What a goodbye it would be if I'd crashed Skylar's car before taking off for good. Talk about leaving a lasting memory.

I gave a short laugh, which came out a little strangled. I twisted my hands on the steering wheel and double-checked in both directions before moving through the intersection again.

By the time I reached Skylar's apartment, I settled on leaving a note. It didn't matter how much I tried to convince myself that the right thing was to wait and give her a proper goodbye. My heart couldn't handle it. Not when I was still grappling with giving up on everything I'd been working toward all this time.

I didn't want to think how much time, how many arguments, how many fearful experiences through the last weeks added up to this moment.

My lips pressed into a tight line as I wrote out the simple note to Skylar. I obsessively checked the front door, my stomach tying in knots at the thought of her walking in before I could escape.

It was the coward's way, but I'd made the choice.

I gripped the necklace as I walked toward the door.

16

Giving In

I clawed my way to consciousness, my mind fighting every ounce of my body's unwillingness to be alert. It was slow and agonizing, painful like my very bones had been pumped full of lead.

When I finally came to, becoming aware of where I was in fits and starts, slumped against Drew's bed—how?—I patted drunkenly at my pocket for my phone.

What time was it? What *day* was it?

My phone screen blinked on and off like it was having a seizure, refusing to give me the answers. Though a vague recollection of driving back to the house floated like a ghost through my memory, I couldn't remember when that was.

I turned to the clock on the wall, but my eyes wouldn't focus enough to read it. Something in my gut told me I was missing something important.

I staggered to my feet, banging into the door before yanking it open and stumbling into the hallway. Evan was walking from the kitchen to the living room and froze halfway when he caught sight of me.

He looked behind him as if I had snuck past him somehow. "How long have you been here?"

I blinked hard and stumbled toward the kitchen to see if I could read the digital clock on the stove, inching closer when the glowing numbers only melded into each other.

Was it Thursday? The day of the meeting with Grace and Carla?

"Where's Drew?" I asked, ignoring his question.

"At work," Evan said slowly, turning so that he could watch me.

I bent over to squint at the clock again, rocking a bit unsteadily, so I set my hands on the counter to keep from falling into it.

For once, Evan's gaze didn't hold the mild antagonism as he stared at me. Instead, his expression morphed from confusion to diagnostic speculation befitting a doctor, despite this being out of his scope of practice.

I couldn't begin to guess what he was thinking, but I knew I probably looked like I was coming down from a bender. It felt a bit like I was.

It took another minute, but the numbers on the clock finally solidified and registered. I was supposed to be at the station almost twenty minutes ago.

"Crap. I'm late," I muttered, pushing myself upright.

I knew I wouldn't make it there without something to stabilize my spinning equilibrium, so I turned to the pantry, pawing at the door. Swaying as I surveyed my options, I searched for something that might level me out so I could get moving. My hand landed on a candy bar, and I figured it was as good a snack as any.

I unwrapped it as I went toward the door.

"Cassidy, wait," Evan said, his voice flush with genuine concern.

My capacity to hold a conversation, let alone explain myself, was at zero, so I ignored him and walked out.

As soon as I was out of his sight, I leaned against the pillar holding up the front porch overhang for a second and shut my eyes, working through my breathing. I took a bite of the chocolate bar, swallowing without taking the time to taste it, and willed it to fix whatever was off after making these jumps, as if it were an issue with blood sugar rather than my brain liquefying. Sugar was always the answer, right?

It did seem to steady me a bit, and I made it down the porch steps without pitching head-first down them, which I counted as a win.

I got to my car and started it up, ignoring the protest of the engine and the violence of the shivering that had overtaken me. It wasn't that cold outside, but there had been a significant drop in my body temperature as soon as I'd become conscious.

I made it to the station in less than ten minutes, which was a bit of a record and probably should have alerted me that I'd been driving too fast. But it didn't dawn on me until I pulled into the parking lot.

Already I felt more stable and less like my brain was trying to escape from the protection of my skull as I did my lopsided jog up the station steps.

I hurried inside, craning my neck to see back into the main part of the station while I stepped up to the front desk to give my name. The uniformed officer seated behind it waved me back since I had been expected over thirty minutes before.

Drew wasn't at his desk, so I cut straight for the conference room he favored for almost all of our meetings. The door was ajar, and I could see his long frame before I was close enough to say anything.

He was leaning against the edge of the table, his legs stretched out in front of him. He rubbed a hand along his chin, and the tension in his shoulders showed the weight of his worry.

He turned as soon as I walked into the room.

"Cassidy," he said, his voice flush with relief as he shot to his feet. He started toward me, his movements becoming stiff and robotic as if he'd caught himself trying to reach for me just in time.

"Where is everyone?" I gave the empty room a cursory glance, breathless from my walk in.

"Carla and Grace had another meeting to get to." He strode forward to push the door closed before turning back to me, sliding his hands along my face to cradle it. "Cass, are you okay?" Worry etched itself into the lines of his forehead while his eyes searched mine.

I felt like I was about to melt. He caught me against him as my knees wobbled.

"I'm sorry I was so late," I mumbled against his shoulder.

"What happened? I called a bunch of times."

I buried my face deeper against him. I didn't want to answer; I didn't want to acknowledge it. Even though I'd already talked through it all with Skylar, this was going to be hard to admit. Not just because it meant truly acknowledging that it was over. But because I had willfully kept it from him.

The comforting warmth of his arms and the way I fit so snugly against him made me reluctant to say anything that would ruin the moment.

Skylar had been right, though. I'd known it as soon as she'd spoken the words. I needed to stop, and now I needed to admit it to him.

But the part of me that worried I would do something to drive him away was shouting so loudly in my head, I couldn't think straight enough to form the words. The fear that I had finally done the unforgivable ate at me like acid, consuming any attempt at convincing myself otherwise. I always thought there was a last straw, and surely this would be it.

Drew pulled back and looked down into my face as my silence stretched and grew heavy with my worry.

It was an effort to keep myself from looking away. I fought the urge to spin out of his arms and put distance between us, to use it as a buffer. I had to stop putting the walls up.

"Cass? What's going on?" he finally asked, probably tired of the pressure my lies by omission had created.

My fingers curled into my palms, and I did look away as the heat burned into my cheeks, my chest tightening.

He waited, and my stomach wound itself into knots.

"I have to stop jumping." My words fell into the silence between us like stones into still water.

He took a breath then shut his mouth, tilting his head. "What? Why? I mean, don't get me wrong. I never wanted you to make these jumps in the first place. But why now? What happened?"

I rubbed my palms together in an attempt to get some warmth back into them. "I've been having issues."

He still had his hands on my arms, so I felt it when he stiffened, his fingers digging ever so slightly. "What do you mean by 'issues'?"

I shook off his touch, suddenly feeling lightheaded again. "Can we sit down? I need to sit."

He said nothing in response and made no move as I lowered myself into a chair. Wariness limned him with a sharpness that made me wince, and my reluctance became a physical wall in my mind, tall and thick. It felt impossible to knock down.

But I needed to be honest.

"You know how exhausted I've been when I get back," I started. "But I've also been. . . losing time."

He sucked in a sharp breath and sat then, leaning forward to rest his elbows on his knees. His intent gaze on my face made me squirm.

I intertwined my fingers, watching them twist together so that I wouldn't have to meet his eyes. "Sometimes I won't remember jumping home. Or even deciding to. I just keep waking up here, in our timeline, at your house."

Drew exhaled loudly through his nose, and I imagined his frustration, maybe even anger. But I didn't want to see it, didn't want confirmation, so I didn't glance up.

"Headaches, dizziness, bloody noses," I continued, though my voice had gotten softer, whittled down by my shame.

His hand moved, and my eyes jerked up to follow it. The trauma response was still ingrained, that hypersensitivity to any movement in high-stress situations. It didn't matter that he'd never hit me; even knowing with absolute certainty he never would, my reaction was automatic.

He paused, then watched me carefully as he rubbed his palm against his ever-present five o'clock shadow. That scratchy sound was comforting amid my unease.

But that wasn't what struck me. It was that he *didn't* look angry or frustrated. It was worry that wrinkled his brow, and his eyes only reflected fear and concern.

I swallowed the lump in my throat. "I ran into another

me. One who works with Edwards, I think. She makes jumps. On purpose." I shook my head as if the thought were absurd. "I asked her some of my questions. She wasn't super forthcoming, but she warned me that jumping too much 'without training' was dangerous."

He started to say something, but I interrupted.

"I know." I threw my hands up in defense, an edge of protection sharpening my words. "I know. You were right. I didn't know enough about this, and I shouldn't have been doing it."

He took my flailing hands to still them, cradling them in both of his. The jolt was a shock to my system, shorting out my brain so that I couldn't think to pull away or continue in my own defense.

"That's not what I was going to say."

It took me a moment to process his words, the thoughts still halted by his touch.

"What I was going to tell you is that I'm sorry it's not working out the way you wanted it to."

I stared at him, uncomprehending now because it made no sense that he was being so understanding. He should be angry. He should be yelling at me that I'd been wrong all along.

Instead, his completely sympathetic expression triggered an emotional response that I couldn't stop. My lip trembled, and I leaned forward into his chest. His arms dropped around me.

Because it sucked, and I was truly angry that I had to stop looking for my answers, give up on looking for my family, quit trying to understand the chaos of being thrust into these worlds without my permission, I felt so defeated.

Bleak despair filled me, the pessimist in me swearing that nothing would ever work out right. I should have been used to it by now, but it still felt unfair.

After a moment, I took a deep, somewhat tremulous breath and pulled out of Drew's embrace. I had to remind myself that he wasn't crumbling before my eyes, and I still had a purpose in the upcoming trial against Creedy. I still had a role to play and something to drive me forward.

It didn't feel like enough right then, but I knew it would be once I got past the mourning period.

He stroked my cheek with the back of his hand. "Thank you for finally telling me."

I tensed, giving him a suspicious glare. "What's that supposed to mean?"

His mouth took on a wry twist. "I knew you weren't telling me everything. I was just waiting until you were ready."

I punched his shoulder lightly, and he sat back with a surprised laugh.

"I hate it when you do that," I grumbled.

He laughed again. "Do what?"

I gripped the front of his shirt, giving him a gentle shake. "All the right things."

He clicked his tongue. "I do believe you said I am the worst."

I scoffed. "You are. It's like you're trying to make me fall in love with you."

His smile was slow and smoldering, and my stomach dropped out just looking at him.

"Maybe that's my plan," he murmured, leaning forward.

My heart launched into acrobatics as he brushed his lips against mine ever so briefly, which was probably a good thing. There was a knock on the door a split-second before it swung open.

We jerked apart as an older man, probably mid-forties,

peeked inside the room. "Oh, hey, Seward. I wasn't sure anyone was using this room. Wanted to do some interviews."

Drew pushed to his feet. "Room's all yours. Ms. Marchand was just heading home." He never took his eyes from my face, and I didn't miss the significant look he gave me on the word "home." I also didn't miss the flush that crept up his neck and hoped the other guy didn't notice.

I stood too, pressing my lips together as I turned toward the door and the other man. He gave me a quick appraisal and then transferred the incisive look to Drew.

I glanced over at Drew too, a nervous flutter starting in my stomach. Drew might have been a hard read, but considering who he worked with, I was dubious our secret would stay that way for long.

The man stepped back from the door to let us pass, his jaw working as he watched Drew put his hand against my back to guide me out and toward the front.

"I think that guy is getting suspicious," I said under my breath as we moved through the room.

Drew didn't turn. "This room is full of detectives. Everyone is suspicious. Hell, *I'm* suspicious."

His attempt at the joke didn't comfort me. The guy had been way too intent on our interactions even in the two seconds he'd watched us. It wasn't as if he'd seen anything worth reporting. We'd pulled apart before he'd looked around the door. Still, I made a mental note to keep Drew at arm's length the next time I came in.

Which reminded me about the meeting we were supposed to have been in with Carla and Grace.

"Has the meeting been rescheduled?"

He frowned as we got closer to the doors outside. "Grace

said she'd let us know."

It seemed like he wanted to say more.

"What?"

He gave a small grimace. "She wasn't happy you weren't there today."

My gut clenched, that old familiar sense of being a disappointment sliding through me like an inky, black toxin. It made me want to go on the defense, my usual reaction to shame.

He must have felt it through the tension in my muscles. His hand still rested on my back, a heat that simmered even through my jacket. "I think it was more than just the no-show. The competency hearing most likely."

It wasn't as reassuring as he probably meant it to be. Unease joined the shame and defensiveness, but I clenched my teeth against the reactive words that billowed within me.

"Try not to stress about it. We'll figure it out." He stopped short of following me outside, and the war in his eyes helped settle the reactivity inside.

I turned a little, taking a step toward the door to make sure we weren't standing too close. It was obvious he wanted to follow me out; he leaned forward then rocked back on his heels, grimacing. His hands flexed as if he were fighting the urge to touch me like he did so often and freely at his house.

"I'll see you later tonight," he murmured.

"Yes, you will."

He flashed me his heart-stopping grin and watched me head out.

17

Stall Tactics

It became apparent to me that rotating my wrist was turning into a habit when I caught myself doing it as I walked the produce section at the grocery store like a nervous tic.

Stopping had been a last-minute attempt at keeping myself together. Nothing forced the tears back into hiding like the threat of someone in public seeing you cry.

So I walked up and down the aisles, collecting ingredients, feeling the pressure of the necklace against my throat like a one hundred-pound weight. Because even though I'd made the decision and had Drew's support and comfort, knowing that I was giving up on something so life-altering felt a little like grieving a death.

The court case against Creedy was before me, and pouring my energy into that would give me something to push forward to. But it didn't mean mourning what came before wouldn't still be necessary.

I didn't want to grieve, though. I wanted to move on, to skip it altogether. Just flip a switch and be done. But I couldn't make the feelings of disappointment and defeat go away just by telling them to.

I had my defense mechanisms for interactions with other people, but I was not as good at protecting me from myself. And if I was being honest, I'd tried to outrun my feelings many times, only to have them catch up to me anyway.

Which meant that this grocery trip of whimsical proportions was a pathetic stall tactic.

I let out a growling sigh, drawing the attention of an older woman a few feet from me. Her side-eye was good motivation to stopper the emotion building inside me again.

I snatched a can of beans from the shelf and moved on, deciding chili was on the menu for the week, and made my way through the rest of the store to get the rest of the ingredients and a few other odds and ends.

Since Drew was not trustworthy in the kitchen, pasta and pancakes being the only things I'd seen him cook with any sort of success, I'd subtly taken over meal prep. I honestly wasn't sure how he'd survived this long.

Any time I was at the house, I made a point of cooking dinner for us. Partly because I wanted to eat decently, and so I knew he did. But also because it felt like I was contributing something instead of loafing. Not that he ever made me feel bad about living there. But feeling guilty was almost my natural state of being these days. Just thinking about it made me hunch my shoulders as I finished my shopping and checked out.

Leaving the store felt like a dangerous game. After my run-in with that one reporter, I was overly cautious about walking into a parking lot. I loaded the groceries into my car quickly, checking over my shoulder repeatedly, and found myself clenched the entire drive back to Drew's house.

I lugged the grocery bags from my backseat, gritting my

teeth at how heavy they felt after my jump earlier. It helped bolster my decision. Feeling weak was something I'd spent a lot of time avoiding at all costs. And if jumping meant weakening my mind and my body, I wanted no part.

I reminded myself that giving up cost me nothing except my answers.

The hair on the back of my neck stood on end as I shifted the bags and shut the car door, and I jerked to look toward the street, scanning as my heart rattled against my ribs.

One of the grocery bags slipped from my hand, landing on the sidewalk with a thunk, but I didn't move, barely breathed, though I saw nothing amiss about the neighborhood.

It was silent and still. No one walked their dog; no one was getting their mail; no cars drove past.

But the feeling persisted.

"Do you want a hand?"

I whirled to face Evan on the front porch squinting at me. Was the panic as plain in my expression as I felt like it was?

"I got it," I replied, my automatic aversion to accepting help from anyone, least of all him, rearing its ugly head.

He frowned and jogged down the porch steps anyway, stuffing the food that had spilled from the dropped bag back into it. He didn't offer to take any others from me, but he kept his pace slow as he walked with me toward the house.

I cast a look around the neighborhood one last time as we trudged up the steps, checking for whatever might have tripped my sense of danger. But still, nothing was out of place.

I needed to stop being so paranoid, so I faced forward again and glanced at Evan out of the corner of my eye.

The muscles along his jaw were flexing, though he didn't look at me, and I wondered what he was thinking about saying that he was ruminating on first. He remained silent as he opened the front door for me, following close behind as I went inside and to the kitchen.

A skittering discomfort tingled through me as I unloaded the bags hanging from my arms, and I wished he would leave me to put the groceries away in peace. I was especially edgy after that creepy feeling I'd experienced outside.

Considering he'd barely said a handful of words to me in weeks and his thinly veiled antagonism the last time we'd interacted, I wanted to run and hide in Drew's room. But I forced myself to be an adult and ignore him.

He leaned against the counter, notably as far away from me as possible so that he was practically in the living room, and watched me start putting things away. I tried to pretend it didn't make me so uncomfortable I wanted to crawl right out of my skin.

"Are you okay?" he finally asked.

I glanced at him as I opened the fridge. "I'm fine."

"You don't look fine."

"Aw, Evan, are you trying to flirt with me?" The biting words were out before I could stop myself.

He grimaced. "I didn't mean it like that."

I straightened to give him the full force of my expectant stare, one hand on my hip. Of course I knew what he was getting at, but he hadn't made it easy for me since I'd been here, so I sure as hell wasn't going to let him off the hook.

"When you came through here this morning, you looked like you were about to pass out."

I forced myself to hold his gaze, though I wanted to look anywhere but at him. "I'm fine," I said again.

He tilted his head a little. "Cassidy, as a doctor—"

I held up a hand. "Evan, I appreciate your concern. I'm fine. Or I will be." I stopped, shocked that I'd let that last part slip out. The last person I wanted to admit having any issues to was Evan.

He folded his arms over his chest and eyed me with the suspicion I was used to getting from him. The downside of giving up on jumping was that I'd get to have these fun little talks with him more often.

I turned back to putting groceries away, working to find something neutral to talk about, to direct the conversation away from me.

But he spoke before I could: "Are you pregnant?"

Heat flashed through my body, and I jerked to look at him, only half sure I'd heard him right. "Excuse me?"

He shifted uncomfortably, but his gaze never left my face. "Are you pregnant?"

I stared at him as anger at the implication of his question slammed through me.

"Why?" I demanded. "You think the only reason Drew would be with me is if he'd gotten me pregnant?"

He straightened like I'd stabbed my finger into his chest, eyebrows jumping to his hairline. "What? No!" A flush reddened his face as he sputtered. "I just—the way you looked this morning, and. . ."

I folded my arms, keeping a mask of skepticism on my face, though I mentally ran through dates and numbers to figure out my actual answer to his question. Because if I was—Oh, God, what would jumping do to a growing baby?

My silence seemed to spark more defensiveness in Evan. "I've seen the way Drew looks at you. His feelings for you are *not* in question. I'm just trying to make sure you're taking care of yourself if. . . you know. . ." He swallowed. Hard.

If.

My heart rate spiked, even though I was fairly certain I wasn't. There was no way—not if my math was correct—but I still had to work hard to not seem fidgety.

I turned my face away, though the worry was slowly constricting my chest. "You don't need to worry about me. I'm fine."

If I said it enough times, maybe he'd believe me. Maybe *I'd* believe me. And it was probably better if I changed the subject before he asked about my entire health history. Or demanded a test as proof.

"So, any news on the house hunt?" It was the first thing I could think of, though being conversational was the last thing I wanted to do.

He was quiet as he measured me for another moment. Then, he finally sighed and looked away. "Put in an offer the other day. It was accepted, so it's a simple matter of jumping through the usual hoops."

My eyebrows shot up, though I didn't know what the usual hoops were. I'd never bought a house. "That's good. Hopefully it works out."

We locked eyes for a minute, like both of us were reading into my words. It was safe to say we all hoped it worked out so none of us would have to live in this awkward atmosphere for any longer. And there would be no more invasive questions.

I busied myself with rolling the extra bags and stuffing them into one to save space and put them in the pantry where I'd designated a spot, all while trying not to go into full panic mode. Drew hadn't complained about me organizing the cupboards, which I'd done a few weeks back. I wasn't sure he'd noticed.

But it made my life easier, and I was determined to keep it up even for my own sake.

I turned to find Evan still assessing me in that doctorly way. Which was my cue to disappear and hide in the bedroom.

Without saying anything, I brushed past him and headed down the hall, feeling his eyes burning against my back. I didn't turn.

In the safety of Drew's bedroom, I allowed myself to feel the full force of the panic Evan's questions had inspired. I pressed my fingers to my sternum, trying to alleviate the pressure building there.

Based on what he'd witnessed that morning and everything that had happened the last couple of months, it was a logical leap for him to make. But my mind went spiraling back through calculations, skipping along the dates in the calendar again, and confirmed that there was no possible way.

Thank God.

I steered my thoughts away from analyzing any element of my relief, my disappointment, my confusion that the complication a child would have added to an already fraught situation.

All of that was just confirmation of what I was about to do. This was just another piece that stacked itself behind the litany of evidence that had been building up to this moment.

The missing time, coming back without deciding to, Evan noticing how I'd looked earlier, bloody nose, the headaches, dizziness, what the other Cassidy had said. . . And yes, the possibility of losing whatever the future might offer me was a motivating factor too. I had to protect myself physically and mentally if I ever wanted to consider. . . that.

Which I didn't right now. Not when I had no idea what I felt about any of it. So I stuffed it deep down and shut it behind a door in the back of my mind, setting my jaw.

Still, I reached up to wrap my hand around the necklace like I was protecting it. Part of me whispered that the smart move would be to destroy it. I couldn't chance it falling into the wrong hands or risk some innocent person coming across it. I knew that there was some element of genetics that played a role in being able to use it, but I could never guarantee who'd find it.

But I had no idea how to go about it, let alone whether destroying it was even possible. I risked some big unknowns if I tried, and I didn't want to put anyone in danger.

My mind danced away from the possibility that I was just not ready to fully close that door, and I reached around my neck to unclasp the necklace in defiance of myself, as if it was some sort of proof that I could detach from it.

I marched to the dresser to pull open the top drawer that had been cleared out for me, pushing aside clothing until I saw the bottom. I lifted the necklace, poised to drop it in, and froze.

The necklace dangled in front of my face, some imaginary force keeping me from letting it go. It swung like a pendulum, a marker of the time that stretched across my hesitation.

As stupid as it seemed, even the idea of dropping it into the depths of my underwear drawer felt so final.

My eyes tracked the necklace swinging back and forth, the realization forming in my head with slow clarity.

I wasn't letting go. I was making a choice.

The life that was here in front of me, that I could grasp and shape myself, was at my fingertips. The things that I could control were accessible only in this timeline.

I had to plant my own two feet somewhere, and though I'd

thought I'd committed to what I was building, I'd yet to stay long enough to start cultivating the roots I'd started to grow.

How much more did the endless branching of universes have to do to knock some sense into me before I finally realized I'd still kept one foot out the door by sliding through dimensions?

The necklace slipped from my fingers, making a dull thunk into the bottom of the drawer with a finality that vibrated through my bones. I pushed all of the clothing over it as if hiding it from view would make me somehow forget it was even there.

<h1 style="text-align:center">18</h1>

Discovered, Dismantled

I glanced up in time to catch Drew coming in from a workout in the garage. He wiped at the sweat on his forehead and looked at his phone, a line forming between his brows as he read the text that had just come in. He sucked his teeth.

"Bad news?" I asked, stirring sauce in a pan on the stove.

My distraction made me splash a little over the side and onto the burner, eliciting a steaming hiss. I muttered a curse as I cautiously wiped around the heat, then looked at him again.

He was frowning. "Grace is asking for a last-minute meeting this afternoon."

My phone vibrated on the counter next to me, and unease curled in my belly as I stared down at my own text message. It was from Carla, alerting me to the meeting. Normally, they asked what times I was available, working around me. This time, I was being informed of the where and when, and it wasn't at the station as usual.

"In an hour," I said, looking up at him again. "Why do I have a bad feeling about this?"

He waited a little too long to answer, his lips forming a tight line. Maybe he was debating about whether to agree or not.

He lifted a shoulder. "Could be nothing."

That answer wasn't reassuring, and an unpleasant tickle ran down my spine. Stuffing his hands into his sweatpants pockets seemed like his attempt at appearing casual, but the uncertainty and apprehension were obvious in the way his muscles bunched.

I tried not to let it get to me as I took the sauce off the burner, then opened the oven to check what cooked inside.

A cloud of heat billowed out and into my face, and I leaned back to avoid the unintentional facial. I pulled the oven mitt from the drawer next to the range and pulled the casserole dish out, setting it on the stovetop. Every few seconds, my eyes darted to Drew's overly still form as I poured the sauce over the chicken. His back was to me as he stared out the front window, hands still in his pockets.

Too casual of a stance for how tightly wound he was. He held a hunter's stillness that set me further on edge.

He turned at the sound of me shutting off the oven. "I'm going to grab a quick shower before we eat."

I nodded. So much for enjoying his day off together. I leaned against the counter, chewing my lip while something in my chest tightened, trying to will my nerves away.

He returned only a few minutes later in slacks and a button down, hair damp, expression overly neutral. Which didn't inspire much confidence, but I pushed away from the counter to serve lunch anyway.

He moved in behind me to help.

"I got it," I said, turning to put a hand against his chest.

He frowned down at me, ready to argue.

"I got it," I repeated with more emphasis.

He sighed then kissed my forehead and left me to it.

I plated the food and brought it to the table, trying not to notice how tight his jaw was clenched as he sat down. I set a plate in my spot, then put his in front of him, but I remained standing for a minute, running my hands along his neck in a soothing massage. It was as much for my benefit as his, but I felt the tension in his muscles that matched the tightness in mine, and they didn't release under my fingers.

He gave my leg a grateful squeeze when I sat, and we ate in silence, both of us too engrossed in our own thoughts to have much to contribute to a conversation.

Whatever this meeting was about, it wasn't something simple. If it was, he wouldn't have been so preoccupied. Or he would have offered some reassurance.

I tried to cling to a small hope that it was good news, but it was feeble and crippled inside me. And some sixth sense told me the hope was futile anyway. Even begging the universe to throw me a bone seemed pointless. A twisted dread languished in the pit of my stomach, rendering my ability to taste my food nonexistent.

"Better drive separately," Drew said as we got our coats on.

I focused on zipping mine up, wondering at the way his words and the meaning behind them rattled in my mind like some kind of premonition. "Right."

They must have struck him too because the look he shot me as we headed out the door made my stomach drop.

The dread only solidified as we drove, growing heavier the closer we got to the DA's office. In the parking lot, I was barely able to hoist myself from the Beast as my muscles protested the weight of my apprehension.

Drew said nothing as he waited for me so we could walk

inside. At least it wouldn't appear strange if we came in together. It had been established that we had a rapport, though we weren't often in public together. Still, it was odd not to touch or be touched by him, especially when I was feeling this way. But this was the last place we'd want to get caught canoodling.

Still, I craved his comfort as the trepidation threatened to make me turn right back around and hide until whatever this was blew over.

We only waited a few minutes in the conference room of the DA's office before Grace Kirby and Carla Ojeda joined us.

Grace was wearing another one of her sleek, tailor-cut outfits that looked poured on. I was convinced she didn't have a casual mode. No matter her mood or environment, she would always look like a fierce instrument of intellectual war. She slept in a suit and stilettos. She read encyclopedias over breakfast, and I doubted she'd ever lost a case. No one would dare go against her. I certainly wouldn't.

Her naturally angular face had a particular tightness to it that made my heart beat unevenly as she divided a look between Drew and me before shutting the door. Carla's usually comforting disposition was marred by a tension that contributed to my uneasiness. She was the only one who sat.

The agitation bouncing around the room guaranteed that I wouldn't be able to relax enough to keep myself seated. Drew was doing his statue impression, eyes narrowed, arms crossed.

"Thanks for joining us on such short notice," Grace began, her voice already holding a note that made me feel defensive. "We have become aware of something that is of great concern in the case against Creedy."

She looked pointedly at Drew, and he stiffened.

The dread I'd felt driving in hit me full-force, even though she'd shot the accusatory glance at him.

The silence stretched, and I realized that underneath Grace's cool exterior and her naturally judging appearance, she was seething. Her features were pulled so taut that looking at her reminded me that she was as lethal as she was lovely. Her anger was cold and beautiful, an ice sculpture in the winter sun, brilliant and hard. Her slender hands were curled into fists at her sides, and the muscle along her jaw rippled.

"Okay, what is going on?" I asked when no one said anything further.

"You tell me," Grace shot back, though she kept that slicing glare pointed at Drew.

I looked at him too, waiting for some revelation to come, but he didn't move or take his eyes from Grace.

"Just what the hell are you thinking?" Grace asked him, the words serrated.

His chin shifted forward a fraction. So he must have known what she was driving at, but I still didn't understand. Frustration whipped through me, and I took a step forward.

"What—" I started.

"When were you planning to disclose your relationship?" Grace turned her stinging gaze to me then, and I shrank back.

They knew. But how?

"It's recent," Drew answered, voice even.

"Irresponsible is what it is," she snapped, rapping her knuckles against the table in front of her.

"Grace," Carla intoned softly, a warning.

Grace took a breath, turning her back to us.

"Is this why you asked us here? To scold us for being in a fully consensual adult relationship?" My defensive tone covered my chagrin fairly well, though the shame still burned in my face.

Grace scoffed but kept her back to us. "Your sex life isn't my concern. Except when it could blow our entire case up."

I took that in, but it didn't click, though fear's cold finger traced down my spine. "What does that mean?"

"It means that we've compromised our integrity," Drew cut in. "I'm a lead investigator on the case. If it gets out that you and I are together, my judgment, my ethics, and my objectivity are all called into question. And your testimony would be tainted."

The words were spoken calmly, but they slammed into me with such force, I practically fell into the closest chair. I'd known that word of our entanglement could be problematic. But I didn't realize how much. I'd figured a slap on the wrist, a possible media frenzy. But to have the entire case against the psychopath who'd tried to kill me crumble because of this decision? That had never crossed my mind.

"We cannot put either of you on the witness stand." Grace's anger had been tempered by the complications voiced by Drew, but I still felt her words like ice pellets striking my skin.

"The trial isn't set to start for some time," Carla said, subdued. It was disappointment, I realized, that had deflated her. She was not angry like Grace was.

"We will probably have to offer a more favorable plea deal to avoid the trial altogether. Because if we push forward with a trial, this will be a weak point they'll use against us. Creedy could get a lesser sentence." Grace turned a steely gaze to Drew. "You could lose your job."

I sucked in a breath, dropping my eyes to the table. Why had he not told me what kind of ramifications were possible if we carried on like this?

Of course, it made sense. No reason for me to have a happy ending. No possibility that I could have what I wanted, be with the man that I wanted. Some outside force would keep us apart, as I always knew it would. So stupid of me to think otherwise.

"We need to discuss your hopes for the outcome here since we might be moving in a different direction." Carla was the only one who remained calm, though I knew I had let her down with my poor decisions.

I turned my head to the side, blinking back tears. Could we get the justice those other women deserved? Because this wasn't only about me. If I had messed this up for them, I would never forgive myself.

"The case still has grounds without our testimonies," Drew said.

Grace raised an imperious brow.

"Yes," Carla cut in before Grace could respond. "We're still weighing the options. And the other victims' families will be consulted about what they want to see happen."

"But our case was largely built on you two," Grace said through a clenched jaw. "If we pretend we didn't know about this lapse in judgment, it *will* bite us in the ass. "

I flinched with every word like she was jabbing her sharply manicured finger into my gut instead of just the air between her and Drew. It was clear she blamed him more than me.

Because I was a victim, maybe she could justify my lapse in judgment. But she wasn't letting him off the hook. Sure, he was more to blame if he knew what kind of danger this put the case in. But he hadn't crossed that line until *I'd* asked him to. He'd given me more than one chance to stop this train, asked me if I was sure many times.

None of that mattered now. The damage was irrevocable, and I felt the uncertainty it created, like the trembling of an earthquake under my feet. How many aftershocks and how bad would they be after this seismic shift? Would anything be left standing?

"So what do we do?" My voice sounded as small as I felt. I was minuscule, shrinking by the moment.

Grace's eyes were burning lasers as they cut to me, and I flinched again. "With the plea deal, we can still try to get a significant sentence, but we'll have to make some concessions to incentivize him to take it. But his attorney's going to push back. We were coming pretty hard at them before, and we've lost some of our leverage."

"Can't you call Harris to the stand instead of me?" Drew suggested. "He's been working the case as long as I have."

Grace's mouth twisted. Her impression of the other detective was as unfavorable as mine, apparently. Not that I knew what his skills were as an investigator, but he'd rubbed me the wrong way those early days in the hospital. And I assumed there was a reason Grace had Drew lined up and not his partner.

"But we still wouldn't have Cassidy. And we have to report to the defense that you two are. . . whatever you are, and we could still get taken down during the trial."

I stiffened, her driving accusations getting old. "Okay, we get it. We messed up."

"I don't think you do," Grace snapped.

"Grace," Carla warned, and Grace's eyes flashed briefly to her. "Maybe we can reconvene when we've all cooled down and have a better sense of a way forward."

I stood, taking that as my permission to leave. I didn't want to be there a second longer, enduring the frustration and disappointment that permeated the room like a noxious gas. I nearly choked on it.

They all looked at me, but I said nothing and walked out. I headed for the elevator, knowing my cheeks were blazing because the emotion was a furnace in my chest. This was like being scolded by a teacher but times one thousand.

I'd made the wrong choice, as usual. But so many other people would suffer the consequences this time. I felt sick.

I stabbed the down button for the elevator.

"Cass," Drew called softly. He was just coming out of the conference room if I had to guess, and it wasn't far. Still, I cringed and jabbed at the button again, not turning.

I slipped into the elevator and pushed the door-close button so he couldn't jump on with me. I needed the alone time the metal box would give me, even if only for a minute. It was blessedly empty.

If I knew him, though, he would take the stairs and beat me to the bottom floor.

How could I have been so stupid? It was obvious now. This was more than a no-no. It put everything at risk. All I'd worried about was my heart—that betraying, selfish, uneducated, fluttering thing.

And damn if it didn't betray me when the doors slid open on the lobby floor and Drew was waiting for me, leaning with one hand against the wall. It sputtered and galloped because he was giving me *that* look.

But it had to end.

19

Heartbroken, In Disrepair

As much as my body reacted to him, I forced it down and brushed past him toward the exit. I had to go, could not be in such close proximity to this man who held my heart in his calloused, careful hands.

"Cassidy." He was not far behind, but I ignored his imploring tone even though my heart jolted, tethered as it was to him, to that voice.

Don't, my mind said when my body threatened to turn toward him.

He caught up with me right before we got outside of the building and slipped his hand around my arm, tugging. "Don't shut me out, Cass."

I whirled, forcing him to jerk to a stop or run into me. "You knew this could happen."

He pulled back slightly at my accusation, more affected by my anger than Grace's. Maybe he sensed the pain under the surface.

"I didn't realize. . . " I shook my head. "I never thought this could ruin everything."

"It hasn't," he started, a little breathless from the knife in my words.

They pierced me too—a clean slice right between the ribs.

"But it's all falling apart." My voice swam in tears, and I took a breath to shore up my walls, to shut the emotions in a padlocked room. "We made the wrong choice."

Hurt flashed into his eyes, a muscle in his jaw feathering. I practically saw his mind grappling for the resolve to push forward. "You regret this?"

A small voice chanted in my head: *No. Never.*

But the irrational side won control of my words. "Don't you?"

He clenched his jaw, shaking his head. "I don't. I can't." He took a step toward me. "And I won't."

Moisture stung my eyes at the strength behind those words, and I blinked a million times to keep them at bay because it didn't make sense.

"But your job, Drew."

"But *you*, Cass." He stepped closer again, maybe sensing my impending surrender.

The way he caressed my name when he said it like that—my heart thrilled to it, but my brain shuddered like a scared rabbit. Ready to run, as usual. I fought the urge to step away from him, to bolt and find some hole to crawl into. And the equally compelling impulse to move toward him tingled along my nerves, my body aching to burrow against him.

"Me," I said, a little belatedly, dubious.

He tilted his head, eyes narrowing, like he was searching for the right frequency to tune into. He lightly gripped the front of my open jacket.

"Don't run off," he said, and I scowled at him, eliciting his lopsided grin that crinkled the corner of one eye more deeply than the other.

I let him tug me closer. "This is bad, Drew."

"It could be worse," he challenged.

"How?"

"You could call this whole thing off, smash my heart into smithereens, and all of it would have been for nothing anyway."

I sucked in a breath, my mind tracing the shape of those words. *Smash his heart.* Was he saying what I thought he was?

"What do you mean?" I asked, my voice just a breath.

"The damage is done, Cass. Ending things now won't change what's already happened."

He was right, of course. My instinct to call it quits wouldn't erase the fact that this getting out would totally derail the case, whether we stayed together or not.

But he'd misunderstood my question.

"That's not what I was asking about."

He cocked a brow as he looked down at me.

It was then that I realized our bodies were pressed together. He'd pulled me fully against him so slowly, I hadn't even noticed. Or maybe because it always felt so right, my mind didn't register the change.

"Smash your heart?" I prompted.

He inhaled deeply. "Ah. That." He shifted a little. Not quite uncomfortable, but not exactly ready to explain himself.

We stared at each other for a long time, probably looking like idiotic lovers from some romantic movie, disregarding any prying eyes that might catch our P.D.A. Grace had already outed us, so what difference did it make now? Except the world at large didn't know. And this could blow up in our faces and ruin more than this case if it got out.

There was no way I was worth more than his job.

Because we had only been a *thing* for a few months. Sure, I practically lived with him, but I could blame the intensity of *my* feelings on having started with a different version of him. What was his excuse?

I felt like I was on the precipice of a cliff, about to jump off. But I was second-guessing that leap because I didn't know if I had any sort of safety net; there were no harnesses, no handholds to grab, with no way to slow the free fall. The ground was a long way down.

And even though Drew was standing right on that edge with me, offering me his hand, I wasn't sure I could doom him to the inevitable destruction that waited for us at the bottom.

My heartbeat kicked up a notch, and I knew I needed a minute. Or several.

I stepped back, and he let me, though it seemed to cause him pain. The wince was a brief flash across his face.

"Cass, don't." His words came out a little strangled.

"I'm not. I . . . just need time to think." I gave him what I hoped was a reassuring smile. "I'll see you at the house."

My smile must not have been convincing because a frown deepened the parentheses framing his mouth. He didn't stop me, though the selfish half of me wanted him to. He was too good, too kind, and I couldn't stand the thought that he was throwing everything away for me.

I trapped my lip between my teeth and backed up, forcing the hand he had on my jacket to slide off. An ache stabbed me somewhere in my middle. It was hard to identify as the pain radiated through my entire body, a spiderweb of grief.

I turned around before he could see the agony on my face.

Because I had to figure this out, to analyze. The space was right. It cleared my head. He muddled it—what, with his undeclared declarations, his molten eyes as they roved my face, his understanding spirit.

Clarity was what I needed. Not the inexorable pull I felt in his presence.

I made it to my car, shivering as the cold leather of the seat seeped through the insubstantial pair of leggings I wore. Admittedly not the best winter attire.

I started the Beast and made my way out of the parking lot, catching sight of Drew as he opened the door to his cruiser. His guarded gaze flashed to me as I passed, and I felt the zing down to my toes.

"Don't be a frigging idiot, Cassidy," I muttered to myself, though I wasn't sure which part was idiotic—that I was almost ready to admit to myself that I was in love with him and nothing else mattered, or that I was opening myself up to this, and it could bring everything crashing down around me.

Hadn't I been steeling myself all this time to testify against the man who'd tried to murder me—the man who'd succeeded in the other timeline? I'd wanted to bring him down. I wanted *his* world to crash down around *him*. I couldn't give that up. Not after giving up on jumping.

But if I walked away from Drew, what did I have left? He was right. The damage was already done, especially to my heart.

Please come back to me.

His words played back in my mind and sent a shock through me; the jolt from the desperation in his voice as his arms tightened around me was almost painful even in memory.

I'd promised him that I'd always come back. At the time, it had been about jumping timelines. But if I wouldn't let dimensions divide us, how could I allow this to?

How often had I been scared, alone, beaten down, and rejected? The fact that I'd experienced none of that with him was not something I could ignore. Was it the stability that scared me? I was so broken, I couldn't appreciate the first healthy relationship I'd ever had?

I pulled up to a stoplight and laid my forehead on my steering wheel, trying to clear my mind.

I had no idea where I would go, but just going felt like the right move. Not that I was thinking of running. Never again. But I needed to get my head on straight, and driving around seemed safest. At the very least, it might distract me so the weight would lift from my chest.

I raised my head a half-second before the light turned green, and I set my thoughts on autopilot, willing myself to let everything fall out of my mind.

I'd been going so hard for the last few weeks that I hadn't taken the breather I knew I likely needed. How long had it been since I'd relaxed, did anything just because?

It was hard to enjoy the scenery when the trees were all naked and brown, skeletal and emaciated. It was no wonder. It was mid-December, and we were creeping toward Christmas already.

Oh God. Christmas.

My stomach clenched, and my breath stopped for a moment.

Drew hadn't said anything about it, but I knew his mom and sister lived in town. He'd spent Thanksgiving with them, after all. I'd opted to make a jump to avoid being invited and the implications that came with it. That had still been early in our relationship anyway.

But so much more had been added to our foundation, expectation to whatever this was, that it felt like it was a bigger deal than Thanksgiving had been.

Would he want me to join them?

The thought lashed me with a new kind of anxiety I hadn't experienced in a long time. The idea of meeting someone's family, someone who was very important to me, wrapped tension around the base of my neck.

What if it was a big family to-do? Evan lived here, and since they were cousins, did that mean his family lived here too? Would they all get together for a meal or some traditions normal people did? And if Evan's family didn't live nearby, would he be joining Drew's family for the day? Maybe Drew and his mom and sister traveled somewhere else to be with a larger group. And what did that mean for me?

My hands twisted on the worn steering wheel as if I could strangle the answers to my questions out of it.

To make the whole thing more problematic, a hollow ache punched at my ribs when I thought of spending a holiday with a family that was not my own. The cold sense of abandonment was a staple fixture for me this time of year. But I felt it more keenly now that I'd experienced two versions of my own family that I would never get to have. Even the broken one I'd most recently had a taste of made me feel homesick. It was part of the reason I'd shifted through realities, searching for them.

I slowed at a stop sign and didn't move for a long time, even though there were no other cars. I'd had no luck in locating the version of my family that had crushed my heart so badly, and it was odd how I missed even the broken, toxic things simply because they were part of the dream I'd always had.

Little Orphan Annie.

Just another example of why I was defective, why it was

so mind-boggling that Drew was willing to throw everything away. . . for me.

A chill shimmied down my spine, goosebumps rippling along my skin. I couldn't let him do that.

But maybe that was it. He was ready to risk it all, but I was too scared to gamble with my own heart, and that obviously made me totally unworthy of his commitment.

I started to pull forward only to be startled by the blast of a horn from an oncoming car. It wasn't a four-way stop, and I'd waited so long, lost in my thoughts, that I'd missed my chance to go.

I took a breath, counting the cars as they passed by until I had an opening again.

One, two, three, four. Remove foot from bake, press on gas.
Stop being an idiot.

I drove for a while, cruising down unfamiliar streets, catching sight of families arriving home from school and work.

And it made the words pulse through my mind like the blood my heart pumped through my veins.

Family. Love. Home. Marriage. Children.

It had been a long time since I'd thought about that kind of future, allowed myself to consider it a possibility, to admit to myself it was something I wanted. And now I was forced to face the possibility.

Even after Evan brought it up a few days before, I hadn't allowed myself to truly consider it. Thinking about it now, really trying to picture it, was like hearing an old song I'd forgotten the words to.

The dream had been sort of feeble to begin with, skewed by a life without a true example. And my time with Callum, someone I had once imagined that life with, had maimed it, twisting and crippling it beyond recognition.

Then being in survival mode, constantly thinking about my next step, how to stay alive—it had been my only focus. And now. . .

Now I had the luxury of thinking about it, dreaming a little. But dreaming felt like an extinct thing inside of me. No signs of life there. Not even a flicker. Too long suppressed, it had given up without me knowing it.

Even this little jolt hadn't shocked it back to life. Not yet.

But would it? Could it?

Maybe if I let it. Maybe if I do this.

My poor little heart started a frenetic rhythm against my rib cage at the very thought, and the argument in my mind restarted.

After driving around for a while, though, I settled into a *wait-and-see* mindset that lulled me into heading toward Drew's house.

It was twilight when I arrived, and the chill bit at my cheeks and snapped up my spine as I walked from the car up the walkway. The windows were dark, so that meant Evan was gone and Drew wasn't home yet. That neither comforted me nor disappointed me.

Like my flip-flopping thoughts and emotions, the dichotomy kept my mind occupied as I trudged up the steps, shifting my keys so that I could unlock the door. Another rush of chills danced down my spine, and my shoulders inched up toward my ears. It was only the cold and my inner turmoil. Nothing more.

I hurried to jiggle the key into the lock, the white cloud of breath in front of my face chasing me like a ghost. My exhale of relief came when the deadbolt clicked, my mind already on getting inside, making tea, and settling my thoughts before Drew got home.

"That's quite the hitch in your giddy-up, Cassie."

Every muscle clenched, threatening to snap my bones, and my brain just *stopped*.

There's no way. No way in hell.

20

Past, Present, and. . .

I should have taken off, tried to run in any direction at all. But no electrical impulses fired as my mind refused to give instructions to my body.

Callum's hand slid around my neck, its familiarity sending a hot nausea rolling in my stomach. He gave it a painful squeeze, just to remind me of the strength there. His breath cascaded in a stifling wave against the top of my head and down my neck, and I felt the heat of his body press closer to me, boxing me in against the door.

He clicked his tongue. "You don't seem happy to see me."

He said it in a conversational way, though I heard his usual tension—that ever-present anger simmering underneath. It buzzed along my skin and sent a fresh ripple of fear through me.

My brain still seemed incapable of coherent thought, and my only movement was the unending shivers that wracked my body as story after story played in my mind's eye about battered women escaping their abusers and then winding up dead because they'd been found.

How? reverberated in my head. *How did he find me here? How would I get out of this? How did I miss him lurking in the darkness?*

"Aren't you going to invite me in, Cassie?" he purred at my ear.

I didn't answer, didn't move. Couldn't. My rapid breathing seemed louder in the tight space.

"Open the door," he snapped when I failed to do anything. His fingers dug into my neck, and I flinched, suppressing a hiss as I fumbled for the knob.

He used his body to block any escape from behind, pushing against me as the door swung open.

Icy dread filled my limbs, and a slick, cold sweat rolled down my spine. I had an insane urge to rub it away.

I stumbled inside on numb legs, struggling to process through the realization that I'd walked right into the hands of my ex-boyfriend, so oblivious. What I'd tried to dismiss as my emotional state and a reaction to the cold had actually been my warning bells going off.

I'd stupidly ignored it and walked right into the hands of the man who'd controlled me for far too long. I knew what he was capable of, and the fear of what he could do began to carve me into that weak, abused woman once more, shrinking and powerless.

I don't want to be her again.

The voice was small. Diminished by the terror that built under my skin, my nerves screaming in recognition of the proximity of the hands that had damaged my body more than once.

Don't be her again.

The words began to pulse through my mind with each speeding thump of my heart, rhythmic and insistent. Life came back to my brain, thoughts slowly reviving and spinning together to build the beginnings of a plan.

I reached for the light switch without thinking, and Callum's hand shot out to wrench mine away, twisting my arm behind my back. A flash of white-hot fire seared through my shoulder. A cry of pain burst from my lips, piercing the silence in the empty house.

"Don't tell me that hurt, Cassie girl," he growled in my ear. "I know you can take that and much more. Or what? Did your time away from me turn you into a whimpering bitch?" He slammed the door behind him with more force than necessary.

I swallowed the pain but not the words that jumped to my tongue. "Hurting me is the only way you've ever been able to make me whimper."

His fist crashed against the side of my head, fireworks exploding in the corner of my eye. The force sent me careening sideways, and I caught myself before my face slammed into the wall.

I kept one hand against the wall to steady myself, never taking my eyes off of Callum as I gently probed the skin around my eye. Definitely tender. No doubt it would bruise.

His nostrils flared. "Always ready with the witty comebacks, aren't you?"

I cursed myself for forgetting how easily my mouth got me into trouble with him. But I reminded myself that I had faced worse—a serial killer who'd already tied my wrists and stabbed me before dragging me into *his* torture chamber. And though everything Callum had done to me in our life together had sent me fleeing across state lines, haunted my dreams, and kept me on edge, there was a part of me that took strength from the previous iteration of myself—that I could, that I *did*, save my own life before.

Callum began to move through the room, barely scanning what was visible of the house. "Hm. Nobody's home."

As if he didn't already know. The smug look on his face, the way his mouth inched toward a grin, told me he hadn't needed to check.

"I saw your boyfriend head off to work a couple of hours ago."

I said nothing, not bothering to correct him, even as my heart rate sped up. If he thought Evan was my boyfriend, he likely felt more confident than he should, and that could work in my favor. It also meant he hadn't done his due diligence.

He took the time to glance down the dark hallway and into the kitchen. So maybe he wasn't as sure as he was pretending to be. His plan might have been to watch me for a while, enjoy the anticipation as it built up, and came across this opportunity when I arrived alone to an empty house.

It was out of character for him to jump in without all of the angles and facts figured out, but he also seemed cagier than he used to be. A thread of tension wound him up tighter than usual, and he moved like a boxer, never standing still. It was a restless energy that vibrated through him, which reminded me that I needed to be very careful.

Maybe it was his stint in prison that had changed things. He was a small fish compared to some, and he'd finally realized it behind bars. Or it might have been the anticipation of trying to find me all these weeks that had made him reckless.

Either way, I couldn't underestimate him. He was stronger than me, and he knew how to hurt without incapacitating, without leaving marks. There were those times he'd lost control, sure. Took it a little too far when he was particularly on edge.

There weren't any weapons on him that I could see, but that didn't matter. The way he clenched and unclenched his fists, the lack of fluidity in his movements, gave away the fact that he was barely restrained. I could tell that he planned to—*wanted* to—use his hands.

"You're so quiet, Cassie girl." He glanced at me, his eyes glinting in the gathering darkness. "Finally learn how to keep your mouth shut?"

He prowled the room but never strayed far from the door, like he knew I'd try for an escape and was trying to keep me from getting access.

My stomach twisted and churned while my mind danced over the options I had since I couldn't get to the door. I remembered the small loaded handgun in a locked box Drew had shown me weeks ago. With all the things that had been going on, he'd wanted to make sure I could protect myself if he wasn't here.

Like he knew something like this might happen.

I inched toward the kitchen while my eyes tracked Callum's movements, flashing periodically to those hands of his, knowing too well the damage they could inflict.

The lock box was on a pantry shelf, tucked far enough back that no one would notice it if they weren't looking for it. I recalled Drew's careful instructions as he pressed the soft black buttons, reciting the numerical combination—a code I would need to remember.

Callum must have sensed my movement because he turned to face me, and I froze, mind and body. He tipped his head sideways like he suspected something was up.

My memory blanked on the code, kicked out by a worry that I'd been caught.

"New boyfriend. Cute little house." His voice was not casual enough to be believable, even to a stranger. A shadow fell over his handsome face, giving his expression a sinister twist.

He couldn't guess my intentions, could he?

I tried not to let the worry paralyze me. If there was even a brief window of time, some kind of miraculous opportunity to reach the weapon, I would have to take it, whether he saw it coming or not.

But I needed to remember the combination first.

I forced the scene to replay in my mind again, letting Drew's words flow over me with the intensity that I felt even now. *"Basic trigger discipline: your finger stays along the barrel the whole time. Even cops don't touch that trigger until they shoot. Your finger moves only, and I mean* only, *when you have made the decision that you are going to pull that trigger."*

Pull that trigger echoed in my mind while Callum's eyes pinned me in place.

I pushed past the words, working my way to the moment Drew had repeated the four-digit code, waiting for the right combination to click in my memory.

"Moved on so easily from me." Callum's lip curled a little, control slipping. "After I came all this way for you."

The words sank into the air, twisting and mingling to create a prickle of guilt in me that shouldn't have been there, and I fought against the pull, that toxic sense of responsibility. It was a stone around my neck, dragging me to the bottom of a pit I had worked hard to crawl out of.

He lifted a brow and surveyed the room again, that nonchalance belying the effort he had put into manipulating my emotions. It was as if he were merely taking in the decor, unconcerned by the way his words tangled me up and threatened to knock me sideways.

I blinked hard, fighting my way out of that quicksand. *Focus on the code.* I moved toward the kitchen again.

Four—that was the first number. I took another cautious step.

Callum's gaze cut to me, and my lungs trapped my breath for a moment.

"Imagine my surprise," he said, continuing his pacing, "when I heard that you were almost the victim of a serial killer."

Violent energy pulsed faster, and I knew I needed to take my chance soon. His expression darkened, and I remembered how I had found it sexy at one time. He was attractive, after all. Hazel eyes that looked almost golden in sunlight, an aquiline nose, a million-dollar grin that could get him out of anything. The bad boy with a heart of gold. Fool's gold, more like.

Breathe. Focus.

Four. . . Three? Yes, three was next.

As soon as those eyes shifted away again, I took another step, the memory of Drew's voice urging me to repeat after him rattling in my head. *Four-three. . . seven.*

What was the last one?

Step.

Drew's mouth shaped the word in my mind's eye.

Six.

I clamped down on the gasp that threatened when the numbers slammed home. But Callum looked at me like he'd heard it, sending my heart thundering behind my ribs.

"You escaped though, didn't you?" His eyes hardened. "You seem to be good at that."

His tone made my insides turn to ice, and he started toward me. He must have decided my flight risk was negligible as he moved away from the door. I took an equal measure of steps backward to his forward, still aiming for the kitchen. He tilted his head, a hint of amusement playing across his face as he looked at my injured leg.

"You left me in my time of need, Cassidy. But it seems like you paid a little for your abandonment."

He continued to force me backward, and my eyes cut to the pantry, then dropped to the knife block. If I couldn't get the gun, maybe I could get to the knives.

Keeping my intentions a secret no longer seemed necessary at this point. Not when I was this close. I needed to defend myself *now*. He caught on to my plan almost immediately, and a terrifying blaze of rage distorted his features before I spun, a thrill of adrenaline shooting through me as I heard his rapid movement behind me.

But I miscalculated and bumped the edge of the couch with my injured leg. The pain sent a shock through me, and I gasped as it gave out. I went down, fear pulsating under my skin, clenching my insides with the realization that my attempt had failed.

The rage on Callum's face morphed, twisting into a terrifying look of vicious glee as I scrambled backward, hitting a wall, and he came to loom over me.

Defending myself with a weapon was now a dead hope.

Just one more thing on the list of all that had unraveled around me. My chance to figure out what had happened to me had disintegrated. The case against Creedy, the one thing I'd found some purpose in, was slipping through my fingers. I'd been scared by the fact that Drew had been so willing to throw that and his career out the window for me, wasn't sure I'd been ready for it.

But now that I could see, now that I could *feel* Callum's desire for violence rippling in the air between us, I knew. That the final thing, and perhaps the most important of all, could be ripped from me, and all I could think was: *No.*

I won't be her again.

A surprising anger lit through me as my unknowns solidified. I didn't fight off a serial killer only to fall victim to this man. And I couldn't let my last moments with Drew stay poisoned by my uncertainty and instinct to pull away when things got hard. It was so stupid that it took something like this—so cliché—for me to realize I didn't want to leave the truth unspoken, that I didn't want to give up on it, on him, on us.

On me.

As Callum moved toward me, the malice took shape in his eyes. He intended to kill me this time, even if it was the last thing he ever did. He didn't care about consequences anymore, not like he used to.

And that *No* echoed in my mind, singing through my body and chasing away the uncertainty, the fear, and the guilt.

I fought to keep my scared-shitless expression in place as I pulled my leg in toward my body, but my lips still curled inward with my determination and the force building inside me. My muscles hummed with anticipation.

Callum came to stand over me, baring his teeth, and the thrill of getting to hurt me glinted in his eyes.

Creedy's face flashed to my mind—these two men who took pleasure in causing others pain were one and the same. They both took lives with relish. Callum liked to take them by controlling every aspect until he was the only one in charge. No one moved without his say-so. In some ways, that was worse. It lasted years instead of days. It was a drawn-out leeching of everything a person was.

A low growl bubbled up my throat as I launched my foot with all the strength, all the built-up rage and bitterness I had, aiming right for his kneecap. The memories of suffering, the damage my body had endured coalesced into this one move of revenge that sought its release in taking him down.

A sick crack reverberated against the walls, and a suspended moment crawled by like a slow-motion scene in a movie before Callum's inhuman scream pierced the air and he crumpled.

The front door behind him burst open, and it had to be my imagination that wood pieces exploded into the air like fireworks.

21

Declarations

Drew already had his weapon drawn as he surveyed the room, not fully coming inside until he'd identified the threat and made sure I was the only other person there.

His eyes blazed as they landed on the "threat" writhing on the floor, his whole body clenching as he visibly wrestled back the rage that flashed across his face and sent a flush up his neck.

He moved inside with his gun pointed toward Callum.

That crackle of wrath made me wonder if he'd lose all sense of morality, ignore protocol, and shoot him right there. The way the muscles rippled along his jaw made it seem like he was seriously considering it.

When Callum became aware of Drew's presence, he stilled, though his breath hissed in and out through clenched teeth, puffing his cheeks with the effort.

Drew loomed over him, carefully out of reach, and pulled out his badge. "Detective Seward. Nice to meet you, Mr. Gallagher." He didn't fully succeed in reining in his anger, his face stony, voice cutting.

I started to drag myself from the floor, but Callum's gaze sliced to me, a brilliant flame of fury igniting in the depths that stopped my progress and my heart for half a second. I felt it scorch along my face, and memories of moments when he'd lost control pressed against my mind. I willed myself not to recoil.

Drew kicked the foot of Callum's injured leg, drawing a howl of agony out of him. "Hey! Eyes up here." The hand around the gun tightened, and his next words came through his teeth: "I swear if you so much as look at her again, I will end you." His voice was low and dangerous, a loose wire shooting off sparks, and a chill ran down my spine.

Drew's finger shifted to the trigger, and his previous words came slamming through my mind again. I realized how ready he was to pull it. The way his eyes flashed almost black made it seem like he was daring Callum to test him, like he was just hoping for a reason.

The desire to have Callum gone permanently from my life and the world was undeniable, though I knew it was unequivocally wrong. But I also knew how bad it would be for Drew if he went through with it.

And even though Callum kept his eyes studiously trained on him, his glare blazed, and the tension sparked. The hair on the back of my neck stood up as I looked at that finger on the trigger. Ready. Willing.

"Drew," I warned, the fear rippling through me.

"Are you hurt?" he asked abruptly, not taking his eyes from Callum's.

I swallowed, trying to focus on taking stock of myself. I didn't trust my legs if I stood and even heard my own jagged breathing in a syncopated rhythm with Callum's pained puffs of air.

"Cassidy," Drew bit out, and I flinched.

Then his finger moved away from the trigger, and my muscles loosened just a fraction knowing he had gained a little more control over himself.

Because I wasn't hurt badly, and because I didn't want to set him off, I gave a quick "no."

He actually looked at me then, apparently not buying it. But instead of digging, and because Callum was grudgingly obeying him, he pulled out his phone to call for backup and an ambulance.

* * *

The police lights flashed in through the front window, painting the white walls in alternating red and blue. It was sort of mesmerizing as I sat on the couch, staring down at the floor, unblinking.

Drew walked to the front door with the last of the officers to shuffle out, stepping out onto the porch to see them off. They'd taken Callum to the hospital a half an hour before to get his leg x-rayed. Then he would be going to jail. I hoped it was broken, that he'd have to have extensive reconstructive surgery, that he'd never walk right again, though I'd said none of that aloud when they'd questioned me.

I winced, realizing it would mean another case to be involved in, possibly testifying to get Callum locked up yet again. The only guarantee was the prison time for violating parole.

I would have to testify to our history and the violence he had intended for tonight—evidenced by the weapon he hadn't pulled on me but had on his person and the mark he'd left like a tattoo along my cheekbone.

Drew shut the door and released a long sigh that sang to the shaken and disjointed emotions jumbled inside of me. He rubbed a hand over his face then turned to me.

I raised my head, finding that his frown had dug deeper around his mouth.

"Well, that was quite the action sequence," I said, a compulsion to fill the silence yanking the words out of me.

He watched me for a beat too long, like he was trying to decide how to respond to my weak attempt at lightening the mood. "Here I was, thinking this time I could do the rescuing. But again, you took care of it yourself."

"I'll let you be the hero next time if you want," I replied, offering a dim smile.

He gave one of his silent laughs, air through the nose, mirthless and dark, and shook his head like he couldn't believe the turn of events. Because the whole thing was as far from funny as we could get.

And some part of me felt the shame of the moment, guilt like some element had been my fault. But it wasn't.

Right?

I pressed cold fingers into my eye sockets, trying to understand the emotions putting pressure against my chest.

I'd put Drew through so much since we'd been together that this was probably unfair. It seemed wrong that I felt the way I did, wanted him and this life together so much. I'd thought my certainty about my feelings for him would wane or disappear now that the danger had passed. Like they'd only been a response to that intense situation.

But they hadn't.

If anything, they'd solidified. The fact remained, and the assurance of its veracity pulsed inside of me with every rush of blood through my body. And it was like that, this knowledge of my love for Drew—a part of my very being, an essential element of life that flowed through my veins.

I gave a tremulous exhale as the realization took a firm hold in my mind. The fear was woven just as deeply into my DNA as the love now seemed. Fear because of what my love had cost me in the past—disappointment, abuse, abandonment, pain, loss.

But I didn't want that to rule me, to keep us from *this* ever again.

Drew had handed me his heart, and I'd almost denied the gift. How could I let myself question any of it? The contrast between a man whose pleasure was my pain for so long and this man, whose solid presence filled me with warmth, safety, and comfort was so stark, I felt like an idiot for being afraid of what that could mean.

My fingers were still pressed to my eyes as I worked through the reality of this truth, but I felt his presence as he knelt in front of me. And then his hands, always so warm and soothing, skimmed down my arms.

I let my hands drop away from my eyes so I could look at him and watched his Adam's apple bob with the force of his swallow as his gaze roved my face, checking for anything amiss.

I placed my palms against his cheeks, and our breath rushed out and mingled together, the tension leaking away with the skin-to-skin contact. The electric current buzzed between us, somehow even stronger than usual, and it sent shock waves through my system that threatened to squeeze the oxygen from my lungs.

He tilted his head as his thumb brushed over the slight swelling in my cheek, and his lips flattened with anger when I let out a hiss at the sting. My guilt came back with a vengeance, bolstered by the reminder of what had taken place.

It took everything in me to cling to the love and not the fear as I faced the uncertainty threatening to overrule what had felt so sure only seconds before. Untangling it all and latching on to what was true had my heart rate spiking again.

"I'm so sorry," I whispered. My shame formed the words, and the anxiety pushed them out.

"Don't." He shut his eyes for a second, taking a breath. "Don't take responsibility for that asshole, or anything that he's done to you. It has never been and never will be your fault."

"But it is my fault that he was here, in your home, exposing you and us to the world, the people you work with. This could end your career."

"This was *not* your fault." He stamped his lips against mine briefly as emphasis. "Besides, I had to self-disclose about our relationship. Everyone knows anyway."

"Wait, what?" A thrill of alarm shot through me as I waited for him to say that he'd been fired or suspended or something. I was ready with the self-blame.

And maybe he sensed it because his expression became even more determined. "I made this choice knowing what it meant, and I don't regret it."

I shook my head. "I just think—"

He interrupted me with another kiss. "Stop thinking," he growled against my mouth before plundering it again.

My eyes automatically fluttered closed as my hands slid to the back of his neck then up into his hair, gripping, clinging for dear life. The need I felt pulsing from him called to me, demanding a response, as the intensity hummed through our connected mouths.

As with a few weeks ago, when we'd been coming down from the adrenaline high of him getting shot, this moment had created in us a desperation to be close, to feel the realness of the other and reassure ourselves that we had made it, and this was undeniably solid.

I gasped for air when he broke away and settled his face in the curve of my neck where it met my shoulder, whispering unintelligible words against my collarbone. His lips moved rapidly along the skin there in what sounded like a half-incoherent prayer. It was as if he was thanking God that we were, in fact, still here, still together, and one enemy poorer.

Then a word caught my ear, the only one that took actual shape in the string of mumblings that danced along my skin.

"What?" I gasped out, pushing him back, so I could look into his face.

He was breathing hard, and his eyes flashed away from mine briefly. It was so unusual for him to be uncertain, and it reminded me of that moment when he'd begged me to always come back to him.

"What did you say?" I asked, a smile pulling at the edges of my mouth. The force of my heart galloping with excitement and nerves was a rhythm whose tempo matched his heavy breaths.

"I said. . . I love you." He tipped his head down, trying to hide the intensity of the feeling from me, even though the half-whispered words seared the air between us.

My smile widened as I felt the last dregs of fear falling away. Nerves still fluttered within me, but it was like a flock of birds taking flight inside my stomach—as pleasant as it was frenzied.

"I love you, too."

He didn't lift his head, but his eyes shifted back to my face, a question in their depths, like he wasn't sure he'd heard me right.

I nodded, confirming for both of us. "I love you, too."

The moment hung suspended as his tentative smile grew, the words spoken aloud becoming a truth that filled the room like a presence.

Then his palm slid across my cheek, a fire chasing the path along my skin where he touched. He kissed me lightly, as if he only needed a brief taste of the mouth that had spoken the words.

But the building emotion inside of me was like a freight train. No, more like a desert seeking hydration, and his lips were my life-giving water. My mouth demanded his, taking what he was eager enough to give.

He wrapped his arms around me, pulling me against him, and our bodies fit together like two puzzle pieces matching up. In one swift motion, he lifted me from the couch, and I hooked my legs around his waist. His hands slid up my back as he walked us down the hall and toward his bedroom.

The door thudded against the wall when he kicked it open, and I fumbled to shut it as it bounced back toward us, all while keeping our lips tethered.

There was a frenzied energy that electrified our connection, adding an extra wildness to every touch, an inferno spreading at an alarming rate. Urgency radiated between us, made my chest ache with the way my heart rioted at knowing that he loved me too; the way he held me tighter against him told me he felt it as well.

Instead of moving to the bed, he pressed me against the nearest wall and braced me with his hips. I didn't even care that I barely had enough space to breathe, trapped as I was between his body and the wall. I had him, and that was all that mattered.

His hands slid over my thighs with a pressure that sent my mind into chaos. Every nerve ending in my body was screaming for him to be everywhere, to soothe the sting of the electric shocks with his hands, his mouth, each part of him.

As if hearing the demand in my blood, his hands traveled every inch of me, drinking in the feel of my body under his palms while his mouth feasted on mine. My fingers laced into his hair, tugging, eliciting a low rumble in his chest, and he pressed me harder into the wall.

The unending zings through my core shot lower, chanting the need I felt building inside of me like an ache. I clenched my legs around him, clinging for dear life as the desire and lust ravaged my system.

"Tell me again," he growled, dragging his teeth along the skin of my neck just hard enough to send a shiver through me.

I barely registered the command and had to process what he'd said. It was an effort to form the words once I understood what he was asking, but I forced myself to whisper them: "I love you, Drew. I love you."

He stilled and pulled back to look at my face, the molten heat flashing in his dark eyes. His next kiss was soft. It didn't match the tempo we'd started with, but it fit the tenderness of his response. "I love you, Cassidy."

I smiled and planted a kiss on the corner of his mouth where it tilted up higher with his answering grin. "Good. Now, don't stop."

He caught my mouth with his again, but he slowed the pace, pushed my lips open with deliberate slowness to let our breath mingle.

"I can never stop," he rasped.

22

A New Hope

I rolled my neck as I leaned against the wall in the archway between the living room and the kitchen, my mug warming my hands, the tea it held warming my throat.

I felt like I needed a long stretch and maybe a massage. My body was spent, having poured out every ounce of my energy into the physical act of loving. It was the kind of pleasant exhaustion that proved I did something worthwhile, like after a strenuous workout that tested all of my limits.

I had never felt this way before, and it was like the tether that bound Drew and me was now made from some unbreakable, yet-to-be-discovered metal. Every pump of my heart chanted his name, working to weave it into my very makeup.

I'd awakened so tangled in him and the blankets of his bed that it was hard to tell where he ended and I began. It was a fitting metaphor for what had been forged between us. I never wanted to unravel our limbs, but life had crept in soon enough.

Work was a master he couldn't put off, and it had drawn him to the bathroom for a shower.

Left alone with my thoughts, my inner monologue had

beckoned me to the kitchen for a comforting mug of tea. I'd tip-toed down the hall, tallying how many days were left until Evan closed on his house and moved out. Two whole weeks.

I'd made my tea, and as soon as I'd run out of things to occupy my mind, my eyes were forced to trace every inch of the living room as I replayed the ugly scene from the night before like I was watching a movie.

Callum's twisted expression, even as he grinned at me, was more grotesque in hindsight than it had been in the moment, the intent in his eyes and the movement of his body more obvious to my mind's eye.

Murderous was the only word to describe it. I'd sensed it, of course. My blood had screamed the truth through my body during our entire interaction.

It would be a while before I fully felt the freedom I now possessed. The invisible hand still grasped me; the itch of pursuit prickled under my skin. I'd been hunted for too long for it to dissipate right away. But he was behind bars, and from what I understood, the violation of parole and the attack on me would keep him there for a long time.

It took a concerted mental effort to start the slow unfurling of anxiety I'd carried within me for so long. It was too ingrained from the years even before Callum had become my personal nightmare.

But one layer was now gone, and I breathed that much easier. *Until the next thing comes.*

I shivered, shutting my eyes as if I could slam a mental door against the pessimist inside my head. I didn't want that to be who I was any more. No more expecting the other shoe to drop.

"Cass?"

His voice was soft and careful, and still I flinched, my eyes shooting open as shocks of fear lit across my autonomic system. Tea sloshed over the edge of my mug, and I hissed as it seared the flesh of my hand.

Drew strode forward to take the mug from me before I dropped it and set it on the closest counter. Grasping my fingers gently, he inspected my hand before his dark eyes shifted to my face. "I'm sorry I startled you. I thought saying your name as a warning would help."

I shook my head, frowning. "It wasn't your fault. As you know, I startle easily."

His brows knit together, my dismissal apparently not alleviating his guilt.

I tried to pull my hand from his, knowing it was a mild burn—not even as bad as a sunburn—but he wouldn't let me.

He kissed the skin where it had blossomed red, then relinquished my hand, his gaze automatically moving to the living room. "I'll sell this house right now if it bothers you."

I huffed a shaky laugh. "Don't be ridiculous."

"I'm serious, Cassidy. If it's tainted by bad memories—"

I slid my hands inside the suit jacket he wore to grip at his hips, moving closer. "And so am I."

He glowered even as his arms draped around me.

My palms traced over the smooth cotton of the white button-down that hugged his trim body. The lines of his abdominal muscles that I felt through the fabric were like a map I'd memorized, the topography as familiar to me as that of my own body. But my touch didn't soften his expression.

"I have a lot more memories of you and me here." I took one hand off of him to point. "That couch is where you told me you loved me."

He lifted a shoulder. "Okay, so you're attached to the couch.

We'll bring it with us."

I clicked my tongue, rolling my eyes. "Oh yeah, sure. Should we live at Evan's house until we find a new one?"

That cracked his black mood, eliciting his introvert's laugh as he tipped his head back for a moment. "I'm sure he'd love that."

"Drew."

He took a deep breath and turned his coffee-colored eyes on me again. The blanket of darkness in his mood had lifted, but he still seemed skeptical.

"We don't need to move." I met his gaze with an intensity I felt down to my toes. "We'll make more memories; crowd my mind with them. And Callum's name won't even be in my vocabulary anymore."

Shivers broke over me when he slipped his hands up my back under my shirt and pressed me closer, the devilish glint coming into his eyes. "I'm on board with making new memories—the kind that will take your *own* name out of your vocabulary."

I gave a surprised laugh, edged with a note of lust that sprang up so suddenly, I was unprepared.

He responded with a low growl, and a tingle shot through me as he lowered his head, bringing his mouth to within an inch of mine. My pulse hammered out my reaction, probably as loud to him as it was to me. Which, of course, made him grin.

"We only have time for one thing. And I want breakfast." And damn, was I breathless.

"What if I want *you* for breakfast?" He nuzzled into my neck, and I squealed, my fingers becoming claws against his stomach.

"You better stop, or you'll be late for work," I warned,

ignoring the lightning bolts shooting straight to my core.

He caught my hands in his, laughing, though that look still burned in his eyes.

"And if you want good coffee, you better get going."

He sighed. "Damn it. You're right. I wouldn't have time to stop before my meeting."

The mention of the meeting made an icy finger trail down my spine. It was the major meeting that would decide steps forward after he'd disclosed our relationship. He didn't seem overly worried about what might happen, but it was a reminder of what our decisions had and could still cost us.

His gaze softened, and he planted a tender kiss on my lips, possibly attempting to redirect my thoughts. "I can't help that I love the way you look in the mornings."

I rolled my eyes, picking up my mug of tea with a steady hand. "Like a disheveled mess?"

He chuckled as he finally headed for the kitchen. "Like my sexy woman."

Warmth bloomed in my middle, and I ducked my head to hide my grin, moving toward the table. "You're still just trying to get into my pants."

He poked his head around the corner of the kitchen, raising a dark brow. "If only."

I snorted, settling into a chair, tucking one foot under me as I curled both hands around my mug.

He set to work on his task, the familiar music of his pursuit of caffeine helping to settle my mind. The cabinet opening, the sound of his favorite mug hitting the laminate countertop, the pop of the lid on the coffee container—all of it formed the soundtrack to my morning that I wanted to play on repeat for the rest of my life.

My thoughts trailed down that path—the idea of permanence—and led me to consider the steps I'd have to take in order to make that a reality.

Only the smallest flutter of uncertainty took flight in my stomach at the reminder that this was new. Because, more than that, it was exciting, and it was all good.

Now seemed like the right time to look into getting a job since I'd given up on jumping. I needed something to keep me busy, and I wanted to show that I was putting down roots and that I could contribute to the household. I knew Evan had been paying rent, and I was determined to at least fill that gap when he left, whether Drew actually needed it or not. I'd been mooching off of him for too long.

He wanted me to feel safe here, wanted to turn this into *our* home, and I would make changes so that we could make that happen.

Starting with the cafe on Main seemed like a good idea. It put me close to the station, and I had a little barista experience. I'd done a brief stint at a coffee shop in one of the towns I'd made a temporary home in during the early days of my flight from Callum.

After all of the things I'd been through in the last several weeks, and the showdown with Callum the night before, I finally felt ready to take the steps to solidify this new life I was building. A job was one stepping stone in that process.

The coffeemaker started to brew, making the telltale gurgling sound I'd grown accustomed to every morning, the warm smell inviting and comforting. I heard Drew's sigh of relief as if he was invigorated by the smell alone.

"I should be home a little earlier today," he said. "Do you have any plans?"

It was like he was reading my mind, though he carried on rifling through the cabinets for his breakfast, unaffected.

I ran my finger along the smooth edge of my mug. "I was thinking of going downtown. I want to see if anyone is hiring, maybe look into getting a job."

The sound of his rustling stopped for a moment, and his analyzing silence created a vibration in the room that made me fidget. I didn't know why he was so unsure about my response. Was I sending a message I was unaware of?

His movements resumed, though more subdued, like he was paying much closer attention. "What kind of job?" His tone was guarded.

I took another sip of my tea, trying to figure out what answer he was looking for. "I'm not sure. Whatever I can get, I guess. Anything to keep me busy."

Drew walked out of the kitchen, his studious gaze locked on my face. "Do you feel like I expect that of you?"

"No," I answered quickly—probably too quickly because his brow furrowed. "No," I repeated with more assurance. "I need to do something besides sit around here all day."

He took a breath. "I hope you don't feel like you have to or that you owe me anything."

"I don't." I stood and walked forward so I could rest my hands on his chest. "Not entirely. That's not my motivation, though I won't lie and say it hasn't crossed my mind."

He frowned.

The desire to make myself clear was a pressure on my mind. I didn't want to hurt him by my pursuit of the topic, but as I'd started explaining, I realized how badly I wanted this for myself.

"Please understand that it has nothing to do with you. It's

something I need for myself. I don't know—to prove I can, maybe." I lifted a shoulder, turning to look at the living room again, my mind playing the phantom scene of Callum prowling the space.

My voice was quieter when I spoke again. "Being with someone like Callum, I wasn't *allowed* to have anything outside of him. Can you believe he was even jealous of my job?"

A scowl distorted Drew's handsome face. "Yes, I can."

My mouth went dry as I remembered the way Callum would rail against the time it took from *us*. As if he'd wanted more time together when what he'd really wanted was to isolate me.

I shook my head. He'd taken too much of my past and had tried to steal my future from me. I didn't want to keep giving him that power.

Drew brushed the hair away from my face, apparently noting the change in my emotional state as he always did. "Then you go do it. I'll support you in whatever you decide to do." He tipped his head to the side, wrinkling his nose. "Unless it's illegal. Can't abide that, for obvious reasons."

I snapped my fingers, grinning. "Damn. That eliminates ninety percent of my job prospects."

"Considering how we met. . ."

I slapped his chest playfully.

The lines fanned from the edges of his eyes as he laughed softly.

"Anyway," I said, turning to grab my mug. "Since I'm going to do that, I need to shower and get ready."

He sighed. "I'll probably be gone by the time you're done."

I nodded, pulling away to walk toward the kitchen.

"Hey." He held fast to my hand, stopping me, and I glanced back. "I love you."

I caught my bottom lip between my teeth as the warmth crept into my cheeks. It was still so new to hear those words. To speak them. But I did it anyway. "I love you, too."

And there was that smile, the one that was just for me.

The warmth spread, blossoming in my core. "You make that suit look good, Detective."

He scoffed and shook his head. "You missed your chance."

I laughed as I continued down the hall.

* * *

I peeked out the window, debating about walking downtown instead of driving. It was one of those brilliantly sunny days that Colorado liked to throw out to make you forget a snowstorm almost killed you the week before. I'd been told it was a staple winter pattern.

I craved the feel of that sunshine, but the old tingle of apprehension pulled my muscles tighter. I even second-guessed my idea of going to the business district at all. Edwards was still out there, and he knew, at least generally, where to find me.

I pressed my fist to my chest where it ached from the crush of fear and anxiety. Tighter and tighter it wanted to squeeze, to lock me in place, its goal to paralyze me. I knew if I let it, I would never leave the house again. That wasn't the life I wanted to build, hiding away in here until every danger passed.

So I made the decision and grabbed my keys.

I wouldn't walk, but I'd be damned if I let the fear run me. I would revel in my new-found freedom from Callum.

I drove with the windows down. The air was a little brisk

as it blew through the car's cab, but it was refreshing in a way that was almost impossible to explain. Like a physical manifestation of my freedom, it was a small defiance against any restriction, real or imagined.

It only took a few minutes to get to Main Street. It was busier than usual, teeming with people who wanted to enjoy the random warm day. I had to watch for bicyclists decked out in their spandex regalia and the mothers with children who could dart out into traffic at any moment.

But it soothed me and chased away some of my anxiety to see the world carrying on in such a state of normalcy. The fact that they could while the craziest things happened to me had once seemed absurd, but I wanted to fight for my own normal, join the mundane day-to-day. I wasn't jumping anymore; running was now a thing of the past. Things with Creedy were. . . as finished as they could be for the moment.

Ordinary sounded good right now, and working in a shop down here, being able to watch the hustle and bustle of the small town fit right in with that image. Drew could come to the cafe on lunch breaks, or I could bring him coffee when he had to work late.

Admittedly, I was romanticizing the whole thing. But the promise of a new day whose birth had been bathed in the glowing warmth of the blazing sun in a clear sky had nudged out uncertainty and pessimism, even if it was only for the moment. The idyllic picture was, of course, contingent upon him keeping his job. But I was pushing that out of my head.

Unable to find anything close, I picked a parking space down the street, glad that I would get to enjoy a brief stretch of the legs after all. I tilted my face up to catch the full force of the sun's rays then sidestepped as a group of teenagers made their way out of the cafe.

It must have been the impending holiday that meant a day off of school. It hadn't registered at first, but the inordinate amount of children around finally made it click. I tried not to let intrusive thoughts take hold at the reminder of Christmas and the big question mark it was in my head.

I sucked in a steadying breath of the crisp air before walking inside the cafe. It wasn't terribly busy, but I still waited until no one was ordering anything to approach the counter, my fingers worrying at the hem of my shirt that hung a little longer than my faux leather jacket. The barista was polite enough, though distracted, as she gave me the paper application.

I filled it out at a table while sipping a chai latte, nibbling at my lip as I tried to remember details I hadn't had to think about in a while. Hopefully my spotty work history wouldn't count against me.

Nervousness fluttered in my stomach as I handed it over, but I knew I had to let it go. I finished my tea and figured I could hit a couple more shops before heading home.

My mind was occupied with rolling through which shops were possibilities as I pushed through the door, so I ended up nearly knocking into someone in my rush to get outside.

"Ooh, sorry," I muttered, ducking my head as I slid out of the way.

"No worries," she replied with no hint of irritation.

I jolted at the voice, twisting to look at her with my mouth agape as she continued inside, totally unaware of my reaction.

I forced myself to move away from the door, but I felt robotic, my legs numb, and I only got as far as the corner where I could still see in through the window. Hopefully, I didn't look as freaked out as I felt at seeing a version of Skylar who knew absolutely nothing about me.

23

Found

I wasn't sure how long I stood there. The way I'd stopped and seized on the sidewalk, staring through the window, probably made me look like a lunatic, and I was glad that Skylar hadn't noticed.

But I was pinned in place by what I saw. Her hair was much longer than the other version, wavy locks falling past her shoulders. Her heart-shaped face was rounder and held a glow that didn't fit with the image I had of her. I realized it was the look of someone unaffected by grief, healthy and whole.

That sent a stab through me.

I was definitely a crazy person for gawking at Skylar in the coffee shop like I'd randomly run into a crush somewhere unexpected, so I forced myself to move farther away, go around the corner, and get my reaction under control.

I'd spent so much time contemplating finding a way to contact her, not landing on anything that seemed natural enough, that it *was* like running into a crush unexpectedly.

Maybe it was the universe's way of giving me the opportunity I didn't know how to manufacture. But I still couldn't figure out what to do with the chance I'd been given.

How did people do this? Making friends sounded so juvenile and ridiculous that I was paralyzed by the question and the possibility of rejection.

It had been so long since I'd had a friend, or even tried to make one, that this seemed foreign. It had never been a conscious decision to become friends with someone before. It happened on its own—being drawn to someone I got along with at work or school or somewhere I went frequently enough to get familiar with them. But even those friendships had been superficial and temporary.

My friendship with Skylar in the other reality had formed unexpectedly and only after we'd been thrust together by such unnatural means. And yet this seemed more outlandish and impossible in comparison.

Would she think I was weird if I walked up to her and started chatting?

Probably. Even the thought sent a wave of anxious flutters in my gut, and I quickly ruled it out.

Should I go in and order another drink, see if we happen to stand next to each other, and strike up a conversation? Did that seem normal?

My life had been chaotic for so long, and the craziness of the reality jumping made it difficult for me to even discern what constituted as normal. But that was my new goal, wasn't it? Be normal?

I started back around the corner and froze again. She was now sitting at a table, looking at her phone. That made her seem way less accessible. I scrambled for a new angle to use in my approach.

Something casual.

But nothing about me was casual at the moment. And I wasn't an easy friend to have. It was probably a futile effort on my part. This version of Skylar might not even be interested in being my friend.

"Well, isn't this cute?"

I stiffened and curled my fingers into my palms, willing that voice to be a figment of my imagination, some trick my mind was playing on me.

"Your tiny friend exists here, and you want to connect with her."

I didn't turn, but I could sense that the other Cassidy had moved closer behind me. I felt the vibration of her barely contained negative energy at my back.

"What are you doing here?" I demanded, ignoring her baiting.

She came to stand next to me, folding her arms over her chest. She was smiling, but it was not friendly. She hadn't taken her eyes off Skylar, who was blissfully unaware of being watched.

"Wouldn't it be so *nice* to have a friendship that could transcend universes?" she said, ignoring my question. "Doubt it would actually work though." She turned to me, that wounding glint in her eyes. "What about this version of you would appeal to this version of her? She'd probably think you're too much work. Or maybe she would be too much work for you."

I shook my head, trying to deny that any of these suggestions would bother me, though I hadn't, in fact, convinced myself any of those things weren't a factor. I hadn't even thought about the possibility that *I* wouldn't like Skylar. It was always an assumption that I was the problem. Because that was usually the case.

Cassidy gave an exaggerated gasp. "But also just being your friend puts her in danger, doesn't it?"

I felt the threat like a chill along my skin, and my gaze tightened on her face as she gave me a serrated smile.

"What danger?"

She scoffed, enjoying her little game. "Just by being associated with you, of course. Every person you care about has a target on their back."

I turned toward her, narrowing my gaze. "Are you threatening me?"

She lifted a shoulder in a noncommittal shrug. "Edwards still has a yen for your blood. And your tiny friend is an easier mark than your boyfriend. I can see why he got that role, by the way." She brought the tips of her fingers to her lips to blow a chef's kiss. Her laugh was soft and sinister when I glared at her.

I tamped down the desire to shove her backward. It wouldn't get rid of her, considering she was there to get the necklace I'd taken from her. "Is this how you thought you'd get what you want from me? Being a bitch?"

She cocked her head to the side, her short locks bouncing against her shoulder. "Can't take a joke, I see."

"Can't ask nicely like a normal person, I see," I retorted.

She snorted, leveling a dark look on me. "That's rich coming from you. Clever trick, by the way, switching the necklace on me like that."

Her eyes flashed down to my naked throat, and I fought the urge to bring my hand up as if to protect what wasn't there. I hadn't worn the necklace for days, but it had been a staple part of my life for long enough that it still felt unnatural to be without it.

But my attempt to give it all up had unexpectedly offered me a modicum of protection. She couldn't do anything to me if she hoped to get what she wanted. She didn't know where the necklace was.

"I gave you back your bracelet, so it's not like I left you stranded." My voice landed harder on *stranded* since it was exactly what she was going to do before I begged her not to.

"You don't get it," she ground out, bringing her attention back to my face. "I can't get to Louisa and Thibald without that necklace." Her face and tone had weaponized, sharpening to slice at me.

I wanted to roll my eyes. As if her tone would make me more willing to help her.

I gave her a mirror image of one of her own malicious grins. "My reason for taking it back is the same as it is now. You're not trustworthy. So why would I let you have it now?"

She took one step toward me. "I have to find them before Edwards does. Remember that guy who has it out for you? He's the one who isn't trustworthy."

"Yeah, and I'm sure you just have a surprise party planned for them," I quipped. "What are *your* intentions? You've given me no reason to trust you. In fact, I find the whole operation twisted and unnatural."

The muscles around her eyes contracted, giving away the reaction she tried to hide from me. "We're in agreement on that. No one should be skipping through dimensions. But this is the situation right now, and I need to get to Louisa. And Thibald."

Her eyes flashed away for the briefest of seconds; I might not have noticed at all if I hadn't made a point of paying attention to any small change in her expression. The way she tacked Thibald's name at the end triggered my already heightened sense of foreboding. Whatever Thibald and Louisa were involved with didn't matter at the moment. I refused to be the one who handed her unfettered access to them.

Because none of it added up.

I leaned forward a fraction. "I'm not interested. I don't want any part of jumping any more. Figure something else out."

I turned to walk away then. It was all I could stand to listen to, and I was counting on the fact that we were in public to keep her from stabbing me in the back, literally or figuratively.

Her desperation was a cold finger along my neck. And maybe because that same feeling had been my own companion for so long, it called to me. But I didn't turn.

Then her words rang out: "I'll make sure no one comes for you again. You can live your life."

That note in her voice wouldn't have made me pause, but what she said had me doing the about-face. Did she know that would be my weak spot? That it was the only thing that would make me consider giving over the necklace?

I glared at her, fully prepared to make her beg. But she sensed that the hook had landed, and she licked her lips in anticipation.

I hated how badly I wanted to believe her. "There's no way you have that kind of power."

Her fingers curled into her palms as she gritted her teeth. She took a breath, deciding on something. "I do. I'm. . . close with David Lee. He runs the whole operation, and I have access points Edwards doesn't. You have my word that I'll make it happen."

I wanted to spit at her feet. "Your *word* means absolutely nothing." I turned around again.

Even if I believed her, which a part of me wanted to, I needed to make sure she actually followed through on her promise. I wanted nothing less. Walking away was my bargaining chip.

She snatched my arm, yanking hard, and spoke through her teeth, "You listen to me—"

I jerked out of her grasp, knocking her back a step with the force. "No, *you* listen. I'm sick of the games, the lying, and the chase. I want proof this ends here and now before I do *anything* to help you."

Her nostrils flared, chin shifting forward a little bit. We glared at each other for a full ten seconds while she worked something out in her mind. I was about ready to walk again, and she must have sensed it.

Her jaw clenched, the friction it caused between her teeth audible. "Okay. I'll get your proof. But I'll need some time to take care of it."

It was obvious that it was time she didn't want to give up. But I didn't care. I had the upper hand for once, the proverbial steak in front of a starved dog. It was intoxicating to be in this position, given that I was usually the one who was a step behind everyone else, especially when it came to all of this. But I wasn't going to budge, not when I had so much on the line. She apparently could tell that.

"You make it happen, then we'll talk," I said, practically spitting the words at her. I had to give her credit for not flinching.

Spinning away, I flexed my fingers in an attempt to dispel the surge of adrenaline I felt tingling through me.

"Wait."

I huffed a breath and turned back yet again.

"Where can I find you?" She curled her lip like it pained her to even ask.

The last thing in the world I wanted was to tell her where I was living. "You found me all by yourself today. You're a smart girl. I'm sure you'll figure it out."

She folded her arms across her chest. "That was by chance."

"But you *were* looking for me," I said, raising a brow, "weren't you?"

The way her eyes danced away from mine for a second was telling.

I tsked. "And you wonder why I believe nothing you've said so far."

"Okay, fine." She took a few steps closer, and I fought to keep from stepping back.

I read a slight threat in the motion, but that might have been from my nerves.

"Fine," she said again. "Meet me at the professor's house in the other reality."

I squinted at her. Seemed like an awfully convenient location to meet. She could easily ambush me there, get as much backup as she needed. But maybe if I had the other Skylar and Drew on my side, I could handle it. That's if they were even willing. It was highly likely Skylar would be. The other Drew, not so much.

There was no guarantee that if we set the meet here, she wouldn't have the means and time to put together an ambush. But it still seemed like a safer option to pick somewhere familiar. My territory, my rules, right?

I debated for a few more seconds before deciding. "Here, at the cafe, tomorrow," I countered.

"Tomorrow," she repeated, her face falling. She exhaled

loudly then grimaced. "All right. What time?"

"One o'clock."

She gave me a curt nod in response, and I felt an absurd urge to shake on it. As if this were a business deal. Instead of giving in, I whipped around to go back to my car.

A small voice, the one that was used to being on edge and poised for self-preservation, whispered to turn and look at her, to make sure she wouldn't pull anything. But she was the one who needed me, not the other way around. I had leverage for once.

So I strong-armed the fearful voice in my mind into silence and stuffed my hands into my pockets.

It was the strangest thing when I sensed her turning and walking away. Was that some sort of weird cosmic tether too?

It sent my mind down a rabbit trail of existential musings, and I wondered if déjà vu was just an alternate version of myself experiencing a similar scenario, like the barriers between planes were thinner when moments were so much the same, and the universe liked to give us a glimpse. And maybe dreams were an intersection point between realities, and the differences between planes accounted for the things that often seemed off, like when I dreamed about concrete facts being different, like my car, or where I lived.

Had I ever had a dream where I had short hair?

I turned to look then, unable to resist making sure Cassidy had truly moved on. Even though she was gone, an unease slithered through me, making me feel edgy.

Admittedly, that came from multiple different directions. Knowing Cassidy wasn't trustworthy, possibly jumping again, fear of what sliding timelines might do to me physically, the wedge it could drive between Drew and me. . .

Obviously, straight up giving her the necklace was what she wanted. And that was an option. After all, if she kept her promise by letting me have whatever proof she'd bring, I could wash my hands of the whole thing. If I hadn't been pulled that first time, none of this would have been my problem in the first place. I could go back to life as if it had never happened at all.

The issue, though, was that it had, and I could never pretend otherwise. And with the unsettled feeling I had about Cassidy's intentions, I couldn't sit by and let Louisa or Thibald get hurt if I could keep it from happening. That was as bad as being complicit in what happened to them. And it seemed worse still because it was another version of me doing it. Anyone else might not think that counted, but I felt it deep in my bones, and I knew I couldn't walk away.

I hunched my shoulders; the discomfort felt like my skin was too tight. It was enough to solidify my resolve by the time I got home, even as the anxiety twisted my stomach.

I had to make a final jump, go with the other Cassidy to make sure she didn't hurt anyone because of what I'd done.

Drew wasn't home yet, and I walked straight to our room. Neither of us had bothered to open the curtains, but even in the dark, the mess of mail and other papers on the dresser attracted my eye. When I'd dropped the necklace into the top drawer there, I'd been hoping to forget it ever existed. Now I wished I had destroyed it. But I still wasn't sure how I would have gone about it. With no idea how it worked, I had no way to know how to incapacitate whatever mechanism made jumping possible.

I still worried that destroying it was as dangerous as jumping, if not more so. I was done playing roulette with my safety and that of those around me. For all I knew, it was some sort of magic, and I'd be cursed for eternity for trying.

Digging through the haphazardly thrown-in underwear, I made my way to the bottom of the drawer where the necklace was buried. Hesitation was a weight in my gut as I stared at it.

I'd never noticed before, but now that I was looking at it and not touching it, there was a faint energy radiating off of it. Was that what had drawn me to it in the first place? Like it sang to the blood in my veins that made it possible to use it? Did other people feel it? Or just ones who were capable of making jumps?

Several minutes ticked by before I took a breath and reached for it. It was warm against my palm, as if it had been sitting against the skin of my throat as usual, absorbing the warmth from my body.

Everything about it felt more dangerous and foreboding than it had before, and I couldn't tell if it was my new perspective about everything, and what I was now risking—my home, my life, my *love*—or if I had simply ignored those warnings before. I hadn't always been in tune with my inner red flag detector, and even now, I didn't trust myself to make the right decisions.

But I'd determined to at least go so that I could warn Louisa. That was as far as my responsibility went.

Right?

Guilt was a snake inside of me, wending its way around my ribs, constricting.

I backed up to sit on the end of the bed, breathing hard against the tightness in my lungs. Curling my fingers around the warm necklace, I put my elbows on my knees, cradling my head.

There was no telling how long I stayed in that position, working through my sense of obligation in this situation, but time didn't mean much when I was already ensconced in the dark room.

It wasn't until I heard the front door open and close that I even moved.

24

With or Without You

Raising my head, I listened for the telltale signs that it was Drew and not Evan. Drew's tread was quieter, his gait longer. He always stopped at the kitchen to drop off his travel mug and set his keys in that bowl on the counter.

I wasn't sure when I had consciously cataloged those things, but now that I was paying attention, I realized I'd filed away so many small details about him as part of the background noise of our life together so far.

I heard the jangle of the keys as he dropped them into the bowl before he called out.

"Cass?"

"Back here," I answered, my voice sounding odd after I'd been quiet and still for so long. Or maybe it was the tension building pressure inside my chest that distorted it.

There went the loping steps down the hallway, faster than usual because he must have heard something in my tone.

His eyes swept the room before landing on me, his brows pulling together as he came all the way inside, jacket flapping at his sides. "You okay?"

I grimaced and looked down at my fist, which concealed the necklace. "We have to talk."

He walked forward more slowly now. "Don't tell me you're dumping me for the other Drew."

A surprised laugh burst out of me as he knelt in front of me, his half-smile in place. The humor didn't fully touch his eyes, though. He was too worried.

I put my hand on his cheek, his five o'clock shadow prickling my palm. "Never."

His smile disappeared, his head tilting. "Then what is it?"

I took a deep breath. "I ran into the other Cassidy."

He stiffened for a second, concern igniting in his dark eyes. His hands came up to grip my arms, and I had a feeling he wanted to check me over. "Did she do something?"

"No."

He narrowed his eyes, taking me in more thoroughly. "Are you actually her and not *my* Cassidy?"

I scoffed, ignoring the giddy thrill at being called *his*. "You're getting really good at the distracting jokes."

"Apparently not that good if you're going to keep being so serious." His lips pursed a little. "Okay, tell me what's going on."

I opened my hand, looking down.

He followed my gaze, and the air rushed out of him. "No, Cass. Why?"

I shook my head, the sudden lump in my throat making it impossible to talk.

After a moment, I managed to swallow the reaction down. "She says she can make it so that no one bothers me again. Really make the jumping, Edwards—all of it—go away."

He gritted his teeth and shot to his feet. "Yeah? In exchange for what?"

"She wants the necklace."

"So give it to her." He must have known it wouldn't be that easy because his voice was tight with apprehension. "Throw the damn thing in her face and walk away."

His agitation made me bristle, the need to defend myself rising with an uncomfortable, blistering heat. I clenched my whole body to keep it controlled.

"It's not that simple." I didn't quite manage to keep the edge out of my tone.

He gave an angry scoff. "Of course it's not." He rubbed a hand against his chin and turned away.

"I know she wants Louisa, and I don't think it's for Louisa's safety."

He lifted his face heavenward, taking a slow, deep breath. The tension was less obvious now, more in check as he turned to me. "What makes you think that?"

I looked down at the necklace in my palm, studying the intricate design carved into its surface. "Something about her specific focus on Louisa. Not the professor; not me. Louisa. I have this sick feeling."

I pressed a hand to my stomach then scooted forward, my own intensity making it hard to sit still. "Drew, I want to be done with this for real. But I can't, in good conscience, throw Louisa to the wolves like that when I *know* something isn't right. This necklace pulls me directly to whatever timeline she's in, within close proximity. I could warn her or something. If I give it to Cassidy with no backward glance, I could be handing over the key to Louisa's death."

"And by going, you could be signing your own death warrant." His arm sliced through the air as if he could knock the very possibility out of existence. "I can't just let you go, knowing you might be walking into a trap. For all you know, her promise hinges on *your* death as well as Louisa's. I couldn't. . . " He swallowed hard.

The emotion clogged my chest in response to his. "What other choice is there?" I asked, my voice choked.

He sat next to me and took my hands, a fierce earnestness in his expression. "You could say screw it and stay here. We can face whatever they might throw at you. Edwards obviously hasn't been able to get to you yet. Creedy and Callum came at you, and you took them down."

I squeezed his hands, but he spoke before I could: "You promised I'd get to be the hero next time. Just let me."

My eyes burned with tears, and I gave a soft, watery laugh. But it wasn't enough. And maybe that was Cassidy's goal—to make the promise too good to pass up. Like she knew what would actually pull me back in.

With all the things we still didn't know, I couldn't leave it to chance.

"What if they send someone else?" I asked. "Someone we don't know to look for? Cassidy and Edwards aren't the only players in this game. And I'm tired, Drew. I'm so tired of looking over my shoulder for the next attack. I couldn't even go downtown without someone sneaking up on me. I want to be free. I want *us* to be free."

He shut his eyes, probably knowing I was right and fighting with himself on agreeing. I put my hands against his cheeks and pressed a kiss to the corner of his mouth, but he didn't melt, barely even seemed to register it.

He didn't move until I shifted closer to him. It was like an automatic response for his arms to snake around my waist as he buried his face in my neck.

"I don't want to," I said. "I want to stay here forever and pretend none of it exists. But it would come back to bite me someday, and not far enough in the future to give us any sense of peace."

He sighed, his breath dancing across my skin. I knew it for the surrender that it was.

"I always come back. I've kept my promise," I whispered.

His arms tightened around me. "I can't just let you go."

"Drew." I pulled back to look into his face, to launch into my argument.

But he rushed on. "Not alone, Cassidy. Please."

I was shaking my head before he'd finished. "What do you expect me to do? It's not like I can bring you with me. Not only do you *not* have the fancy-ass blood type, but you're an anchor."

His hands dropped against his thighs in frustration. "Isn't there some way to warn Louisa without jumping?"

I blew out a breath. "I don't know! I—" I cut myself off, an idea starting to form.

He tilted his head, watching my face as the wheels turned in my head.

"Okay. I might have an idea."

25

Darkness Is a Monster

As we drove, the sun dipped behind the mountains, casting glowing orange fingers up into the sky like it was holding on for dear life. By the time we arrived, night had crept in like candle wax swallowing flame, dousing any trace of warmth, and whispering a chill into my bones.

The townhouse was lifeless, its windows dark, but we sat watching for a long time to be sure, neither of us speaking. It was hard to tell whether the curtains were just closed or if no one was inside. But the darkness of the house next to all of the others with blazing Christmas lights and lawn decorations was stark in contrast, more foreboding than it normally would be.

It was a long shot to come, expecting that Louisa was here, like that day over a week ago. But she had been inside then, and a small hope persevered that she would be again, keeping all the lights off because she knew someone was looking for her.

The part of me that wanted this to be over clung to the possibility that I could successfully warn her, count my duty as fulfilled, and go home. No backward glance. But I reminded myself of the truth I'd learned about putting stock in foolish hope.

"You ready?" Drew asked. His low voice felt harsh against the simmering silence.

I could barely make out his expression in the darkness of his car, the streetlights and shadows taking turns caressing the shape of his cheekbones and jaw.

"I think so." I tightened my grip on the note in my hand, vaguely worrying about the sweat from my palms ruining the message it contained. The paper was already damp.

Was it enough? I wondered for the thousandth time since we'd set out on this errand. Would it count as the right amount of effort? I grimaced as none of the guilt and responsibility melted away like I wanted it to. Because this was not a sure thing.

But even if I jumped with Cassidy, there was no guarantee I'd be able to warn Louisa in person either. Or prevent what might come next. And I could very well be putting myself in danger for a lost cause.

"We can go back home," Drew suggested when I failed to move or say anything further.

Even though I was still locked down by uncertainty, frozen by all the questions, all the doubt, and guilt, and the unfair burden of it all, I couldn't turn back. I had to make sure I covered all my bases in case something happened. If, by some miracle, Louisa came back here before Cassidy used the necklace to find her, I would have done right by her.

My hope was that, if she wasn't inside the house, she had left a door or window unlocked because it would make this whole endeavor way easier. I wasn't holding my breath, though. I still wouldn't know where to leave the note so she would find it anyway. If only I knew more about her, maybe I could figure out the best option.

It was looking more and more futile, but I had to try.

"I'm ready," I said, my voice steadier than I expected it to be.

We opened our doors simultaneously, and I was grateful for the darkness to keep us hidden, though that meant it kept possible threats hidden as well.

I gasped, almost jerking away when Drew reached for my hand as we walked across the street, my nerves too frayed by everything swirling in my mind. Usually his touch soothed, but the extra electricity that always sparked between us sent my system into overdrive.

I found myself scanning the shadows obsessively, looking for movement or human shapes. My mind played tricks on me, and I flung myself against Drew several times before my brain made sense of the things I saw.

A tree, a lawn decoration, a bush.

Darkness would hold a special kind of terror for me for the rest of my life after everything I'd been through, and I hated that my mind flipped through images of my torturers to taunt me.

"Cass, take it easy," Drew whispered as we approached the front porch. "You're okay. I'm with you."

I jerked to look at him, realizing my breaths were punching in and out of my lungs, and my death grip on his hand was likely cutting off his circulation.

I forced myself to loosen my hold and my clenched muscles to release. It took every ounce of my effort as I went one by one, concentrating on each individual muscle.

We walked up the porch steps, my eyes trained on the corners the light didn't permeate, searching for a crouched body, an attacker ready to strike. But nothing moved; no noise punctured the silence.

I pulled the screen door open and tried the knob, deciding against knocking or ringing the bell. That hadn't worked super well for me last time. Locked, as I suspected it would be.

"I don't know where to leave it that she'd find it," I said, my voice a tight cord of anxiety that snapped on the night air.

Drew released my hand and opened the storm door himself, crouching to feel along the bottom of the wood for a gap.

"This is an older house. Did you see a mail slot last time you were here?" He rested his elbow against one knee and squinted up at me.

For the life of me, I couldn't remember. Not that I'd paid attention. Why would I? My inability to recall wound my nerves tighter, and my hands curled into fists.

"I might have missed that detail since I was running for my life and being dragged through realities." I couldn't keep the bite from my tone. "You're the detective. Isn't that the kind of thing *you* should notice?"

He rose from his crouch, ignoring my anxiety-induced sarcasm, and scanned the frame around the door before searching the edges with his hands. He grunted when he came up empty.

"You could leave it stuffed between the door and the frame," he suggested. "Inside the storm door, it wouldn't be as noticeable."

I chewed my lip. It didn't seem like a great option, but there weren't many in the first place. Especially at night when I couldn't scope out anything better.

I blew out a breath. "Okay, fine."

I opened the storm door and reached to stuff the note in, gritting my teeth as I worked to wedge it in as tightly as I could between the inner door and the jamb. I pulled my hand back haltingly, an unsettled feeling chasing me.

It's not enough, my mind chanted, but I let the door float closed on the hydraulic hinge.

My hand-scrawled note about Cassidy getting the necklace and her dubious intentions upon possibly finding Louisa seemed like a weak attempt. It was a pitiful, half-assed effort to shed responsibility.

As we turned to head to the steps, I tried not to glance back. The sense that the message was too weird and cryptic twisted my gut with invisible hands, wringing unendingly. She wouldn't get it in time or wouldn't see it at all. Someone else might find it before she could. All the reasons pressed against my mind and tangled into the knot in my stomach.

This was supposed to assuage my guilt over what might happen to her. But the burden grew heavier with every step we took, and I felt myself dragging as we went down the steps to the walkway.

Drew glanced back at me, alerted by my reluctance, and took my hand in an attempt to comfort me.

It will be enough, I chanted. *You are not responsible for what happens to her.*

Shivers ran through my body, the pressure of what I knew to be the truth making me feel sick.

A man's voice sliced like a knife through the darkness. "You better not move another step."

26

Looping

My hands clawed at Drew's arm of their own volition, and he swung around, pushing me behind him as he faced the duplex next door. A porch light flashed on, and the hulking form of a man materialized from the shadows. It wasn't Edwards, but his size sent a thrill of fear through me anyway.

"I'm a police officer. State your name and business," Drew said, his hand moving to his gun.

The man's expression was hard to make out with the light blazing behind his head, but his hesitation was palpable. "You got a badge?"

Drew extricated his arm from my grip in order to get his ID while keeping a protective stance and a free hand for retrieving his weapon. He inched forward to hold the badge up, and the man stepped forward to inspect it. Light fell across his face, illuminating a suspicious but overall kind-looking visage. He had wide, warm eyes and a softly lined face that helped settled my heartbeat.

"Detective Seward," Drew informed him.

He gave one tight nod after inspecting Drew's badge. "Sorry, detective. There have been some shady folk around since my neighbor's been gone."

Drew looked at me and stuffed his badge back into his pocket. "Do you know her well?" He tipped his head toward Louisa's house.

The man lifted a meaty hand. "Not really. We say hello when we happen to be out at the same time. You know how it is these days."

Drew acknowledged that with a nod. "Tell me about the people coming by."

He scratched the back of his head. "A couple dudes, some woman, an older guy. I'd seen him before—he's her dad or something. But he was acting pretty cagey too, which was weird. Didn't used to be like that."

That sent a thrill through me. "How recently did you see them?" I asked, too eager to wait for Drew to ask the question.

His jaw tightened like he wasn't a fan of me interjecting, but he didn't say anything as the man's attention shifted.

His eyes sharpened on my face, and I realized I might look familiar if the woman he'd mentioned happened to be an alternate version of me. It seemed more than likely the other Cassidy had made an appearance. No wonder Drew wasn't happy I'd spoken up.

"It's been off and on for a few weeks now." He transferred his gaze back to Drew. "I saw the girl who lives here a few days back, so I don't really know what's going on."

Another zing of excitement shot up my spine. So maybe there was hope that Louisa would get my note, and I sent up a prayer that she would make one last visit before tomorrow.

"I've been keeping an eye out for lurkers," the neighbor said, interrupting my thoughts. "Sorry about confronting you. You were acting kind of suspicious."

Drew waved him off. "I appreciate your efforts. Much prefer that to apathy. Do you mind if I take your name in case we have more questions?"

"Darryl Faber."

"Thanks, Darryl."

The man gave a quick nod, his eyes sliding to me again, and he noticeably didn't go back inside as we continued to the street, across, and to the car.

I felt Drew's eyes on me across the roof as we both reached for our respective door handles. In the darkness, I couldn't quite tell what his expression was trying to communicate, so I climbed into the cab to wait for whatever it was he wanted to say.

But even then, he remained silent as he started the engine and pulled away from the curb.

I gnawed at my bottom lip as we drove, the silence getting heavier and heavier as we went. It was like he was ruminating on the same things I was. That there were too many unknowns, too many things we couldn't guarantee.

But he wouldn't feel the culpability that I did, and he probably didn't sense that what we'd done tonight wouldn't be enough, that I still needed to show up the next day.

I didn't want to broach the subject because I felt the fragility of the moment, his brittle mood, my flimsy sense of control. But we had to talk about it, and I needed to make a plan. If I had some sort of strategy, maybe I wouldn't feel like everything was spinning out of my grasp.

"You're still going," he said, shattering the building pressure and my already-crumbling façade of composure.

I even flinched. For once, his ESP didn't make the irritation bubble to the surface. I was grateful that he knew me, could tap in when I couldn't figure out what I wanted to say.

He raked a hand through his hair, his universal sign of distress.

I spoke before he could say anything else. "I have to, Drew. Don't you want this to end for good?"

He blew out a breath, a resigned, unsettled sound. "Of course I do."

Having him bring it up gave me some sense of certainty. Or it gave me enough to manufacture it until it became genuine. I wasn't sure. It didn't matter.

"I'll meet her at one tomorrow, with the necklace." My hand went unconsciously to the pendant that rested against my throat again. Since my encounter with Cassidy earlier that day, anxiety about separation from it had prompted me to keep it as close as possible. It had become like some precious jewel, and I only felt secure if I knew exactly where it was. It was my bargaining chip.

"I'll meet her," I said again. "Make sure she gives me what I need. I'll give her the necklace. We'll part ways."

He grimaced. "Do you even know what it is she'll have? How do we guarantee she keeps her promise? She could give you some kind of decoy or something we have no way of analyzing to see if it's real. What if she's playing you?" His words shot out in quick succession.

They were all valid questions, all logical concerns.

"What if?" I repeated, my voice sounding as defeated as I felt. It was a question that would lead nowhere except to deeper and more debilitating uncertainty.

I sighed, shaking my head. "Those are questions I can't answer. I guess we have to trust that things will work out.

If there's a chance at breaking the hold this whole jumping universes thing has on me, I want to take it."

He pulled into his driveway and turned the engine off, staring at his hands on the steering wheel for a full minute.

"Cass."

Before that tone could seep into me, pull me to his way of thinking, I plowed forward: "We'll go together. You can drop me off and hang back until I need you. I don't want to scare her off. She never said I had to be alone, but the deal was struck that way, and I want to make sure it all goes smoothly."

I added silently that I didn't want to risk him getting hurt. Or worse. My mind flinched away from thoughts of what exactly could be *worse*. I didn't want to think it, so I wouldn't voice it.

"Cass," he said again, his voice falling heavier on my name, a full argument already in his tone.

I twisted in my seat, and he turned to meet my gaze. "Please, Drew. Can we just do it my way?"

His lips flattened with displeasure, but he nodded grimly. I wished that gave me a sense of relief, but it didn't. Chills cascaded down my arms, and there was an endless flipping in my gut.

But we got out of the car and walked toward the house anyway. Despite the tension between us, Drew tucked me against his body, reminding me that it was where I belonged.

Belong.

That word echoed in my mind in a ceaseless rhythm for the rest of the night.

27

Hangers On

"I don't like it." Drew glared out the windshield.

"Zero percent surprised," I replied, pretending I didn't feel like an army of ants was marching in my stomach.

"Cass." He shook his head, grimacing.

"I'll be fine," I said, trying to believe my own words. They sounded convincing enough out loud. "We got here early so I could scope it out." I leaned forward, twisting my fingers absently in my lap as I surveyed the area.

After our visit to Louisa's house, my muscles had coiled up, and I was still waiting for them to release. I knew it wasn't likely they would any time soon. The tension headache was already slicing away at the back of my skull.

"I still think we should say 'screw it' and get out of here," he muttered, the extra gravel in his tone giving away how unhappy he was about the situation.

Everything inside me screamed to agree. After all, giving up the necklace felt like some sort of betrayal of this other girl I didn't even know. But for all I knew, Louisa was a crappy human being and didn't deserve my efforts to help her.

I reminded myself that I could back out if things didn't feel right.

"Let's just see how it goes," I murmured.

My fingertips tingled with anticipation and discomfort. For the millionth time, I debated about doing exactly what Drew suggested. But if this was a simple enough trade, and it meant I could be free, I needed to try. Right?

I'd have to trust that the note would be enough. Louisa was already jumpy about visitors to her house. Surely she'd be all right if she was as cautious as she had been when I'd dropped by two weeks ago.

I reached for the door handle, forcing myself to trust the plan. Hand the necklace over, get whatever Cassidy had for me, go home, live happily ever after.

I got out of the car with an increasing sense of dread moving like sludge through my veins. When I heard Drew's door open too, I jerked to look at him as he rounded the front of the car.

This wasn't what we'd agreed on. Or rather, what I'd told him I wanted him to do. But he *had* agreed. Well, nodded. Grudgingly. But still.

I stepped off the curb and marched forward to ward him off. He shook his head against the argument that sprang to my lips, his eyes hard.

Fear sprinted through me, igniting the anger I always latched onto as a deflection. Because the last time he was with me during a showdown like this, he'd gotten shot.

My fault.

I pressed a hand to his chest to stop him from walking farther, fighting to keep from shoving him backward. "This isn't what we talked about," I hissed.

He bared his teeth. "New plan. I go with. Something isn't

sitting right."

I stiffened, chafing against the idea of, one, being dictated to, and two, putting someone I loved in danger.

His fingers wrapped around my wrist, and he pulled my hand from his chest, backing me up onto the sidewalk. "The hero, remember? You promised."

Fear, anger, panic—it all twisted and filled me, nearly choked me, threatened to blind me. "I *need* to go alone."

"Like hell you do," he snapped.

"Drew—"

"No. There's no good reason for you to go in alone. I didn't hear that as any part of the agreement with the other Cassidy."

I scraped my bottom lip with my teeth, biting back a cutting response. Fighting my natural inclination for resistance snapped my muscles tighter across my shoulders. But he was right. Not about him being the hero—because that was just dumb machismo, and he knew it.

His lips had become a pale line, and realization finally dawned in my thick skull.

"You're mad," I said flatly, shocked.

He huffed through his nose. "Yes, I'm mad! I was trying to give you the space, let you figure out you don't have to do this alone—that you *shouldn't* do this alone. To ask me to come with you. But here you are, walking right into the danger without a backward glance, like none of this fucking matters." He stopped, breathing hard. Then: "Like it wouldn't kill me if something happened to you."

I swallowed, struggling to find words, recognizing we'd hit that point—the moment that he would decide he'd had enough. My stupid habit of using self-sabotage as my vehicle to protect myself had ruined everything to the point of no return.

As if he sensed my inner turmoil, he cradled my face. "You can't keep doing things without letting me all the way in. I know it's a process, and I *will* keep hanging on. But it doesn't mean I won't be mad when it happens again."

That last word made me flinch. He knew me too well.

"I love you, Cassidy. And I will keep working because I want this. I want us. But please." He shut his eyes briefly. "Please stop shutting me out."

I took a shaky breath. "I'm sorry." My shoulders slumped. "I know I've been awful about it all. But I'm so scared of losing you too." I stopped, looking down at the zipper on his jacket instead of meeting his eyes. "I see now that losing myself doesn't only affect me any more. That will take me a bit to get used to."

It should have occurred to me sooner, given the state the other Drew was in after "losing" me. It wasn't fair to either of them, but at least I could control some aspect of it with this Drew. I could keep myself safe, protect the little life we were building together.

"I'm sorry," I said again.

He took a cleansing breath then brushed a loose lock of hair out of my face. "I forgive you."

We stared at each other for a minute before I broke the trance.

"We better get moving. We lost our early lead."

Drew's gaze sharpened as he looked around, reaching for my hand the same moment he started walking. "I don't mind staying out of sight, just in case. Let her believe you came alone, but I'm not going far."

I wanted to throw out a snarky comment about his *gracious* offer, but I let it go in favor of keeping the peace. It wasn't worth fighting about when we'd recently resolved a much bigger disagreement.

He released my hand as we neared the corner, and he continued walking forward as if he'd always planned to go inside the coffee shop. It seemed a wasted effort considering the other Cassidy knew what he looked like already. Or claimed she did. That could have been a ploy to get a rise out of me, which was very on-brand for her.

I waited a full minute before rounding the corner myself, finding that the other Cassidy hadn't arrived yet.

I sat at the nearest outdoor table, my jitters quickly translating to a leg dance that made the table rattle. I forced myself to stop bouncing, remembering how the other Drew had scolded me for my jiggling not so long ago.

But I couldn't fully relax. I shifted incessantly as I scanned the street, and my jaw started to hurt from the clenching. Only when I caught movement would I stop moving, unsuccessfully trying not to look as unsettled as I felt.

After a while, I checked my phone for the time, finding that she was already late, and my belly tightened in response. I pulled my jacket closer around myself as the breeze picked up. Its icy fingers cut right through me, magnified by the frigid fear building inside.

The sun was shining, but it couldn't melt what sat heavily within me: something was wrong. As usual.

We'd made no backup plan, no alternate meeting place or time. I didn't know how long I was supposed to wait. There was no precedent for this. And knowing that she was taking a risk by doing what she'd promised made my intestines tie in knots of dread.

The door opened behind me, and I twisted to look at Drew. He didn't meet my eyes as he moved to sit at a table far enough from me that the casual observer wouldn't guess we were together if they glanced over.

He brought his to-go cup to his lips to cover his mouth as he spoke. "She's late."

Hearing it spoken aloud dropped another stone in my gut. "Yes."

I twined my fingers together to keep them still, my eyes crawling the length of the street again. The cold wind had chased a lot of the pedestrians inside, and I knew it would start to look questionable that we were both sitting out here.

Another ten minutes crept by, and I'd started to shiver from cold and nerves.

"What do you want to do?" Drew asked, spinning in his seat, not bothering to hide his interaction with me now.

I tipped my head side to side, debating. I'd waited long enough for her to arrive, even running behind. "Let's call it. I'm going to go to the bathroom and then I'll meet you back at the car."

He scanned the street, squinting, before his gaze settled on me again. "I'll get it warm for you."

I nodded once and stood, nibbling the inside of my cheek as I went inside. I briefly debated about ordering a hot drink but decided against it as I headed off toward the restroom. It was easy enough to make tea for myself at home.

I shoved my hands into my pockets when I got outside, shrugging my shoulders as if I could keep the warmth from inside the cafe in my body by sheer force of will. But the drop in temperature leeched the heat too quickly.

Cassidy being a no-show was irritating enough, but her tardiness forcing me to sit in the cold for longer made me even grumpier. I focused on that feeling instead of the—probably misguided—worry that something bad had happened to her.

I rounded the corner, my muscles loosening a little when I spotted Drew's car waiting for me, promising the warmth my body craved.

An unexpected force knocked me sideways, and it was how I imagined getting hit by a linebacker in a football game might feel. My mind had no time to process the blur of the world around me as I staggered into shadow until my eyes registered the brick walls around me. I realized I'd been shoved into an alley between two buildings.

I blinked to get my own face into focus as it sneered before me.

"What the—" I managed before Cassidy slammed me back into the brick wall, punching the air from my lungs.

"Sorry I was late," she said.

She definitely didn't sound sorry. In fact, there was a distinct twist to her face like she was fighting back anger.

"Welcome to the party."

A chill shimmied up my spine at the second voice. Male. Familiar. I cut a wide-eyed glance toward Edwards, who was giving me a faint smile. Smug.

"Grab your necklace," he said to Cassidy. "A deal is a deal."

I glared at her, a flame of rage licking down my arms and into my hands as I curled them into fists.

I should have known. How stupid of me to believe she would actually follow through on what she'd promised. Drew had been right. I should have walked away, denied her what she'd asked, and left the rest up to chance.

"Don't move!"

We all jerked to look at Drew and terror bulleted through me as he stood at the mouth of the alley, his weapon drawn.

He'd positioned himself so he could easily duck back behind the wall, but there were no guarantees.

Images of him on the ground, unconscious and bleeding, flashed through my mind, sending my heart punching against my rib cage. The panic took hold, making my mind wheel to the only idea I could come up with. I grabbed the necklace, rubbing my thumb over the design.

Everyone's attention snapped to me as soon as the pressure built, the ringing sound beginning like a siren call to our blood.

"No! Cassidy!" Drew's voice was already warbled.

I tried to break the other Cassidy's hold on my jacket, but her grip had turned to iron around the lapels, so I pushed away from the wall and rammed her back with the force of my fury, aiming for Edwards so I could knock all three of us into the next timeline.

Anything to keep Drew safe.

I bulldozed forward, knocking into Edwards, and he went down. I kept pushing until I slammed Cassidy into the opposite wall while the air swirled around us.

And then I remembered: Drew was an anchor. He could lock me into this reality.

Already, in the midst of the tornado of shifting planes, I felt it. It was a much stronger physical presence, a hand yanking me in his direction though he wasn't touching me. He wasn't even close.

But I'd never experienced that tether quite like this before. I fought to stay on my feet while the air compressed around us, the world rippling and flashing in my periphery.

A scream tore through me when a lightning bolt of pain shot through the center of my body. It was like I was about to rip in two with Cassidy's corporeal hand gripping my jacket, pulling me to a new plane, and Drew's soul-grip holding me in place.

The ringing in my ears buried the sound of my own voice, and it felt more like tumbling this time, as if I'd been knocked off course from being pulled in two directions at once.

My consciousness blinked out, like someone pulled the plug on a computer without shutting it down properly. A full-system darkness, no activity, no electrical pulses.

The process of rebooting was slow and painful.

My brain staggered under the pressure of a headache that raged like a juggernaut in my skull when thought started to flicker back on.

I gradually registered that something had changed. It was a slow process of cataloging everything around me. The stagnant air, the dim lighting, the feel of the ground beneath me—hard concrete—but I wasn't cold like I should have been if I was still outside. That's where we'd been when Drew—

Oh, God. Drew.

I tried to sit up, to move, but I seemed paralyzed. Panic coiled in my gut as no part of me responded to what my mind was screaming. Was I stuck in here, unable to communicate or control my own body? Had I turned into some kind of vegetable, trapping my consciousness in some crazy coma limbo?

But no, my eyes were open, and I was staring up at a ceiling with crisscrossing metal rafters that loomed high above me. I blinked once. Twice.

The first sound I finally heard was my breath sawing in and out of me, and I realized I was nearly hyperventilating.

"Welcome back to the land of the living."

I jolted, electrical shocks firing through all of my nerve endings like a cut live wire, wild and dangerous.

28

Cassidy Vs. Cassidy

The headache that knocked around in my skull dulled behind the thrill of panic that snapped up my spine at the sound of my own disembodied voice. But it seemed to ignite the connection between my brain and my body because I curled my fingers into my palms exactly as my mind willed.

Lying on my back was too vulnerable of a position—I couldn't gauge where the other Cassidy was or where Edwards might be—but my mind was still sluggish even after everything started to click back into place.

If I had my way, I would have jumped to my feet, ready to defend myself.

But all I managed was a groan as I rolled to my side and pushed myself up to my hands and knees, trying to get my equilibrium settled. Rough concrete bit into my palms, sending my eyes wide as I stared at the unfinished floor. The details settled in my mind, and it dawned on me that we were in a warehouse. Again.

My eyes wheeled for my doppelganger, but all I could see was empty, shadowy space. Was this the same warehouse?

My breath came out in pathetic gasps.

"You sneaky, little *bitch*." Cassidy's voice was a jarring reverberation against my brain.

There was a brief pressure against my side, and I tumbled sideways, landing on my back again. I blinked, bringing her enraged face into focus above me. She'd knocked me over—not that it took much effort—and her hands curled around the front of my jacket.

"Your little boyfriend is an anchor!" As if to drive the point home, she lifted me up and then slammed me back down against the floor.

I curled upward to keep my head from smacking the hard ground.

Her accusation gouged into me, but instead of weakening me, it lit a fire in my bones that radiated through my blood, clearing my mind of cobwebs. I chopped at her elbows, forcing them to bend, and she grunted, falling into me. I used her surprise to roll both of us so we switched places. I straddled her stomach and pressed her into the floor with a forearm at her throat.

"You have no room to accuse me of anything! We had an agreement, and instead of keeping your word, you didn't show up." I gritted my teeth.

"An agreement, my ass." She blew a lock of short hair out of her eyes, her breath puffing into my face.

"You brought Edwards there to ambush me!"

She snorted. "And you left a little love note for Louisa."

I stiffened, pressing my weight more heavily into her.

"We both know you had an agenda just as much as I did," she choked out.

I shook my head as if that could stop the truth of the

accusation.

She smirked. "Seems we're not as different as you'd like to believe, are we?"

"I'm *nothing* like you," I spat, wishing the denial would settle deep enough to stop the infection of uncertainty she was injecting.

"No?" There was a strange, manic glint to her eyes, like she was strengthened by the effect her words had on me. "What lengths are you willing to go for the life you want?"

"You know *nothing* about my life." I tried to keep the edge in my voice, but it was already weakened by the poison of doubt.

"Oh, I know a lot more than you think. Your whole 'woe is me' bit is pretty classic. But then you start dragging your little man candy's name in the mud, offering up the necklace for your own selfish gain."

I sat back like she'd slapped me, taking my forearm from her throat. It was enough to give her a window of escape, and she shoved me off of her, spinning away and out of reach. We glared at each other across a chasm of animosity.

Her words continued to echo in my head, a taunt tinged with the bitter edge of truth.

How long had this company been keeping tabs on me? How much could they possibly know? Or was it deeper than them? Was *she* learning all the angles of my life for a specific purpose—for them or for her own reasons?

I had to shut it down—my doubt and this line of thinking. She was trying to throw me off, to distract me. None of it was true.

I shook my head. "It wasn't—"

"Wasn't it, though?" she interrupted, tipping her head to the side, basking in the hold her words had over me. "You just want to live your life, right? Move on?" A theatrical little pout. "Did you ever stop to think about what giving it all up means? Who that *affects*?"

No. That wasn't right. I wasn't hurting anyone by bowing out, letting things fall as they were *meant* to. My meddling was what had messed things up—for the other Drew, Skylar, my family, *me*. . .

"You didn't even consider it, did you? How you would stop at nothing to get everyone to leave you alone. Sounds like the textbook definition of 'selfish' to me."

I wanted to argue with her, to throw out the letter as proof that I wasn't in this only for myself, but that's what she'd contaminated with her accusation. To her, it didn't matter that I had been trying to help someone else. She would taint it with the fact that I had to deceive *her* to accomplish it. No good deed goes unpunished.

She took in my expression and laughed, a bubbling, tortured sound that drove the poison in deeper.

My breaths shot in and out of my lungs, painful with the contagion. "I can't believe you're spinning this to make *me* seem like the bad guy." My voice was barely above a whisper.

She leaned toward me. "We're all the bad guy, Cassidy. At some point or another." Her taunting smile wilted. "Some of us just know when to admit it and use it when we need to."

I placed my fingers against my temples. It wasn't wrong to want to live my life; it wasn't wrong to want the hurt to stop—mine and Skylar's and Drew's and anyone else's whose life I was messing up.

As if she hadn't caused enough damage, she kept going, giddy with power. "What about other victims of Creedy's? There are more realities where he's still killing."

Pain lanced my heart, a guilt-tipped sword. "Stop it."

"Or ones in which Callum has control of some other woman who has no means of escape. What about them?"

"Stop it!" Desperation and agony shot the words out like a cannon, but it only gave her more fuel.

"And what about your family, Cassidy? Don't you want to *fix* them?" She gave an exaggerated pout. "Or was it that you wanted to fix yourself? Because we both know you're still broken. Unloved and unlovable."

I lurched forward to grab her, but she cackled and spun away from my reaching hands, staggering to her feet.

"Admit it! You could have destroyed the necklace before. But you were keeping it. Why?"

I stared at her, chest heaving, uncertainty continuing to brew. She was naming all the things that had been nagging in the back of my mind, things I had barely realized were there, but they'd been lurking the whole time, casting my decisions in the shadow of doubt.

Why *hadn't* I gotten rid of it? I'd stopped wearing it, but I'd left it whole and functional, right where I would easily find it if I ever needed it. I didn't actively decide to keep it as a backup plan, but wasn't that exactly what I'd done?

"You weren't truly giving it up, were you?" She smiled as if she could read my mind. "Did you want a reason to jump again?" I was shaking my head, but she was on a roll: "Try one more time. Just to see, right? Or maybe to run from it all. That's what you're good at, isn't it?"

"No," I gasped, trying to claw my way back to what I did know of myself and the decisions I'd made. I'd questioned, I'd been scared and unsure, but I'd allowed myself to love and be loved. Finally. I knew the difference now.

As if the thought triggered something across planes, I felt the jerk in my core much stronger than usual. My hand was there, pressing into my stomach before I'd registered it, my eyes wide in shock.

Cassidy's malicious taunting stopped, her own expression going sharp with recognition as she stared at my hand.

Her eyes jerked back up to my face, and she spoke through clenched teeth: "Give me the necklace. Now."

I ignored her demand, too bewildered to care about all of her stupid attempts to derail me. "What was that?"

She gave me a sour look.

"What was it?" I bit out, the words hammering against the tension between us.

Her lip curled back. "Your anchor." She narrowed her eyes on my face, analyzing. It was like she was seeing me for the first time, changing her assessment of the situation. "I didn't realize his pull was that strong," she added, mostly to herself.

That strong, I repeated in my mind. What was she saying? That Drew could pull me back by sheer force of will? Or was it a natural characteristic of an anchor?

It had never been so powerful before. Certainly not enough to feel like he could drag me back. But this made me wonder if he actually could.

"Is that normal?" I asked, desperate to know more, to understand what was still so unfathomable. Still so many questions.

A grating sigh sawed out of her as she threw her hands into the air. "I don't know!" she ground out, taking a breath before continuing. "Usually anchors are places."

"Like this warehouse?"

She squinted at me, a suspicious glint to her expression.

The question was mostly rhetorical, and I didn't need that answer as much as I wanted the others. "Can a place pull you back?"

She hesitated for a moment. "No," she said grudgingly.

I watched her closely. "So why can a person?"

Her eyes flashed away from my face, and she shifted her weight. Was it my imagination that she seemed uneasy?

Her gaze swung back to me, and she held out her hand. "The necklace."

I curled my fingers around the pendant, which drew her gaze. "Answer the question."

"I don't know!" She shifted again, rubbing her hands down her thighs. "It's. . . unusual, okay?"

"Unusual," I repeated, skeptical.

She huffed. "It was only a theory. No one I know has actually experienced it."

I watched a flurry of emotions dance across her face even though she fought to hide it. But she was me, and I knew what I was seeing in her expression, even behind a veil of false bravado—realization, sadness, pain. And finally, her shoulders dropped as she deflated a little.

My experience with DeMarco and Edwards gave me an idea of what type of people were involved in this whole operation. I couldn't see anyone being attached so strongly to any of them that they would be anchors, but admittedly, I had only seen a certain side of them.

And it was hard to believe she could possibly have anyone in her life, let alone someone as an anchor. And maybe that was why she'd deflated, realizing that no one was so attached to her that they could pull her back, would even want to.

It painted her taunting in a whole new light. She knew what

triggers to use because she felt it all too.

"The necklace," she said again. The fierceness in her voice sounded manufactured this time, like the desperation to cling to her original plan was losing its power over her. But she must have felt like she had to follow through.

"The proof," I countered.

She did that analyzing appraisal again but made no move to hand it over, whatever it might be.

"That was the whole agreement," I reminded her.

"Yes, it was. But your little side mission wasn't part of that agreement." Her voice was so much more subdued, I didn't realize what she'd said at first, that it was even an accusation.

I wanted to understand the change in her demeanor. But even with all the questions I could see reflected in her eyes, the fear that she would never actually hand the file over burned in my gut. It would never be over until I had it.

"Edwards wasn't part of the agreement either," I shot back.

Her eyes shifted.

"Were you even planning to hold up your end of the bargain?"

She shot me a glare but didn't defend herself, which made anger flare inside me, and an idea formed in my mind.

I lifted the necklace from my throat, yanking slightly, betting on a bluff I had no basis for yet. "I swear if you don't give me some answers, I will destroy this thing."

Her jaw clenched, and she jammed her hand into a pocket. "The proof, the flash drive—" she held it up— "is legit. Every file they had on you was erased and only exists here."

Okay, that confirmed what I didn't know. It was entirely possible to destroy the necklace, and it must not have been very difficult if the threat worked that well.

I opened my mouth to demand to see what was on the drive, but another jerk in my core caught me off-guard, and I staggered, clutching at my stomach as if I'd been shot. That time, it was almost painful—though not as bad as I imagined a bullet wound would be. Definitely not as bad as being stabbed.

Cassidy reached toward me as if she'd had the impulse to help and looked horrified when she realized what she was doing. She pulled her hands back so quickly against her body, it was like she'd touched a hot stove.

I felt the yank in my middle again, and a surprised cry of pain scraped up my throat. I put my hand against the closest wall to steady myself, a little bead of sweat tickling at my hairline.

"He's going to pull me back, isn't he?" I gasped.

She barely moved, staring at me with wide eyes. Her refusal to give me an answer was telling.

I didn't need her confirmation as the tug came again, sharp and insistent. Clenching my teeth against another cry of pain, I wondered if it had been him the whole time, pulling me back to our reality without either of us realizing.

"He's not taking my anomaly anywhere."

It was a man's voice that came from the shadows, and we both jerked to look. She was as startled as I was, which told me she wasn't expecting him.

He stepped out of the darkness, shadows clinging to his face and making the lines around his eyes and mouth more pronounced. But my gaze dropped to the gun in his hand.

29

Turntables

My lungs throbbed painfully, reminding me that I'd held my breath for too long. As if my body hadn't been through enough, depriving it of oxygen was one more item to add to the litany of abuses it had suffered recently.

I shouldn't have been surprised that Edwards was here. I'd known it must have been coming. But we were so engrossed in our own conversation, I'd forgotten that I should have been paying attention to the rest of the room.

Cassidy didn't seem shocked at his appearance, even if she'd been startled initially. So she'd expected him to catch up with us eventually. Was everything before this just a distraction to keep me occupied until he got here? And why hadn't he come through with us the first time?

The way she was staring at him now made me question what exactly they had set up. There was more animosity in her gaze than I would have expected for someone who was supposedly in cahoots with him.

"Surprise," Edwards said with a smile. His gun was trained on me, but he was looking at Cassidy.

I caught the way her hand tightened around the flash drive as if she were trying to hide it. Did he know she had it? Was he aware of the trade we had agreed to make? Or had she kept everyone in the dark about her real intentions, using each of us for her own purposes?

This whole thing was turning into a bigger question mark.

"You're late," Cassidy said, irritation the only emotion I heard in her voice.

Uncertainty spiked my blood, a cocktail of panic and adrenaline that heightened all of my senses.

I'd had a glimmer of hope that she was at least questioning things, that maybe I could convince her to stick with our trade and call it good. But Edwards' appearance sent that hope spiraling into a suffocating black hole, strangling the life out of it.

She walked to stand closer to Edwards, though notably not *next* to him. If anything, she seemed to position herself like she was facing a potential opponent, not like a partner, and certainly not like a friend. So maybe the alliance was tenuous at best. But I hated that I was still so out of the loop, that I couldn't discern the truth of the situation.

I grimaced when Drew's pull sent another sharp stab through my gut. It wasn't as strong this time, not as close to knocking me off my feet, but it was there, demanding and painful.

"I had a little trouble finding you." He looked at me, eyes tightening. "I wasn't sure where exactly you might have ended up. That anchor sure threw a wrench in things, didn't he?"

My stomach dropped. It sounded like he was saying Drew had caused something to happen. Like Cassidy and I were sent to an unexpected location because of him. The two of us had been physically connected when we'd made the jump, whereas

Edwards had not. Perhaps that made a difference. When we'd jumped, I'd had a sense of something being different. Like maybe something had knocked me off the usual trajectory.

Drew caused all of that?

"Well, here we are," Cassidy replied, her own gaze shifting to me. The intensity of it blistered my skin, and another wave of uncertainty washed through me. There was some unnameable thing in her expression.

Did she want me to do something? Or was she trying to tell me something?

"Now that you've delivered on your end," Edwards said, "I can deliver on mine."

Cassidy stiffened; some part of this was unexpected. A small shot of sick relish released into my bloodstream to see her experiencing at least a fraction of what I was going through.

Edwards stepped back into the shadows, the outline of his form the only thing that was visible, then moved toward us again. The light that fell over him was like someone pouring paint over his face.

Clearly unwilling, a man staggered out from the hallway at Edwards' prodding.

I choked on a gasp and fought the urge to take a step back.

A dark line of blood trickled from his hairline, and his eyes, normally bright with otherworldly intelligence, were dim with pain and weakness. His hands were bound in front of him, and Edwards forced him to kneel in front of him.

"This is not exactly the delivery I was looking for," Cassidy bit out, shooting a disparaging look over Eli Thibald.

Edwards didn't flinch. "It's a step closer than you were. You think she's not going to try to find him? To help him?"

"You are such an idiot," she muttered. "No wonder you

always play the lackey."

This time, he rose to her bait. He strode forward, his expression twisted with rage. Because I'd been on the receiving end of that kind of fury, I tensed up in anticipation. But she was unprepared—maybe because she'd never seen what that kind of emotion could make someone do—when he pistol-whipped her across the face.

The sound seemed to vibrate along the silence her shock created. Or maybe it was my nerves that felt the echo.

She glared at him, touching her hand to her lip to wipe the blood where the gun had broken her skin. There was a phantom sting along my own mouth, my experience with the same injury an indelible memory.

"Don't forget who holds the gun in this scenario," he growled. "You might be David's little *pet*, but his influence doesn't reach as far as you think it does."

While the two of them scowled at each other, I tried to catch Thibald's eye. I wasn't sure if Edwards was aware of the fact that Cassidy hadn't taken the necklace from me yet. And since I still had it, I knew I needed to at least try to help Thibald escape as well. After all, hadn't that been the whole point? So he wasn't Louisa, but he was their link to her, and this felt like the right thing to do—the assist by proxy.

I gripped the charm in my hand, ready to slide my thumb over the familiar ridges, but Edwards raised his gun at me, his eyes following a half-second later. Cassidy and Thibald shifted their attention as well.

"Not this time," Edwards growled.

I froze, my gut clenching. If the necklace wasn't made of such stern stuff, I would have crushed it with the way my hand clamped around it.

Apparently, he wasn't as incompetent as he seemed or as Cassidy intimated. Or he'd learned his lesson. He held out his hand for the necklace, and everyone in the room tensed up, particularly Cassidy.

It might have been her ticket to Louisa, but it was my way home. Dread filled my core as I debated my options.

Cassidy licked at her lip almost absently, but she intentionally caught my eye, giving the smallest nod. She was at least a smidge more trustworthy than Edwards because I knew a little better what to expect from her. At least I hoped so.

But whatever her plan was, I didn't have much of a choice anyway. Not with a gun pointed at my face. I reluctantly dropped the necklace into Edwards' open palm just as another tug wrenched in my core, taking me by surprise. I staggered sideways, sucking air through my teeth.

Edwards jerked, his lip curling back like a snarling dog. Then he tilted the gun in his hand as if in question, taking me in with suspicious appraisal. "That is quite the pull. I knew he was an anchor, but this. . . "

"Yes, I've heard all about how unusual it is," I snapped, the pain giving an edge to my words.

"Has he pulled you back before?" Edwards asked, his eyes calculating. His question seemed academic, and the other two watched me for my answer, just as eager to hear it.

"Why? Looking to do an experiment?" I asked, going against my better judgment in goading him.

He smirked darkly, though it looked like another snarl. "Being a smart ass must be wired into the DNA," he said, glancing at Cassidy.

I said nothing and looked at Thibald, who was still watching me intently.

Cassidy seized the opportunity my silence afforded. "I'd rather be a smart ass than a dumb—"

Edwards whipped his gun in her direction, and she stepped back this time, having learned her lesson. She still looked pleased with herself, and I wondered if it had been an intentional distraction.

Then I felt it—some shift in the atmosphere, like the tether to Drew was working. The buzzing in my ears, faint, like a bug flying around my head, gave me hope that I'd be gone in a moment. I willed myself to give in to the tug across planes. If I could just get back, we could go with the old plan. Start over, go on the defensive when the time came.

Being pulled versus jumping was an entirely different experience. All those times I'd been unconscious for hours afterward made it clear it was a more jarring experience physically. Even now, I started to feel light-headed and ethereal, like I was fading from this plane of existence.

Until Edwards clamped a hand around my wrist, and everything snapped back into focus like all the weight of gravity shoved my consciousness back into my body.

I gasped.

"That connection really is quite powerful," he murmured, tilting his head.

So Edwards could function as an anchor himself. Or block the energy somehow?

"David would find that quite fascinating, wouldn't he?"

I caught the way Cassidy's expression darkened and realized Edwards was talking to her. It was the second time he'd mentioned David in conjunction with her, and I wondered what sort of relationship the two had.

As if he sensed her discomfort, Edwards turned ever so

slightly in her direction. "Has David ever pulled you back?"

Thibald shifted then, drawing my attention, though the other two were too locked in their power struggle to notice him.

Thibald's eyes had sharpened on her face, a realization dawning that I hadn't quite figured out yet.

"Shut your mouth." Her voice was low, but it held a purring danger, and something twanged on the air, making the hair on the back of my neck stand up.

Edwards didn't seem to notice. Or didn't care. "David has you fooled with his little lover's routine, but his attention has been divided since the day his baby girl disappeared. And he might not see it, but I do. You hate the little bitch for keeping him from giving himself fully to you."

Her whole motivation was a romantic relationship with David Lee, a man who was likely as old as my—our—father?

Ick. And I thought I had daddy issues.

Whatever flimsy agreement Cassidy and Edwards had made appeared to be crumbling before my eyes, and I wondered what exactly the endgame was here. Was he trying to convince *me* of something? Get Thibald on his side? Or was it really some stupid spite war?

"You," Edwards said, using the gun to direct Cassidy over, "hold her here."

Grudgingly, she shuffled over, taking hold of my wrist in Edwards' stead so he could put his hand on Thibald.

"We've got a nice surprise for your boyfriend," Edwards said proudly.

Cassidy's face changed then. This had not been part of her plan, and it didn't seem like that's what Edwards had promised—if they had indeed made some sort of bargain.

"Still trying to get ahead, then, are we?" Cassidy asked, the taunt she'd once directed at me now saturating her words to Edwards.

His eyes narrowed on her face.

But even with his focus on her, she was sneaky, her hand sliding down to mine. I stiffened, though I realized I needed to keep the surprise off my face. It was an effort not to look down and draw attention to myself or what she was doing as she pressed the flash drive into my palm.

So she was throwing herself in with me, even though I no longer had the necklace to offer her. It put the two of us against Edwards. The question was if Thibald would help.

When I looked at him, I caught him staring at my hand now curled around what Cassidy had given me. His gaze flashed to her face, calculating.

Trustworthy? his eyes asked.

"This wasn't the plan," Cassidy said.

Her voice had edged toward desperation, and it elicited a strange reaction in me. It was like my adrenaline was responding to my own voice, even disembodied, because a new flood of fight or flight kicked my pulse into overdrive.

I wasn't sure what her plan was or how to help. My theory about some kind of cosmic connection seemed to be dying a quick death. It was stupid that being forced to interact with another version of myself didn't come with freaking telepathy or something.

With Edwards pretty well focused on her for the moment, though I wondered if that was her goal: make an opening that I could squeeze through.

"Yeah, you think I'm going to let you have Louisa, knowing what I do?" Edwards sneered at her. "The point was to get in David's good graces, not give you what you wanted. You thought I had some sort of vendetta against your doppelganger just because DeMarco was blinded by his hatred for you. I'm not that short-sighted."

"What were you going to do to her?" Thibald demanded, his voice a croak that made me jump.

We all looked at him, but he was focused on Cassidy.

She glared at him. "What difference does it make to you? Isn't the point to keep Louisa away from her father?"

Her words left a grimy feeling along my skin. The deflection was very clearly not a denial, and I found myself questioning again. What *was* her motivation? I'd had a sense it was nothing good, but the fact that she wouldn't come right out and say it was suspicious.

"The point was to protect her," Thibald said. He sounded so defeated already.

"At any cost, apparently," she countered.

Thibald sucked in a breath like she'd punched him in the gut.

"None of us have clean hands," Edwards interjected, clearly exasperated by the arguments taking place.

"Some dirtier than others," Cassidy said to Thibald, apparently wanting to get on everyone's bad side.

He lurched to his feet, disregarding Edwards and the gun. I suspected it was deliberate when Edwards stumbled backward, and Thibald spun, catching me and Cassidy off-guard, using his bound hands to knock the gun from Edwards' grip.

Without thinking, without even looking at Cassidy, I sprinted for the weapon as it went sliding across the floor. A blazing desperation to get there first flared through my body. Not one person there was trustworthy, and I needed it all to end. I needed to get the upper hand.

But my frenzy to get there first was mirrored and magnified by my twin out of time and space, and we crashed together as if yanked by an imaginary string. We slammed to the floor, grappling for the gun.

My nails scored her wrists and hands, and she kicked, landing a blow in my still-healing leg injury. I clenched my teeth against the cry of pain that blasted up my throat.

She grunted, twisting as I clutched at her jacket, my arm muscles straining in my efforts to pull her back or use her body as a ladder to reach the gun first.

And then a heavy body fell on top of us, and I shrieked as sweaty hands pawed against my back, gripping my hair and yanking my head backward.

I glanced back at Edwards' twisted expression, face shiny with sweat, and caught sight of Thibald's crumpled form several feet behind him. Ice shot through me.

Then the telltale sound of a bullet being chambered in the gun echoed through the room. Edwards and I froze. My stomach dropped to my toes as Cassidy staggered to her feet, her chest heaving from the effort of reaching the weapon first.

"Stand up, my pretties," she huffed, gesturing with the gun she held with both hands.

I couldn't move until Edwards did, so I waited, though my eyes caught on the glint of metal half hanging from his pocket. It was only a small length of the chain from the necklace, but it was enough.

As he pushed himself up, I twisted my legs, knocking him back down and eliciting a glare. But it also gave me the window to hook the chain with my finger, allowing the necklace to slide out of the pocket as he got to his feet. I didn't even have to pull.

I stuffed it into my own pocket right before I rolled to my

stomach and climbed to my feet after him.

"You think you've won," Edwards growled. "But David will find out. He'll know what you've really been planning. I will—"

The sound of the gun firing ricocheted with such force, I didn't hear Edwards hit the ground, though I watched him topple, flopping down like he'd lost all of his bones.

Shock yanked the gasp out of me as my chest constricted. I didn't even realize the tugging had started in my core again until I staggered sideways.

"Go!"

Cassidy's voice was muffled and distant, and I looked at her without the ability to truly process what she was saying or why.

"Get out of here."

The words rattled in my head, the echo hitting harder and louder, making me flinch.

"You have the necklace. Get out of here. Then destroy it."

I blinked. "Destroy it? I thought you wanted it?"

Her eyes dropped to my pocket where I'd stuffed it. A strange look twisted her features. "Just go. You can be free or do whatever the hell you want. Merry Christmas."

I squinted at her, not trusting what this meant. Would she come after me later? Or would someone else?

"I swear to God, Cassidy." She marched forward, jerking the necklace from my pocket and stuffing it into my hand. "You know jumping is easier on you than getting pulled through. Go before he yanks you back."

I didn't want to miss my opportunity when she was being inexplicably gracious, so I rubbed my thumb over the ridges, summoning this stupid, physics-defying power that had torn everything I knew down to the ground, exposing the cracks in the foundation.

As the view in front of me became obscured by a cyclone of sound and light, the buzz crawling under my skin, the pressure in my ears threatening to burst the drums, I was filled with a dichotomy of abject sorrow and peace.

Staring at this other version of myself, knowing she was hurting, knowing what she was choosing by giving me the necklace, I could see how the ability to jump ripped everything apart, was a defiance of all that was natural. But it also offered the chance to rebuild a life worth living.

I hoped she chose to build something new.

And then everything went black.

30

Return To Me

A voice tight with anxiety broke into my awareness, but my brain couldn't parse the words that tumbled out. Cold concrete at my back pulled the warmth from my body as a breeze bit at my cheeks, coaxing me to full consciousness.

Hot hands against my face urged me to open my eyes, but my mind was slow to obey, my body outright rebelling against anything I tried to tell it to do. I knew on some level that I *needed* to open my eyes, to move, but I couldn't exactly remember why.

"Cassidy?" It was a man's voice, muffled but familiar enough to begin breaking through my stupor.

A moan was the closest I could get to forming a response.

An expelled breath of air brushed along my face like a sigh of relief, and part of me settled into that sense of relief too.

I became aware of my hands clutching at something. No, someone. A warm, muscular chest, familiar against my palms, like my hands belonged there, had explored this body many times.

I gasped as my eyes shot open, and Drew's arm slid under

my back, lifting me up and against him, crushing my hands between us, and the relief became complete.

"Thank God," he breathed, rocking me slightly as he held me almost too tightly.

But I would never complain, never ask him to stop holding me. Even as my sluggish brain struggled to comprehend, to remember everything that came before this moment, it registered on the deepest level that this was where I was meant to be.

The moment stretched, pressing against me with the weight of questions I felt brewing under the surface.

Finally, Drew released some of the pressure with the first one: "Are you all right?"

I sighed, taking stock of my throbbing head, the aches in my body. But the comfort only he could inspire thrummed through me and made all of that seem distant, if only for this moment.

"Getting there now," I mumbled against his shoulder.

"Where is the other Cassidy?" His voice was tight with concern, but he didn't release me yet.

Where *was* the other Cassidy? My brain sputtered, fought the process of remembering. "I–I don't know."

Drew pulled back, searching my face. "What do you mean you don't know?"

I rubbed at my temples as if I could massage the memories back in. "Uhhh. She-she sent me back? Told me to go."

"And Edwards?" Drew asked.

I shook my head, trying to knock something loose. "Uh, dead?"

His eyes probed mine. Looking for proof of life? Was I brain-dead? I felt brain-dead.

He lifted his brows when I said nothing further. "Are you asking or are you telling?"

I squeezed my eyes shut as the headache pulsed against my skull. It wanted revenge for making my brain think.

"Cass?" Drew pressed, his fingers on my arms digging in a little.

I waved my hands in the air as if to dispel the mental haze coating my brain. "Telling. I'm–I'm telling."

He frowned, his eyes roving over my face. He didn't relax, didn't seem comforted by what he saw.

Some distant voice in my mind told me that I should probably be worried about that, but my brain was not computing beyond *oxygen in and out.*

Abruptly, Drew muttered an oath under his breath, pulling his sleeve over his hand and dabbing at my nose.

I realized belatedly it must have been because it had started bleeding. I pushed his hand away from my face so that I could check on the bleeding myself.

The shiny crimson on my fingers didn't inspire as much panic as it probably should have—as it clearly did in him because he was moving, pulling out his phone.

"It should stop soon," I said, my voice a little too clinical. I didn't want him making any phone calls, especially of the emergency variety. He hated hospitals; I hated fuss.

His eyes followed my hand as I brought it back to my nose, trying to stanch the flow, his worry winding around me like the wintry breeze that made me shiver.

His lips became a thin line. "I don't like it."

"Zero percent surprised," I quipped.

He didn't smile, but he raised a brow. "You must be okay if you're making jokes."

I shrugged then winced as a rippling ache radiated through me. "I'm not okay yet. Not until you take me home."

He was still intently watching my face. "I will gladly take you home if it means you'll stay there."

"Deal."

He huffed a mirthless laugh and pulled me into him again, anxiety a vibration in his body that I could still feel. Talk about a role reversal.

He pulled back again, doing another once-over, eyes tracing my face in slow assessment. He could see that the bleeding had stopped, but he didn't seem satisfied.

"Can you walk?"

"Probably." I shifted and grimaced when the aches in my body again made their presence known. "Eventually."

He frowned, then shifted to a crouch, tossing my arm across his shoulders and slipping one of his hands behind me and the other under my knees.

I sucked in a breath and clutched at his jacket. "You are *not* carrying me out of this alley."

"The hell I'm not." He lifted me with a grunt. "It's my day to be a hero, and I'm damn well going to live it up."

I scowled as he hiked me up against his chest, cradling me like a freaking damsel in distress. And he was *basking* in it, barely hiding the smile I saw tugging at his mouth.

And damn if it wasn't the littlest bit sexy to have him carry me across the street to his waiting car. I could let him have his hero moment. But only this once.

"Don't let this go to your head. It's a one-time thing," I warned.

He smirked. "Me being the hero? Or me carrying you? Because you seem to like that."

I scoffed, though the warmth crawled across my face. "I would rather not need a hero at all from now on."

His expression darkened, and I regretted bringing down his mood with the reminder. "Let's hope you don't. Not because I dislike it."

"Obviously," I interrupted, raising a brow.

He set me on my feet when we reached the passenger side of his car, supporting my weight as he opened the door. I dropped into the seat and let him fuss over situating me, if only because I was tired and cold, and it seemed to make him feel better.

He said nothing else until after he'd started the engine, but I felt his unspoken words blistering the air between us. His expression was too compressed, giving away just how many thoughts were spinning in that head of his.

"Cassidy let you go," he said slowly, not looking at me as he flipped on the turn signal and checked behind us.

I leaned my head back against the headrest. "I don't know exactly what her motivation was, but, yeah. She took out Edwards then told me to go. She even let me have the necklace."

He glanced over, his eyes tightening.

"I'm going to destroy it," I assured him.

And still, his silence was a physical presence, a tangible question mark searing the air. "Is that what you want?"

I didn't hesitate. "Yes."

The string of tension running through him didn't loosen. Did he not believe me? Or was he worried I would regret the decision at some point?

"Look," I started, fishing in my pocket and turning a little in my seat. "She gave me this flash drive. I assume it has whatever information about me the company—or whatever—had."

His eyes shifted from the road only briefly to the drive I held up. "There's no guarantee—"

"No, it's not," I interrupted. "But the fact that she gave it to me, let me keep the necklace, and told me to go makes me think we can at least count this as a win. And I said I was done. That was a promise."

Air huffed through his nose as he took my free hand. I watched him move it around over his knuckles then flip his hand so that our palms connected, and I shivered at the electricity that pulsed along my skin.

But apparently he wasn't convinced because his mouth pinched as he shook his head. "If you give it up—"

"No regrets, Drew." My voice was firm with the knowledge that I spoke the truth. Every cell in my body sang the tune of absolute certainty.

He smiled a little, sighing, and I knew he must have been thinking about that moment only a few days ago when he'd said something similar. But the conviction was strong, zinging along that unyielding tether between us.

I wondered if he felt it that way too—more than just our electric connection. But maybe because I had always been the loose satellite, I was the only one who felt the pull like he had his own gravity.

I almost told him about the tug between timelines, the way that whatever had happened between us had become stronger. But it didn't seem like the moment, and I was tired. Too tired to explain anything or ask any more questions.

So I settled on the next best thing, which really encompassed the whole concept.

"Hey," I said softly.

"Hm?"

"I love you."

31

Flash

I almost laughed when I emerged from the hallway. Drew would have been the picture of leisure if not for his scowl.

He slouched back in his chair at the table, an arm draped over the back and one long leg stretched out in front of him. His coffee sat on the table in front of him, tendrils of steam coiling in the air with sinuous allure, but it appeared to be neglected.

"What's with that face?" I asked, walking into the kitchen to find a mug of chai waiting for me. I suppressed my grin and picked it up, bringing it with me to the table since he hadn't answered my question.

Drew raised his eyes at my approach, expression unchanged. Dark and broody. Admittedly sexy.

"Thank you for my tea," I said, placing a hand on his shoulder and leaning down to kiss his frowning mouth.

His scowl deepened.

I laughed. "Dude, what is your deal?"

He sat forward, placing his arm on the table, and stabbed a finger toward the other end. "That thing is driving me crazy."

I didn't need to look to know what he was pointing at, but

I did anyway, finding the flash drive sitting in the exact spot I'd left it. Even though I had no interest in learning what was on it, I still hadn't gotten rid of it, even after destroying the necklace. Which might have said something about my unconscious feelings about it.

I didn't want to delve deeper into what might be behind that fact. What I wanted was to bask in the removal of one more impediment to the new life I planned to immerse myself in. Project Turn Cassidy Into A Normal Girl was priority number one.

"You really don't want to know what's on it?" He turned a scalding eye on me, incredulity blatant on his face.

I raised a brow and sipped my tea. How he'd managed to learn the exact ratio of cream to sweetener I preferred, I had no idea. But he'd yet to mess it up. He was spoiling me by making it for me every morning. It made up for the fact that he usually spilled the cream and forgot to wipe it up or left the mess from the whole process sitting out on the counter most days.

"Must be the detective in me," he muttered, curling his fingers around the handle of his mug as he returned to scowling.

I waved my hand. "If you want to look at it, feel free."

He jerked to look at me, skeptical and suspicious. His evaluation of my neutral expression didn't seem to convince him. "You sure?"

I lifted a shoulder. He hadn't asked me before, so I'd never said anything about it. And maybe I'd been waiting for him to. It took this moment for me to realize I had chosen not to look at it as some sort of proof to him—and probably myself—that none of this mattered anymore, that I was well and truly done. I could feel it in myself that I'd wait however long it took to convince us both of the fact.

Now it was Drew asking the question, doing the digging, so I had no reason to feel guilty. I'd proven to myself that I could leave it in the past if I wanted to.

But it would be nice to at least know what sort of information David Lee and his cronies had on me. Especially considering how much Cassidy had known about my life and background. That still sent a flurry of anxiety through me because someone had been watching and researching me without my knowledge.

What was it about me that attracted these creepy weirdos? Step one in Turn Cassidy Into A Normal Girl would be to ditch any connection to a life that lent itself to collecting stalkers like stamps in a passport.

I set my chai down as if it were a gavel ratifying the decision into law, then walked to the charging laptop on the side table next to the couch. Unplugging it with a dramatic flair helped me dispel the nervous energy as I turned to carry it over to Drew. He accepted the computer, never taking his eyes from my face. It was like he was waiting for the "just kidding."

To prove my point, I went to retrieve the flash drive and handed that to him as well.

With a deep breath, he turned to set the laptop down and open it, inserting the flash drive while I rested my hip against the table, pretending that anxiety wasn't coiling in my stomach. My grip tightened on the handle of my mug as the light from the screen illuminated Drew's face. I forced myself to study the angles and planes of his features that became sharper under the harsh light.

I suddenly felt like someone was revealing secrets I wasn't ready to share, even though he knew all of them already, had held them in his hands, and loved me anyway—despite or because of those dark, jagged pieces.

Whatever was in the document that had opened to him pulled out his analytical cop face and edged his expression. Watching that familiar change in his features brought me unexpected comfort. I reached out without consciously deciding to, running my thumb over that crease between his brows as affection welled inside of me.

He didn't look over, but his face softened and one corner of his mouth tipped up.

Like a balm to my nerves, the realization that he was here despite everything soothed any remaining uncertainty inside of me. After each of the things I'd put my faith in had crumbled or was snatched away from me, one thing had remained: him.

My anchor to the end, he had never once wavered, even when I had.

Here was this steady, unmovable man in the midst of everything spiraling wildly out of control in my world. And I'd gotten scared, almost giving it up. Maybe since I'd never been able to hold anything steady, let alone myself, or because I'd never had anything so stable, I'd turned to the spinning because it was all I'd known.

Even after I'd almost run away, driven by my fear, he'd still remained, pulling me back into the steadying warmth with his gravity, reminding me that as much as things changed or fell apart or disappointed me, he would be there as my mooring.

After years of failing to fit in wherever I was, then months of being on the run, getting pulled through multiple realities. . . I'd finally found where I belonged. But it turned out it was never a place. It was a person.

I belonged with him, wherever that would bring us or take me, and a blanket of peace settled over me—pleasant, soothing, and totally foreign and familiar simultaneously.

I slid my hand across his shoulders and leaned against him, pulling his focus from the screen. He tipped his face up to look at me, his first real smile of the morning warming me to the core. What a smile did for that handsome face would always undo me.

I lowered my head to press my lips to his.

There was no frenzy in the way my nerves responded to our proximity. It was a slow igniting of my senses as his arms twined around me. He pulled back after a moment, looking at me with a slight question in his eyes.

"What was that for?"

"I need a reason?" I smirked. "Because I love you."

He grinned, seeming to forget what was on the computer screen.

I gave him a sly look. "And because you're picking me up from work today so you can help me find a Christmas present for your mom."

His arms tightened around me. "Am I?"

A thrill of anxiety skated through me, even though I could tell he was teasing. "I need you!"

He puffed up his chest. "To carry you through the store like a big damn hero?"

I punched his shoulder lightly.

"Fine," he said with a laugh, not even slightly chagrined. "But only if you bring me a fancy coffee."

I snorted. "What fancy coffee? You like it black."

"Yeah, but you have all those expensive brewing machines and whatnot. What good is having a barista for a girlfriend if I don't get free coffee?"

I shook my head. "I demand a coffee tax, then."

His gaze sharpened with suspicion. "What's that?"

I pressed my mouth to his in a slow kiss. He gave a contented sigh when I pulled back.

"I love you, Cass," he murmured.

I rested my forehead against his. "Never stop," I whispered.

"I promise I won't."

32

Little Orphan Annie

"You'll be fine." Drew took my hand in his.

I grimaced, unsurprised that he could tell I was nervous. Not that it was hard to guess. Anyone would be nervous in my shoes under even the best of circumstances.

He brought our clasped hands up to press a kiss to the back of mine and shot me his smug grin.

Probably because I was glaring at him. It would always be simultaneously annoying and comforting to have him read me so well.

"Deep breath," he said, pulling in air as if he could calm my nerves by proxy.

I just arched a brow at him. "Don't patronize me."

He held up his free hand in surrender, still grinning. "I'm trying to help."

I wanted to pretend I wasn't nervous, rely on that tough exterior I used to call on at any sign of emotional danger. But I didn't want to start off on the wrong foot. I was supposed to be Normal Girl Cassidy, and I genuinely wanted to make a good first impression. Because, for the first time in a long while, this actually mattered.

"Are you ready?" He made no moves, content to wait as long as I needed, even as I started to shiver.

Definitely not was what I wanted to say. But because it was cold, because it wouldn't get any easier, because Normal Girl was my lofty new goal, I gave him one solemn nod.

But even Normal Girl Cassidy was still grappling with Little Orphan Annie Syndrome, and a pinch of grief nipped at my heart for a moment.

Drew gave my hand a squeeze and reached for the knob, not bothering to knock. He poked his head around the door to look inside, as if to make sure the coast was clear.

Heavenly scents wafted out, their escape immediate and enticing. If anything, I could survive meeting his family if it meant I could eat whatever it was his mother had cooked for us as the big Christmas meal. Unless the smells were making promises they couldn't keep.

Based on Drew's cooking skills, I wouldn't have put much stock in the smells. But I'd had the frozen dinners his mother made for him. And if her reheated, pre-made meals were any indication, I was about to have my taste buds knocked out and kept in a happy coma until the new year.

Drew stepped inside, tugging me behind him like a reluctant puppy on a leash.

The front room was straight from a Christmas catalog. Crackling fire—okay, not crackling because it was gas-powered, but the effect remained—fluffy, flocked greenery on the mantel with hand-made stockings stuffed full of goodies hanging at intervals, and a big tree with white lights in the corner displaying handmade and nostalgic ornaments that made my throat tighten.

The presents under the tree made me nervous to add the gifts I'd brought for his mom and sister. Nothing at the store had felt quite right for his mom, so I'd done a pencil drawing of a picture of the three of them I'd found in his room. And he'd assured me the earrings he'd helped me pick for Della would be a hit, but faced with the possibility of her actually seeing them made the panic run rampant.

I spun to face him and clutched at his jacket. "Is this a bad time to tell you I want twelve kids and to live in a big ass fixer-upper house out in the boonies?"

He tipped his head to the side, smiling. "Twelve is a good number."

"Drew!" I whispered.

He rolled his eyes. "Stop trying to scare me away to get out of meeting my mother. Put the presents under the tree and relax. My mom will love you."

He gave me a little push, and I curled my hands around my purse, which held the gifts. I reluctantly walked forward, laying the wrapped items with the others already under the tree.

He held his hand out to me when I turned back, and I chewed my lip as he tugged me behind him again.

"Ma? Dell?" he called, peeking down a wide hallway.

"Is that my boy?!" a woman's voice crooned from the recesses of the house.

Drew's grin exploded when his mother emerged from the aroma-shrouded kitchen.

Her hair was almost black except for the silver she'd left in gorgeous swaths throughout. The wavy locks were pulled back into a French twist so her lovely and gently lined face was entirely visible.

She floated forward to embrace her son with a soft smile. He wrapped his free arm around her, dropping his chin on top of her head in a comfort ritual that simultaneously warmed and stung my heart.

She pulled back, tipping her face to allow him to kiss her cheek before stepping to the side so she could look around him at me.

It was stupid that I wanted to scoot further behind him to hide. I had never been "bring home to mom" material, and my mind began to shout all the reasons why—I was emotionally stunted, difficult to deal with, a family-less wreck with nothing to offer but a tarnished past and a sarcastic mouth.

Drew squeezed my hand, which he hadn't relinquished during their hug. His nonverbal reminder that he was still there with me made the scared rabbit feeling disintegrate, even if the nerves continued to buzz through me.

"Mom, this is Cassidy." He pulled me forward so he could drop my hand and slide his arm around me. "Cass, this is my mom, Shannon."

I lifted my hand to shake hers, but of course she had to take me by the shoulders and pull me in for a hug like the classic, perfect mother she probably was.

The Little Orphan Annie inside of me sighed with contentment.

"It's so nice to meet you, Cassidy." She gave me an extra squeeze before releasing me and slipped her arm around my waist, pulling me from Drew's grasp and walking us toward the kitchen.

"Hey! That's mine!" he protested, but he was smiling when I glanced back at him.

"I hope you're hungry," Shannon said, ignoring him.

He winked at me and mouthed "love you" before I turned back around.

"It smells amazing," I said, genuine warmth in the words, though I still heard my nerves underneath.

"Hopefully it tastes as good," Shannon said with a self-effacing smile.

"Ma's a genius in the kitchen," Drew said proudly.

I raised my brow at him. "So what happened to you?"

Shannon snorted, giving my shoulders a squeeze. "I tried, but that boy could not even boil water properly. I gave up."

"Hey!" he protested.

"That explains why he cooks bacon wrong." My smile was uncontainable, though it froze for a second when we got into the kitchen. I spotted the girl sitting at the island, a veritable smorgasbord in front of her. Girl was not the right word. She was a grown woman, though she was younger than me.

She had the same dark hair and eyes as Drew, her face more rounded and feminine. She was a striking beauty, though she held herself with the quiet shyness that suggested she didn't know it.

"Still?" Drew's sister asked, shooting him a teasingly reproachful look.

He shrugged. "I'm incorrigible."

She tsked, then transferred her attention to me as she stood. "Hi. I'm Della."

I took her offered hand. "Cassidy."

"Drinks?" Shannon asked, opening the fridge.

"Beer for me," Drew said, holding out a hand while simultaneously stuffing a loaded cracker into his mouth.

I shook my head. "Nothing for me, thank you." My stomach was too twisted with nerves to accept anything, let alone a drink.

Shannon handed the beer to Della, who passed it to Drew.

"I can't believe you force her to eat your floppy bacon," Della said as he popped the top off.

"Better floppy bacon than floppy something else," Shannon quipped just as Drew took a sip of his beer.

Which he choked on, spinning to the sink to hack and cough and spit while Della guffawed.

Shannon tossed her head back and cackled, enjoying her son's reaction more than the rest of us, and I wondered if she had timed it for that exact reason.

It only took a second for my shock to wear off before I started laughing too.

"Think that's funny, do you?" Drew said, turning to me, his eyes narrowed in mischief.

Which never boded well for me. I took in the beer dribbling down his chin and realized his intentions a fraction of a second too late. He grabbed me by my waist and yanked me against him, attempting to kiss me with his wet beer mouth. I squealed and wiggled in his arms, heat seeping into my cheeks because his mother and sister were watching.

But I heard their laughter behind me and wiped my face against his shoulder, letting the anxiety pool out of me in the comfort of his arms.

Then I dried his mouth and chin with my sleeve, and he grinned down at me. I realized his goal was to loosen me up. Which had probably been his mother's aim as well.

I gave him a lighthearted glare and punched him in the arm so he'd release me.

"Ah, true love," Della sighed, which made the fire burn into my cheeks again.

"Damn straight," Drew agreed, dropping an arm around my shoulders.

Epilogue

Interview

One Year Later

"Should we set the scene?" Drew sat back against the arm of the couch, stretching across the length, and pulled out his phone. He shook it theatrically, like he was snapping a floppy newspaper open.

I groaned. "Please don't." I was curled up on the opposite side of the sofa, and he settled his feet on either side of me.

"She paints a very vivid picture. 'The vibrant red of Cassidy Marchand's hair isn't the most striking thing about her, even though it is what set her apart all those months ago—'"

I kicked at his shoulder, and he laughed, catching my bare foot with his free hand. Despite my protest, he continued to read aloud, skipping to the interview.

Ellen Davenport: It's been quite a ride for you over the last year, it seems.

Cassidy Marchand: In more ways than one.

ED: How so?

CM: It's a lot to deal with.

He paused, lifting his eyes to my face. "Almost gave that one away."

I quirked a brow but said nothing as his thumb rubbed the

bottom of the foot he still held. At least I was getting a foot massage out of this torture.

ED: Are you satisfied with how the trial went?

CM: I made peace with the possible outcomes before it ever started. But, yes. I'm glad he's behind bars for the rest of his life.

ED: You made peace? Is that in reference to the fact that you and the prosecution decided not to have you testify?

CM: . . .

ED: The defense had a field day with your detective on the stand. I assume that was one of the factors at play.

CM: It had some influence.

ED: You and the detective are still together.

CM: Yes.

ED: What was the thought process there?

CM: It's not a thought process. I love him.

He stopped again and smirked at me. "I can imagine how you said that."

I pursed my lips, trying to remain unaffected, staring way too intently at my fingernails.

"It's unfortunate she doesn't give us a little insight into that."

"What?"

"Your tone."

I snorted. "Unfortunate for who?"

"Anyone and everyone, obviously."

I rolled my eyes while he turned back to his phone to continue reading.

ED: Obviously that's not how it started.

CM: No. But nothing happened until well after Creedy was arrested. Even after the initial court proceedings. It wasn't an intentional thing, and it wasn't something we sought. But it did happen. The timing just wasn't ideal.

ED: He handled the cross-examination well. It was pretty brutal.

CM: He was prepared for it. No amount of aggressive and pointed questions could take away the fact that he's a good man and a good detective.

ED: Do you think the doubt cast by your relationship influenced the outcome of the case?

CM: We knew it could. But that part was out of my hands. It took some time to be okay with it; I can admit that. Because it was never only about me.

ED: You're talking about the other victims?

CM: They deserved justice too, to have their stories known. It didn't matter what happened to me, or the decisions I made.

ED: But your story matters too. You still bear the scars of what happened. Not just physically.

CM: It's all less painful knowing it's over. The most important part was for people to see what kind of a monster Gavin Creedy is.

ED: I'm sure. I think we all breathed a collective sigh of relief when that verdict came down.

CM: He's where he belongs, and that's what matters.

ED: Did you want a stronger punishment?

CM: Did you?

ED: It's not about me.

CM: . . . If I let myself dwell too long on what he put me through, I might get stuck in a cycle of wanting revenge.

ED: A normal reaction for anyone in your position, I think.

CM: *Sure, but it's not a place I want to stay. He's in prison for life. That's enough for me. Living my life is what's important now. And I have the freedom to do that.*

ED: That's a great perspective.

CM: *It's the choice I've made.*

ED: I'd imagine that's a daily decision.

CM: *Sometimes.*

ED: You have a somewhat troubled past, don't you? Your ex-boyfriend was recently imprisoned as well.

CM: *He was.*

ED: Is there a pattern there?

Drew huffed an irritated sigh. "This was supposed to be about the Creedy trial."

I gave a shrug, untouched now that the whole thing was over, but I remembered the flush of anger and the effort it was to keep it at bay.

CM: *Not anymore.*

ED: Turning over a new leaf, so to speak?

CM: *You can call it whatever you like. I call it moving on with my life.*

ED: It's admirable to see you push forward.

CM: *. . .*

ED: I appreciate the perspective you've given. I know people have been very interested to hear from you and understand your side of things.

CM: *That's been obvious.*

ED: You were fairly camera-shy before. Why give an interview now?

CM: *It's over, and it's less sensational now. I'm far enough removed that it's not as hard to talk about it.*

ED: So what's next for you?

CM: Build a life I can be proud of. Move forward, like I said. That's the choice I'm making now.

ED: Any news as far as you and the detective are concerned?

CM: No.

He raised a brow. "No news?"

I gave him a coy smile. "She doesn't get to announce it as if anyone deserves to know about us and our life."

He lifted his hands in surrender, returning my smile. "No actual complaints. Obviously, she would have seen it."

"And she was kind enough not to put it in anyway." I fiddled with the band on my left ring finger, the sparkle of the small, oval diamond catching the light. I still caught my breath every time I looked at it.

He acknowledged that with a dip of his head, a little grin pulling at his mouth when he caught the look on my face. "I told you she played fair. One of the few I'd give the time of day to. At least you acknowledged that you love me in a national news article."

"Yeah. You're welcome for that."

He yanked on one of my toes playfully.

ED: Okay, fair enough.

I interrupted his reading. "Please stop torturing me."

"Don't you want to know how it turned out?"

I shook my head. "I got to see it before it went to print. I don't want to relive it."

The left side of his mouth tipped up. "Fine. I'll stop." He

locked his phone and set it aside.

I sighed. "Thank you. I don't want to be in a bad mood for dress shopping."

"God forbid," he teased.

I stuck my bottom lip out. "Seriously. I'm going to be nervous enough having all three of them there."

He laughed. "Why? They all love you."

I wrapped my arms around myself. "Because it's a big deal, and Della and Skylar have *very* different ideas about what I should get."

He narrowed one eye at me. "You sure it's not cold feet?"

I scoffed. "Don't be an idiot."

"What a nice thing to say to your fiancé." He smirked. "I'm sure you'll have fun."

I gave a melodramatic whimper.

He chuckled, opening his arms, and I crawled forward to lay my body over his. His warm arms wrapped around me, and I settled my cheek against his chest. That heartbeat was a comforting and well-known rhythm, and a peace settled into my bones.

"Can you sneak me pictures?" he whispered.

"Hell, no. Your mother would kill me."

Acknowledgments

Self, you have the greatest support system that anyone could ever ask for! I'm not sure how many times I could say it before anyone really grasps how truly grateful I am for the encouragers I have in my corner.

But there are so many.

Before I even started this author journey, I have to thank those who read my early works and told me I should pursue this. I had never planned to publish. Then, when I did consider it, I figured later. Maybe when the kids are older. Maybe someday, after I have many more stories to share with the world.

But then I played around with a cover, for fun, and discovered how amazing it looked. And I thought, "Why not try it?" But I only planned to do it for my own bookshelf to boast my name. I figured maybe my best friend and my mom would be the only ones to buy it.

And here we are, a year and a half later, and I'm still meeting people I don't know who have read my book! What a wild ride.

So thank you to those who read and pushed me. Thank you to those of you who reach out to me and tell me you've read (and loved) my books! Thank you for writing reviews and sharing with your friends.

As for my specifics, as always, Mom and Dad. Brandon, my handsome husband and inspiration for all things swoony. Alyssa, my bestie for the restie/soul sister. Cheyenne, Lucy, and Mandy for the writing time and support and dance parties. Cheyenne, particularly for the snacks and coffees and merch. Kase, for your input and keeping my work more honest. Bestie, for being the overseas bestie I never knew I needed. Ania, for starting Quill & Cup and striving to create a space for women who write. Samara, for being one of my favorite people to talk deep with. Karin and Liz, for being my early readers and lifelong friends. Caitlin, for being my earliest writing partner, spanning two decades of friendship—whoa. Danielle and Meredith, for being awesome, for being fans, for being early readers and plot hole noticers.

And Jesus. Because I love Him and I know He loves me, even if I cuss a little. You gave me this little writing gift, and I'm trying to use it. Thank you for blessing me with the gift, with everything that has come since publishing, for giving me the people I've named here, and for Your love.

About the Author

Tracey Barski lives in Colorado with her dreamboat husband and their two adorable and precocious children. When she's not writing or wrangling tiny humans, she works as an editor and proofreader. For fun, she likes to pretend to be eighty years old, crocheting and watching Hallmark movies. She can also be found reading or singing loudly to any song she knows the words to. Find her on Instagram and Facebook, as well as at traceybarski.com, to find out about her upcoming books! If you enjoyed the books, please reach out! She loves to hear from readers! And don't forget to post reviews on Amazon and Goodreads!

You can connect with me on:

🌐 https://www.traceybarski.com
📘 https://www.facebook.com/authortraceybarski
🔗 https://www.instagram.com/authortraceybarski

Subscribe to my newsletter:

✉ https://www.traceybarski.com/contact

Also by Tracey Barski

The Alternate End of Cassidy Marchand
Cassidy Marchand is abandoned, on the run, and out of money. She soon discovers she has entered an alternate reality. The biggest hitch? Alternate-reality Cassidy is not only dead, she's been murdered.

Resurrecting Cassidy Marchand
Cassidy Marchand thought the alternate reality thing was done. But then the father who abandoned her as a child and the mother who died when she was eight walk into her hospital room, and she realizes she must be in the wrong universe. Again.

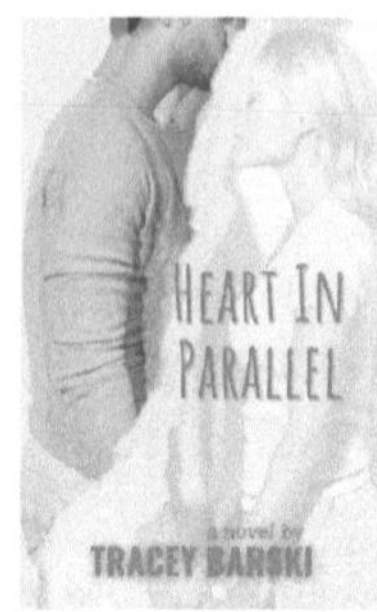

Heart In Parallel

Luke Pearson and Erin Baylor wake up to a world—and a life—that's not quite right. Desperation and grief mix as they join forces to search for a way to send Luke back where he belongs and to find answers to her brother's murder.